A Corner of Universe

For Hank —
So great to
meet you!
Rebbie

A Corner of Universe

Rebbie Macintyre

FIVE STAR
A part of Gale, Cengage Learning

GALE
CENGAGE Learning

Detroit • New York • San Francisco • New Haven, Conn • Waterville, Maine • London

GALE
CENGAGE Learning

LIBRARY OF CONGRESS CATALOGING-IN-PUBLICATION DATA

Macintyre, Rebbie.
   A corner of universe / Rebbie Macintyre. — 1st ed.
     p. cm.
   ISBN-13: 978-1-59414-859-0 (hardcover : alk. paper)
   ISBN-10: 1-59414-859-7 (hardcover : alk. paper)
    1. Married women—Fiction. 2. Pregnant women—Fiction. 3. Physician's spouses—Fiction. 4. Marriage—Fiction. 5. Domestic fiction. I. Title.
   PS3613.A272543C67 2010
   813'.6—dc22   2009041456

First Edition. First Printing: February 2010.
Published in 2010 in conjunction with Tekno Books.

Printed in the United States of America
1 2 3 4 5 6 7 14 13 12 11 10

For the women who taught me about family:
Phyllis, Shannon, and Heather

ACKNOWLEDGMENTS

Thanks to my editor, Gordon Aalborg, and my first readers, Keri Clark, Lisa Olexy and Judy Barnes. And thanks to the concentration camp survivor whose words about forgiveness during a television interview were the seed for this story.

CHAPTER ONE

Parched for my husband's attention, thinking to look wildly sexy—even though my waistline had already expanded by over an inch—I wore a too-tight dress and too-high heels to the Mechin Foundation banquet. I realized my mistake as soon as I tripped up the steps, popped off the spike heel from its thin sole and split my dress up the back seam—all within eye-shot of Cal's luscious new partner, Dr. Melissa Delany.

The steps led from the entry into a cavernous foyer which brimmed with glittering people, doctors and their wives, mostly, and when I fell, my palms had slapped the marble floor. The cocktail chatter came to a sudden and unanimous stop. I froze, looked up into dozens of eyes that stared down at me with expressions ranging from shock to amusement. For one instant, I could have literally heard a pin drop, but instead, with a muted pop, something akin to the sound of a dainty passing of gas, one final stitch of my seam gave way.

Melissa Delany hurried to my side. "Are you all right?" she said.

My husband, who had been talking with several German partners of the Mechin Medical Foundation, wrapped an arm around my waist and pulled me to my feet. He looked at me with alarmed concern, but the cleft between his aggravated eyebrows was as dark as a charcoal line.

"I'm fine," I said. "My shoe."

And as smooth as her glossy lips, Melissa Delany whisked up

the pencil-like heel, gracefully excused us and led me limping down the corridor.

"I have an extra pair of flats in my locker," she said. "What size are you?"

"Eight," I said.

I had been a size eight, I insisted silently, at least until four weeks ago, the day I learned I was finally pregnant. Now, my toes jammed even a size eight and a half.

I glanced over my shoulder to Cal who stood hands-on-hips staring after us. The party behind him had resumed its merry buzz, and, as I watched, a coworker tapped him on his shoulder to resume his conversation. Melissa Delany supported my elbow as we walked away from the crowd.

"My sister said her feet grew a full size with her first baby," she said. "I'm not in obstetrics, but I think that's pretty common. My flats are a nine. Maybe we can stuff some toilet paper in the toe."

I stopped and slipped off what was left of my stilettos. They were several years old, so at least I hadn't plunked down a couple of hundred dollars just for this party only to have gotten ten minutes worth of wear, but still, they had been great shoes. I padded down the cold marble hallway gingerly swiveling my right hand at my side. A strained wrist to add to my humiliation. The first few weeks of my pregnancy had already impacted my ability to balance. I felt like the little bubble of fluid in a carpenter's level; a fraction of movement and the bubble would slide off center.

The physician's locker room at the clinic was entered through a common room that held vending machines and a couple of cots, bare and lonely, shoved against the far wall. Gray metal folding chairs were scattered loosely around Formica tables which were dotted with half-filled coffee cups, Snickers wrappers and wadded napkins. Melissa pushed open a door labeled

Women and led me to a wooden bench placed between rows of lockers. The space reminded me of my high school locker room where teenage girls giggled and squealed as they ran to and from the showers. The astringent smell of antiseptic soap stung my nose and made my eyes water.

Melissa knelt in front of me and slid on black ballet flats she'd pulled from a locker labeled with her name. I knew she was probably trying to be nice, but doing for me what I could well do for myself reeked of condescension.

"You don't have to do that," I said. "I'm perfectly able to change my own shoes."

She bounced to her feet with a grin. "Done. And they fit perfectly. You might be one of those pregnant ladies whose feet expand after all."

She smiled at me, sincere and friendly. "Cal told me the news a couple days ago. Congratulations."

How did he seem, I wanted to ask. How was he when he told you? Excited? Put out? Disappointed?

But I sealed my mouth. Melissa Delany was not my confidant, and she certainly didn't need to speculate about the state of my marriage. Besides, Cal said he was happy about the news, so I should quit doubting him.

Five weeks pregnant and I was already making myself crazy with hormonal insecurities.

The banquet was a celebration for Mechin, the foundation my husband worked for, and marked a new phase of their business. A phase Cal was ecstatic about. A phase I dreaded.

When we'd met, Dr. Cal Sterling, my internist husband, practiced medicine in a clinic in downtown Chicago he owned with two other doctors. During the first year or so of our marriage, he'd gradually shifted his focus to the business end of managing the clinic. He'd developed unique accounting procedures, combined them with the new technology and several new models for follow-up patient care. The practice was fantastically successful and soon the partners opened three more clinics. Eighteen months ago, a group of international investors, Mechin Global Foundation, approached Cal about providing his expertise to set up six new clinics in Uganda, a country they'd targeted as being receptive to foreign money and medical intervention. Leaving behind his partners, he took the offer with Mechin. The career change meant a salary reduction, but Cal was ablaze with the possibilities of his new position, of helping needy people gain access to medical treatment.

It was important work. Wonderful work. Work that ate our lives.

An hour after I'd changed into Melissa's flats, I stood next to my husband in the foyer near the cocktail bar while he talked to one of the new doctors, a radiologist that recently had been hired. He was a single man without a date and I wondered if he was alone because he had an annoying habit of snuffling then wiping his nose with his cuff of his shirt, a gesture that would probably not endear him to the Chicago singles crowd. The noise volume had increased several decibels from when we'd first arrived and every so often, a burst of raucous laughter would echo around the stone pillars. Cal was his usual reserved self, nursing a glass of champagne that fizzled from the bottom of the stem. I sipped my club soda.

The radiologist once again swiped his nose. I looked away to hide my smile and saw Lucinda what's-her-name gyrating toward me. She stopped, giggled a little and leaned toward me like we were best-friends-forever girlfriends sharing a secret.

"I heard you made a grand entrance," she said. She gave an evil little smirk and lifted her martini glass to take a mincing sip.

I shifted my gaze and gratefully smiled at Darcy Jenner who

was pushing her way through a press of suited shoulders. Darcy was a friend, and although her husband worked for Mechin in the same capacity as Cal, as an internist, Ian managed to balance the demands of the job with his role as husband and father to their four children. I admired Ian and Darcy, and in moments of self-pity—sitting home in front of the television while Cal worked late into the evening—I envied them. Darcy, dressed in a very sensible loose-fitting silk dress and jeweled gold flats approached with a sympathetic smile in place.

"Hello, Lucinda," Darcy said. "How are you feeling?"

"Feeling?" Lucinda said.

"I'd heard you had a problem with your foot. What's the name of that thing that old people get? Gout?"

Lucinda snorted and flipped her hair back as she stomped off. I covered my mouth to muffle the giggles.

"She deserves it," Darcy said. "So smug that she runs all those miles. I mean, who cares?"

"Oh Darcy," I laughed, "really. You are so bad."

"Well. She's so superior. So righteous about her freaking running and her tofu. I'm over her. What did she say to you that she was looking so superior about?"

"She'd heard about my grand entrance."

"Good news travels fast, I suppose." Darcy laughed, placed a friendly hand on my arm. "You remember what happened when Jordan was born?"

I'd heard the story before, and she knew I had, but she wanted to comfort me, and I appreciated that from her.

"The night of the falling waters," I laughed.

"Yes. In the middle of Ian's graduation reception, a cast of thousands, in attendance. My water didn't simply break. It exploded. Gushed. Flooded all over dining room rug." She shook her head. "God it was awful. So believe me when I say

13

that breaking a heel off your shoes is minor league compared to that."

"I'm not so sure about that. I also split my dress up the back," I said.

She arched a look over my shoulder to examine my backside. "I'd never even know it."

"Yes. In addition to being a Harvard law school graduate and having a medical degree from John's Hopkins, she happens to be an incredible seamstress."

"Melissa Delany?"

I gave her a smirk, but was sorry the instant it lifted my mouth.

"She's really very nice, Zoe," Darcy said.

"I know. I know she is. She's nice and brilliant and single and stunning with a perfectly upturned nose."

"You're stunning. And your nose is regal. Like a Roman empress."

"Oh, that would be me. A regal, already very fat, Roman empress." I laughed at myself. "I guess I'm feeling just a tad insecure right now."

Darcy patted my arm again. "Take it from a woman who's been preggers four times. Don't pay attention to the stupid stuff that comes flying through your hormone-saturated brain. It's all bullshit."

I laughed. "I was just thinking about that earlier, how I'm only a few weeks along and already I'm feeling the changes. God. I'll never make it all the way through and stay sane."

The last time I was pregnant, I miscarried inside of a few short weeks; now, as thrilled as I was to finally be pregnant again, I had never experienced the heaving mood swings and the sense of being physically off-kilter.

She laughed again. "Sure you will. And after this project gets launched, Cal will have more time to be at home."

"I hope you're right."

She nodded, patted me again. "Trust me."

Yes, I told myself. Trust what Darcy said. It made sense. And her advice wasn't tinged by pregnant lady urges.

"We're leaving in two days for Bermuda," I said, grinning, "and come back next Tuesday."

"Hey, that's right. I'd heard that. You're staying in the Mechin condo?"

"Yes."

"Ian and I did that last year. It's right on the ocean. I slathered myself with oil and baked all day. The kids had a ball. The pool is beautiful."

"I've heard."

"A nice benefit we get with Mechin," Darcy said. "This will be a great trip for you and Cal. Before you get too big and have to stay put."

My spirits soared. Yes, we'd have a wonderful time, just the two of us. A second honeymoon.

The night ended with my feet swollen, the makeshift stitching in my dress strained to the point of re-bursting and Melissa Delany's size nine shoes pinching my feet. We drove home in silence, Cal animated and ready to tackle the world, me ready for the comfort of my bed. My head bobbed with the motion of the car, the heat under the dashboard warmed my feet, the music from a Natalie Cole CD soothed me and the flashing headlights of passing cars sent me into a kind of trance.

When we were only a few blocks from our home on Universe Street, Cal turned off the music and cleared his throat. "Uh, Zoe, there's something I need to talk to you about."

He pulled into our driveway, turned off the ignition. The clicks of the engine were the only noise, other than my husband's careful breathing. He lifted his arm and rested it across the back seat, cupped my shoulder in his physician's palm.

"You remember when we first started dating and I told you about Danielle. Danielle Bennett."

"Your college girlfriend? The one who got—"

My throat closed suddenly, and I felt heat rise into my face. Despite the icy November air of the Chicago night, I was warm.

Cal nodded. "Yes. The one who got pregnant."

"I remember," I said.

Cal had confessed the story during one of our first passionate nights together. He'd offered to marry his girlfriend, although clearly out of obligation, but Danielle had refused. A few months later, she married a man who agreed to adopt the baby. Cal was positive that despite Danielle's quick alternative, the child was his. A "near miss" he'd labeled the incident. A near miss that had allowed him to finish college and medical school unhindered by the burden of a wife and child. "Have you heard from her?" I asked.

"No. I heard from him. The boy. Well, young man now. He's twenty-one and his name is Seth."

"He called you?"

"No. He came by. Today. At the clinic." Cal's laugh broke through the car. A laugh that was not exactly forced, but nervous. Cal did not like surprises, and I could just picture his stunned expression when his son introduced himself.

"But . . ." I stumbled a moment, then tried again. "How did he find you? Did his mother tell him who you were?"

"Yes. His father died a few months ago. The man who adopted him. Danielle told Seth about me then."

"But, my God. What a shock. At his age, to find out the man you thought was your father wasn't really your father. Poor kid. That was wrong of his mother, to do it like that. Where does he live?"

"In Minneapolis, or somewhere near it. To tell you the truth, I was just so blown away I could hardly keep track of the conversation." He shoved his palms through the tight dark curls that hugged his scalp.

"But Cal, this is unreal. He wanted to come see you? To meet his biological father?"

"Yes. I mean, like you said, it had to be pretty shattering to find out his true parentage at twenty-one years old."

I shook my head in silent sympathy. A girl I'd gone through high school with had been adopted when she was ten by a loving family, our neighbors from the next farm over. At fifteen, despite the best the family could give her, she turned restless and depressed, constantly bemoaning to the other girls about her lack of knowing who she was. At seventeen, she finally ran away, never to be heard from again. The family had been devastated. I couldn't imagine what a person would feel suddenly finding out everything he'd believed to be true was in fact a lie.

"He's not staying very long in Chicago," Cal said. His voice brought me back to the present.

"Did he leave home, after his mother told him?"

"I don't think it was like that. He didn't seem to be upset with Danielle, kind of casual about it. I wondered if he'd suspected it all along. Anyway, he's just passing through town then heading out to California for some kind of school. Like I said, I was finding it a little hard to concentrate."

The leather in his seat rustled as he turned in his seat to face me. His grip on my shoulder intensified. "He seemed like a nice kid, Zoe. A real nice kid. He's only going to be here for a few days, then he's off to this school and from there, he said something about living overseas. Mexico, he said, or maybe Brazil. It's some kind of a scuba diving school, I think."

He paused. The clicks of the engine had stopped and now

17

silence engulfed us along with the clouds of our cold breath that fogged the interior of the car.

"Start the heater for a minute," I said. "I'm cold."

The windshield was white with our vapor, and I looked out the side window; the neighbor's cat crept though the firethorn hedge that separated our house from the neighbor's, the Reckarts. Like a shadow, he slithered underneath the hedge and was lost in the tangle. I wondered if he'd find a safe and warm haven someplace. Neva, the girl who lived there with her mother, took care of him, but only haphazardly. Obviously, a cat out on a cold night like this would not be well tended.

"Thing is," Cal said. He cleared his throat. "Thing is, Zoe, is that Seth is only going to be here a few days. I don't know when or if I'll even see him again."

The heater hummed, circles of clear glass began to form through the fog on the windshield. Cal massaged my shoulder with one hand and drummed on the steering wheel with the other. He was in profile to me; the light from the streetlamp lit one side of his face and glinted in his dark eye.

My mother had a saying she'd repeat to me from time to time, when the tension between Dad and her would crescendo enough so that we'd sit at the dinner table in tense silence. Later, when my father had been safely ensconced in front of the television and we were washing the dishes, she'd talk to me woman to woman, even though I was only twelve or thirteen. "Marriage is fifty-fifty, Zoe," she'd say. "And most of the time, the woman works both halves."

We'd laugh, and she'd talk about how hard being married was, but how fulfilling. "The alternative is being alone. And I don't want you to be alone, sweetheart. You're my girl, and I want you to have a home and a family."

I'd fought that notion for most of my teen years and through my twenties, vowed to make my own life as a career graphic artist, build a top design firm in Chicago.

But that was many years ago—before Cal, before the ALS had twisted my mother's limbs and squeezed closed her throat. Before she died.

Now, my husband sat next to me in a warm car and stared out into a cold night, and I thought about working both halves of my marriage.

"You want to cancel our Bermuda trip," I said.

He turned toward me, the gratitude soft in his eyes.

"I'll make it up to you, honey. I promise. We'll go right after Christmas. I'll talk to Walter and see if we can get the condo sometime in January. We'll go then, I promise."

My hand flew up between us, palm forward. "Stop. No promises, Cal."

"I mean it. I promise we'll go in January."

But I closed my eyes, shook my head. I would not set myself up for disappointment. I'd heard too many times in our three year marriage how he'd do one thing or another, but no sooner had the words been said and he'd come to me with a change in plans: A special Sunday we'd set aside for a day at home watching football on television would vanish in the demanding throes of his work. A special dinner I'd prepared would grow cold, the candles stayed unlit, because he had to attend to last minute demands from the clinic.

"No promises," I said.

By the light of the streetlamp, I saw his mouth turn down at the corners, the insulted jut of his chin.

"You'll see. I'll make it up to you," he mumbled.

And I knew he meant it. He really would try to make it up to me. Or rather, he'd want to try to make it up to me.

His lips pressed together and he stared at his lap for a moment, then turned up the heater.

"You warm enough?" he said. He glanced at me, touching

me with his eyes to measure where I was, see how I would respond.

And as usual, the vulnerable little boy expression he unconsciously wore tugged at my sympathy. He was a good man, a man who was dedicated to medicine, a man who had been there for me when I needed him. Now, here he was, trying to balance all these spinning plates: his position with Mechin, his lust for accomplishment, a newly pregnant forty-one-year-old wife, and now a grown son who'd dropped into his life.

"Cal." I took his hand that rested on my shoulder, brought it to my lips. "It's all right. We're okay. Of course we have to cancel the trip. You don't get to meet your son every day. And especially since he'll be leaving the country. It's okay. We'll get to Bermuda."

He grinned at me, clearly relieved, gave me a wet full kiss on the mouth, turned off the engine and trotted around the front of the car to get the door for me.

I would go up to our room and unpack my already packed suitcase—a suitcase that had been ready for a week. Tomorrow, I'd call my biggest client, Griffin Uniforms, and tell them I'd be available for meetings to design their spring campaign graphics after all. I'd cancel the kennel where I'd reserved a spot for Goldie. And I'd call my friend Sabrina and tell her we wouldn't need her to look after Hattie.

Hattie. Cal's eighty-eight-year-old grandmother had lived with us a year, and we'd never left her before. Even though she'd smiled and clapped for us when I told her about our Bermuda trip, I sensed an unease, even with the arrangements I'd made for her to go to Sabrina's.

"I'm not a child," she'd said. "I can stay here by myself."

I'd hugged her, breathed the rose scent that was a part of her. "I know you're not a child. You're a remarkably young vibrant woman, but I'll feel better about you staying with a friend."

Now, with the cancellation of our trip, she'd be pleased, although she'd never tell me. She had too much class for that.

So, for Hattie's sake, it was good we weren't going. And Cal could spend time with his son. It was a small sacrifice, I told myself, one of my times to "work both halves," as my mother would have said. For my husband, I would be accepting and gracious.

My mother would have been proud of me.

CHAPTER TWO

I contentedly worked from my home office the next day design-
ing new layouts for the Griffin Uniform catalog, but when dusk
descended outside my loft window, Cal called to say he'd be
home late, and depression oozed through me like I'd swallowed
curdled milk. I knew in the pit below my heart we would never
have our vacation together. Dejected and brooding, I turned off
my computer, went downstairs and retreated to the one room in
the house where I could find solace: the nursery. I'd adjusted
the handmade quilt across the arm of the antique rocker in the
corner when from outside the shuttered window, dry twigs
snapped under footsteps. My spine tingled, and I instinctively
placed my hand on my stomach. The firethorn hedge separating
our house from next door rustled. I held my breath a moment,
then let it out.

Of course. Neva Reckart, creeping around between the
houses again. I opened the shutters, turned the lock, lifted the
window and leaned into the wintry air.

The hedge's serrated leaves had ensnared her pink sweatshirt.
She gaped at me and with pudgy fingers, tugged her shirt free,
bursting a few of the berries. With a puzzled frown, she
examined the crimson blotches staining her shoulder and her
fingertips, then swiped her hand down the side of her jeans. The
branches snapped when she pushed her bulk through the woody
snarl.

"Neva," I said. "What are you doing? If you want to come see me, just knock on the back door."

Her mouth opened and closed a few times. "I'm sorry, Zoe. I'm sorry. I just . . ."

Frantic eyes searched for an escape.

Irritation nipped at me, but I forced the frown from my face. "Did you want to talk to me?"

A smile plumped her cheeks like she'd stuffed two jumbo jawbreakers into her mouth.

"I just wanted to look in the baby's room, that's all. It's so nice in there. It's a nice place for a baby. Honest. I didn't mean anything bad."

"I know you didn't, but it scares me when I hear noises outside the window. Would you like to come inside the house, into the room here and look around?"

She shook her head, swirling lank brown hair across her face.

This was the third time within the last two weeks I'd caught her sneaking around between the houses, standing on tiptoe to peer over the firethorn bushes in order to catch a glimpse into the nursery window. Even though I'd spent time with Neva over the course of the three years we had lived on Universe Street, she remained timid.

"Okay," I said. "But do you understand what I mean? You're always welcome here, but I don't want you sneaking around. Understand?"

I caught myself speaking to her with the same tone I'd use with a ten-year-old. She was socially unskilled, not mentally retarded, I reminded myself; and at eighteen, she certainly wasn't a child.

She smiled up at me. "Okay. I won't do it anymore. I have to go. See ya."

"Bye, Neva."

She thrust through the way she'd come and finally stumbled free of the hedge; a few needle-tipped glossy leaves clung to the pillows of her shoulders. The evening shadows swallowed her and she disappeared from my view. A second later, her feet pounded up the wooden steps of her own front porch.

Leaning further out the window, I surveyed the neighborhood. It was the week after Thanksgiving, so holiday wreaths decorated the old-fashioned green lampposts that lined our street. Cal and I had purchased the two-story home on the on the corner of Universe and Stargazer three years ago, just before we'd been married, and had felt lucky to get it; the prices were just beginning to spiral out of our reach. The neighborhood was circa 1920s, close to downtown Chicago, still dotted with a few haggard bungalows and saggy-roofed two-stories like Neva and her mother's, but mostly populated by people like ourselves who put every extra nickel into restoration. I breathed in the sharp air and enjoyed a moment of quiet. No traffic rumbled across the old bricks, but in the distance, the yells of the neighborhood boys echoed as they played football. Boys and football and winter evenings. I placed my hand on my still-flat stomach; if I had a boy, I'd like for him to play neighborhood football on these streets.

I closed the window, locked it and surveyed the hedge through the wavy glass of the original ninety-year-old pane. Who ever heard of a teenage girl being a peeping tom?

But Neva was a misfit, and I felt sorry for her. One evening about a year ago, a rare evening at home with my husband, I'd told Cal I wanted to have her over to have dinner with us. He choked down the vodka cocktail he'd been drinking.

"You're kidding, right? She looks terrible, Zoe, with that oily hair and all that acne. Not to mention she weighs about three hundred pounds."

"Oh, so you never had acne as a kid?" I said.

"Sure, but jeez. Why do you want to have someone like Neva Reckart here? For dinner?"

"I feel sorry for her, Cal," I'd explained. "She has no life. Only her work at that burger place. And I don't think her mother pays any attention to her."

"How do you know? Have you been spying on the neighbors while I've been slaving away?"

He'd laughed as he said it, but it rankled me. "I have not been spying," I said. "It's just very obvious she has no kind of life. No classes to go to or hobbies or friends. She walks past the house to the bus stop in that awful Burger Barn striped uniform and if I'm out, she always stops to talk. She's lonely. I feel sorry for her. I'd like to be kind to her. What's the matter with that? I thought one of the reasons we decided to move to the inner-city was to be a part of community and get involved with our neighbors. Well, Neva is a neighbor. And if a little kindness can help her, what's the matter with that?"

My intensity had risen as I'd spoken, and my husband, seeing he'd managed to stir up the hornet's nest of my emotions, had gently laughed and kissed me on the forehead.

"If it makes you happy," he said, "we can have her over for dinner." He'd kissed me again, then grinned at me over his shoulder as he trotted down the hallway to the kitchen. "Just let me know when you plan it so I can work late."

I hurtled one of the throw pillows from the sofa at him, but narrowly missed his head.

I still felt sorry for Neva, and I still wanted to have her for dinner, but somehow, I simply hadn't made the effort. I renewed the pledge to myself. I would invite her over. Maybe not dinner, but at least for a visit. And a tour of the baby's room, from the inside rather than through the window.

Turning to the dresser I'd painted with stars and comets, I lifted one of the newborn Pampers from a small wicker basket and cupped it in one palm. It was hard to believe a baby's bottom would be so tiny. I replaced it and meandered around the room. A few weeks ago, I'd begun my occasional day-dreamy inspections. It seemed to help calm the fear that would tear through me without warning like a monster cyclone swirling across the Midwestern plains: Fear for the survival of my marriage.

I was thirty-eight when Cal and I took our wedding vows. A week later, my mother died. I got pregnant a few weeks afterwards, decorated the nursery, and a month later miscarried. In the two and a half years since, while I prayed for a child, my husband prayed for success in his career.

Six months ago the Mechin project was supposed to have been finished, but it wasn't. And even though he worked out of the Mechin office in Chicago so he didn't have to travel, he still toiled hellacious hours—sixteen to eighteen hours a day, six days a week. On the seventh day, usually Sunday, he cut back to a mere eight or ten hours.

A black mood drifted at the edge of my consciousness. I wound the key and the star-and-moon mobile hanging over the bassinet chimed "Twinkle, Twinkle Little Star." Behind my eyes, a dull headache pulsed to life.

Enough.

Cal was a good man, he'd make a good father. This Uganda project would end someday, hopefully very soon, and he'd be able to devote more time to us and our home life. I was not going to allow my surging hormones to sink me into a morass of depression. I would not let my imagination get carried away with fear.

From the front of the house a car revved. It idled a moment more and then stopped. A door slammed.

I flipped off the light, closed the door behind me. My hurried footsteps tapped along the hardwood floors as I made my way down the hall to the living room. Through the picture window, I saw a black BMW, expensive and slick, parked at the curb. A man swaggered up the front walk. I rested one knee on the sofa which sat under the window and tilted one of the slats of the wooden blinds to get a clearer look.

I prided myself on being an accurate people reader, thanks in part to Hattie, who had mastered the art. I'd learned to note the revelations that come with unconscious body movements: a pull on an earlobe or a crease between the eyes that's quickly smoothed in the presence of others: and this young man's body language was unmistakable. His confidence bordered on arrogance. His open leather jacket swung from side to side, and his shoulders swiveled like a linebacker's whose muscles were taut from practice.

He crossed the wrap-around porch in two steps. The old buzzer-bell droned, and Goldie's paws clicked as she trotted from the kitchen across the living room to the foyer. As a mellow ten-year-old Labrador retriever, she didn't bark, but she still liked to satisfy her curiosity about who might be stepping onto her property.

The bell pierced the silence again. I opened the front door.

His eyes skimmed over me and he flicked a smile in quick appreciation. I'd seen that gesture before, the eye movement and smile, from Cal. A phrase shot through my mind: "Spitting image."

He was the spitting image of my husband.

"Hey. How ya doin'?" His voice vibrated from his chest, rumbling and broad as his body.

I stared at him.

"Is this the Sterling residence? Dr. Cal Sterling?"

I managed to nod.

"Well . . . um, is Dr. Sterling here?"

I shook my head.

"Oh. Well." His eyes darted in back of me, settled on my face and his smile changed the world from gray to sunlit, just like

Cal's. He stuck out his hand. "Seth Pruitt."

I watched the hand for a moment, noted the hair on his wrists not yet thickened and curled with a man's growth, then scrutinized his face. Handsome. His hair was much lighter than Cal's, ginger-colored—streaked either by the sun or an excellent colorist—but identical in texture and mass to Cal's. He'd pushed the loose waves behind his ears. I shook his hand and looked into dark eyes. Gypsy eyes. Cal's eyes.

"Sorry," my visitor said. "Didn't mean to scare you. I guess you don't know who I am." His hand dropped to his side. The floorboards of the old porch squeaked a little when he shifted his weight.

"Yes, I do. Sorry. I thought Cal would bring you home with him. Or I thought he'd be here. I mean, I didn't expect to see you without him here." I laughed at myself, stepped back and opened the door for him to enter. "Come on in."

He lumbered through the doorframe, and I closed the door behind him. He hitched up his jeans a little and surveyed the foyer and adjacent living room.

"Nice place," he said.

"Thanks."

I followed his gaze through the mostly-restored foyer.

"What's up there?" He gestured to the wooden railing above us.

"My office."

A set of stairs led from the foyer where we stood to my office loft. The nursery and Hattie's room were downstairs, and a second set of stairs off the back hall went to two bedrooms upstairs, the master and the guest room. I'd painted, stained and plastered my way through about half the house, but it sat now in a state of partial-renovation. Cal's career change had tightened our budget.

I focused on him again. "Would you like to sit down?"

He shrugged. "Sure."

"Can I take your jacket?"

"Oh. Sure."

The buttery leather whispered when he shrugged out of it, and I smoothed it a little before I hung it in the hall closet. Expensive. When I turned back to him, he was adjusting the sleeves of his blue cashmere pullover.

I led him through the foyer into the living room, one of the rooms that I'd mostly finished. It glowed with polished wood floors, gold area rugs and burnished overhead beams.

"Nice," he said and nodded approvingly.

He sat on the sofa. Goldie sniffed his boots a moment then sauntered back to the kitchen. I sat in my chair-and-a-half beside the cold fireplace and examined him a minute more. The jacket, the scuffed leather boots, the defined and pumped muscles visible beneath the cashmere sweater, the fashionable dark stubble shadowing his jaw told me he gave serious attention to his appearance. He'd honed his good looks to the present day standard of gritty sophistication.

I drew the afghan I kept on the chair arm over my lap. I'd start a fire later; when this young man had entered, he'd ushered in the chill of the evening.

"So," he said.

He grinned. One knee crossed over the other and his arms spread-eagled across the back of the sofa. "Sorry to just drop in like this. I did leave a message with Cal that I was coming. I mean, I kind of figured if it wasn't okay, he'd call me. I left a number. But he didn't call, so I came ahead."

A cramp in my lower stomach squeezed then loosened, and I placed my hand there.

"Cal didn't mention it, but don't worry about it. He'll be home, uh, later," I said.

"Oh. Well. I did leave a message. I wouldn't have come here

29

without doing that. Uh, sorry, I didn't get your name."

"Zoe. Zoe Sterling."

"You do know who I am, right? Hey, you okay?" he said.

"Yes. Yes, just fine." I stood. "Excuse me. I think I'll go call Cal, see if he can get home early."

"What time does he usually get home?"

Not until after eleven, and sometimes not until two or three in the morning, but I didn't say that now. The same old issue with Cal: his fiendish hours. Meetings, he said, much needed communication to set up the medical clinics in Uganda. With an eight hour time difference, midnight and later here corresponded to morning meetings over there.

I left him there, walked down the hall to my favorite room of the old house. The kitchen had been the last of my projects before the money-crunch. Weathered beams spanned the ceiling and a six-burner gas range sat in the center island. The counter tops were marbled granite in gold, black and brown, and on the far side of the kitchen, the stone extended to include a breakfast bar. I used two rattan stools for seating, one of which was now occupied by Hattie, who perched there like a miniature ancient bird. A glass of red wine rested in front of her.

It was her usual place this time of the evenings, a habit she'd developed so we could chat while I fixed dinner. Liquid black eyes followed me as I crossed to the kitchen desk, another functional extension of the granite. She tilted her graying head and spoke in her still-thick Slavic accent.

"I heard someone's voice in the living room. Who was it? What's the matter?"

"Just a second, Hattie. I need to call Cal."

I grabbed the cordless and jabbed the numbers that would connect me to Cal's cell phone. After three rings, I heard his voice.

"This is Cal Sterling. Leave a message."

"Hello, Cal. I hope you can come home earlier than you thought. Your son is here." I clicked off and replaced the receiver in its cradle.

I glanced out the kitchen window to the thickening night. Lifting the lid on the stew pot I'd set on the stove earlier in the afternoon, I inhaled. The aroma of rich meat, oregano and cooking sherry I used in the recipe told me it would be delicious. I replaced the lid then turned to find Hattie watching me.

"Cal's son? What do you mean, Zoe?"

I shook my head in sad acceptance. Cal should have told his own grandmother about Seth, about her great-grandson, but typical of Cal, he'd let it slide, no doubt caught up in his frantic schedule.

I stood next to her stool, hugged her thin but surprisingly solid shoulders and smiled down at her. "Why don't you come in the front room, Hattie. There's someone you'll want to meet."

I made brief introductions, and we settled in the living room: Hattie into her chair, our newfound relative in the middle of the sofa and me tucked back into my chair-and-a-half. Seth grinned at us, back and forth, while Hattie watched, amused, the laugh lines deepening around her eyes.

Seth spread his arms open and rested them across the back of the sofa; his hands flapped like he was drumming to a beat of music only he could hear. I wondered if he was nervous, which would be understandable, or if he was simply one of those young people filled with jittery energy.

"This is a cool neighborhood," he said. "Not like Chanhassen. That's where I'm from. Minneapolis. In the suburbs. But even in the city there's still nothing to do. It's way dead."

Hattie spoke from her corner. "I think most young people feel that way about their hometowns. No matter how exciting or unexciting they are."

31

He looked at her for a long moment, and I thought he might argue with her, but a sudden smile and a shrug of one shoulder proved me wrong. "Yeah, maybe. But Minneapolis is definitely not Chicago. I drove around for awhile before I came here." He nodded to himself. "Yeah." He looked at me. "You're not too far from some clubs and all, are you?"

"No," I said with a laugh.

This young man was not like his father. Cal was so serious and had been labeled by most of his classmates as a brainy nerd. He described himself as a shy introvert; he was seventeen before he went on a date, and his first sexual experience was at twenty with Seth's mother. Did Cal see any of himself in the ebullient stylish young man? Or did he see his mirrored image, a version of himself minus the serious intellect?

"And your folks?" Hattie asked. "Are they still in Minneapolis?"

He cleared his throat and his arms dropped down to his lap. His fingers clasped together: restrained, subdued. When he spoke, his voice had lost the too-loud, too-buoyant tone of a person who was trying hard to make an impression.

"Uh, my dad died in September. I mean my legal dad. My adopted dad." He shrugged. "You know. And Mom still lives there, but she left the day after Thanksgiving for a cruise with a bunch of her friends. A month long. Australia and all down in there. I'm happy for her cause Dad's death really hit her hard."

"I'm sorry for your loss," Hattie said.

"Yeah, he was a good guy." He slapped his hands on his knees, like an exclamation point at the end of a chapter in his life. "And, I decided, why don't I give my real dad a call? Mom had kept his old address and stuff, and he's all over Google. He wasn't too hard to track down. The famous Doctor Sterling."

I arched an eyebrow at the fib. His account of discovering his biological father was different from what he'd described to Cal, but I figured if that topic was to be broached, it was best left until later.

"So, Cal said you were on your way to California for school," I said.

"Yeah, I'm moving out there. Going to a dive school out there."

"Dive school?" Hattie asked.

"You know," he made a motion in the air of a breast stroke, "scuba diving. I'm going to be a dive instructor. Work in a resort in Cancun. I have a friend who's there now and he says he can get me on there. It's awesome. Diving and girls and stuff."

Hattie nodded her understanding. "Have you been to college?"

He crossed his leg and his foot jiggled for a moment then stopped.

"Nah. Wasn't for me. I mean, I took a couple of courses at MCTC, that's a community college in Minneapolis, but I'm twenty-one now. No way I'm going to wait four years for some degree."

He stretched his arms over his head and yawned quickly, then flopped them down to the sofa again.

"Yeah, diving is great." His jocund bellow echoed slightly in the room. "I've already been on four dive trips with this sports store I worked at in Minneapolis. Mexico is great. I can't wait to go back there."

"When does your school start? In California," I asked.

"Oh. Well, not till January. But don't worry. I won't stay here that long." He grinned again. "This other guy has an apartment in LA that I'll be living in. I can go out there anytime. Hey, that reminds me." He scooted forward on the sofa, ready to get to his feet. "Can I use your phone? I gotta call Burton. He's my friend in Mexico."

I felt the surprise on my face. "Oh. Sure. I, uh, I don't know how to dial internationally, but, go ahead."

How much was an international call? I had no idea. Cal called to Uganda, to the Mechin directors over there, but he'd always done it from work.

"I guess you can't call on your cell, right?" I said. "Your plan doesn't cover it?"

I wasn't trying to be rude, to make a big deal about a few dollars on a phone bill, but at the same time, I didn't want to keep silent.

Seth stood, hiked his jeans and walked around the coffee table to stand in front of me.

"Naw," he grinned, "I got a cheap plan. Is the phone in the kitchen?"

"Oh, yes. Yes, just follow the hallway there. You'll see it on the desk to your left."

What had I left out? Bills? A bank statement? "Here, I'll show you," I said.

I led him down the hall, his booted heavy steps following, and at the desk, I whisked a few open pieces into the top drawer. I felt a little foolish, there was nothing of consequence, but at least it was off my mind.

He thanked me, granted me a devastating smile. Despite myself, I felt the tickling flattery of knowing I was being admired.

Back in the living room, Hattie and I talked about Cal, Seth, Hattie's feeling that family was family, and therefore should be encased in a common cocoon. I started a fire in the fireplace, closed the drapes against the deepening evening, returned to the kitchen to turn off the burner under the stew. Seth was splayed out in the desk chair, his long legs stretched in front of him, his boot tapping on the baseboard—leaving a black mark, I noticed. He glanced at me and tossed a quick smile of recognition my way while he kept up his banter about a girl his friend was evidently dating. He'd been on the call for about twenty minutes. I returned to the living room, sank into my chair by the fire and talked with Hattie about where we could buy yarn for a baby afghan she wanted to knit for me. Another twenty minutes passed, and I heard Seth heartily calling good-bye, promising to talk to his friend in a couple of days.

Forty-five minutes on an international call? Not on my phone, I thought.

Seth sauntered into the living room, came over to my chair and placing one hand on the back to steady himself, leaned down toward me. His face only inches from my own, he smiled, a soft smile that reminded me of Cal.

"Hey," he said. His voice was low and husky. "Thanks for the use of the phone."

Heat bloomed in my chest, rose up my neck and seared my face. I was that little bubble inside the carpenter's level again, off balance and sliding to one side. His breath smelled of peppermints, like the candy I kept in a bowl beside the phone. For one absurd instant the thought flashed through my mind that he was actually going to kiss me, but in the next moment, he stood and walked away. He inserted himself on the sofa where he'd been before.

I deliberately slowed my breathing, tried to make sense of my muddled emotions, and a few moments later, I heard the back door open and shut, the jangle of the car keys as Cal dropped them into the dish on the table beside the back door.

"Zoe?" he called.

At the threshold, he stopped in his tracks and surveyed the room in silent amazement. His wool coat sparkled with the evening's dampness. He reached up to lightly pat his hair, an unconscious gesture derived from his worry about his receding hairline.

Seth strode around the coffee table still wearing the engaging grin that assumed his father would be delighted to see him. His hand extended outward, ready to shake. They stood face-to-face like mirrored reflections different only in age. Identical pairs of black eyes held steady.

Cal's low, clipped tone highlighted his words. "And so you just decided to show up?"

"Well, yeah," Seth said. He shrugged and the hand fell to his side, but he kept his easy smile. "I figured you knew I was coming. If you didn't want me to, you knew how to get a hold of me. I left my cell number on the message."

Cal's jaw worked, the sure signal that he was chewing his emotions, trying to keep them under control. "I didn't think you'd just—" He broke off and hurried over to me. "Zoe."

He knelt in front of me, held both of my hands and brushed my lips with his own.

"I'm sorry, sweetheart. I'd thought he'd wait."

I grasped his cold hand in my own. "It's okay, Cal. It's fine. Sit down. Here," I moved to get up, "let me get your coat."

The gratefulness I felt in seeing Cal was exaggerated; the discomfort a few moments ago still clung to me like thick cigarette smoke. Had I over-dramatized Seth's body language and thanks for the phone? I glanced to Seth's face. The smile he'd had in place when he'd seen Cal had faded a little. He was disappointed at his father's reaction. He was really very young and I had undoubtedly read too much into his mannerisms. Yes, another hormonal surge, no doubt.

Cal stood still and glared at his son. "Your message said you'd wait to hear from me. I didn't think you'd just come here without a call. Just waltz in here."

Seth cast around the room like he was waiting for someone to save him. The silence lasted a long moment, and when he spoke his voice had turned deep and hard.

"Hey, don't worry about it. You don't want me around here, I can leave."

From the corner of the room, Hattie's thickly accented words sliced through the tension. "There is no need to be hasty, young man. It's the nature of families to argue."

In the silence that followed, I stood, threw the afghan over the back of the chair and went to Cal. I touched the cold velvety wool of his sleeve.

"It's all right, Cal. Let's talk later. But for now, it's all right."

The poor kid. The only father he'd ever known died only a few months ago. His death had obviously left Seth emotionally adrift. Then his mother had dropped the bomb on him about his biological father. Couldn't Cal see this? Was he really so insensitive? I turned to Seth.

"Hattie's right. Don't be upset. Your father is just surprised to find you here, that's all." I turned to Cal. "Isn't that right, Cal? You're just caught off guard."

Cal looked from Seth to me to Hattie, and his face relaxed into a grin. He extended a hand to Seth.

"No hard feelings? Okay?"

Seth grinned back and quickly shook hands.

Hattie rose from her chair. "We should go eat now. A big thing has happened and we should eat."

She stood, small and hunched, a wise old matriarch issuing an edict. "The world can change at the flip of a coin."

We followed her mincing soft-soled footsteps down the back hall.

CHAPTER THREE

After dinner, Hattie retreated to her room, Cal and Seth settled in the living room and I, being the chief cook and maid, remained tethered to the kitchen. Thirty minutes later, I folded the dishtowel on the rack and punched the button to start the dishwasher. It whirred to life.

When I opened the back door to let Goldie out, cold air swirled into the kitchen. I watched her from behind the window in the door, then cracked it open just wide enough to let her back inside.

When I'd had the kitchen refurbished, I'd insisted on including a walk-in pantry, and as I entered it now, my mouth watered in anticipation. Spices and a tantalizing mustiness pervaded the small closet, and I inhaled deeply. Floor-to-ceiling shelves lined three sides and on one shelf, a wine rack held one lonely bottle. I reached up to the second shelf on the right side and felt for the glass jar in the back corner. I counted out four dark chocolate drops. I adored chocolate, and could easily let the cravings control my life; but I'd found that just four or five treats a couple of times a day were enough to keep the need at bay, like holding a ravenous dog at the end of a tight leash. The foil wrapper clicked softly as I unwrapped the first one; I popped it in my mouth and closed my eyes to savor its creamy denseness. Heaven. I dropped the other three in the pocket of my baggy sweatpants.

I took a tea mug from the cabinet, filled it with water and set it in the microwave to heat. Leaning against the counter, I crossed my arms over my chest and tuned in to the rumble of male voices coming from the living room. Cal and Seth were discussing who they favored in professional football. That's nice, I thought, for them to share that interest. In recent months, Cal hadn't allowed himself the luxury of watching a football game for an afternoon, but in the first year of our marriage, we had enjoyed it together almost every Sunday during the season. I'd curl up with him on the sofa, a platter of wings and cold beer at our finger tips, and we'd cheer our way through a game. Now, with the Mechin project, his attention was occupied by everything but me. Even with a new associate to help him . . .

Melissa Delany.

Don't do this, I told myself. Her qualifications were perfect for the job, and I would not stoop to deny any woman a career opportunity just because she was beautiful.

I bit down and the last morsel of the chocolate compressed in divine intensity. I fished in my pocket for another one, unwrapped it and savored the goodness all over again. I deserved a reward for my attitude about Melissa Delany.

The bell dinged and I retrieved my steaming mug and added a tea bag. I switched off the light and walked down the dark hallway holding the mug with both hands. Its warmth soothed my cold fingers. Goldie ticked along behind me then climbed the stairs to the second story. She'd head to our bedroom and curl up on a blanket I kept in the corner nearest the bed. She knew the routine.

In the living room, Cal and his son shared the sofa. They faced each other, Cal's arm stretched across the sofa back as if he was silently entreating his son into his life. After dinner, Cal had changed into his "fancy sweats" as I called them: a luxurious black cashmere sweater and matching soft trousers that pulled on and tied like terry sweat pants. He looked more relaxed than I'd seen him in months. Seth leaned back into one of the upholstered pillows, his arms crossed over his chest. They stopped talking, something about the Bears, and looked at me. Cal smiled, but he obviously wanted to stay connected to the conversation. I had the distinct impression I was interrupting.

"I'm going up to bed," I said.

"Okay, sure, Zoe. I'll be up in a minute. I guess Hattie got to bed all right."

I lifted my eyebrow at him. "Same as usual."

The house proceeded with a routine of which my husband was unaware.

He glanced at Seth and smiled. "Okay then. I'll be up in a little bit."

"Seth," I said, "I think you have everything you need in the guest room and the bathroom. If you're missing something, feel free to open closets."

I climbed the steps to the second floor and started toward our bedroom but paused at the open door to the guest room. Seth's laptop sat on the desk in front of the window, the green lights glowing. Sweaters and jeans spilled out of his open duffle bag on the bed. A sweatshirt lay crumpled on the floor. The open closet door revealed a pair of shoes and two pair of boots he'd flung inside. A canvas suit bag hung from the rod.

So, I thought, I guess I didn't have to worry about him making himself at home.

I'd left the light on earlier in our bedroom and its hominess welcomed me. After my mother's death and my miscarriage, I'd felt entitled to indulgences, and this was the one room in the house where I'd wanted to splurge. I'd gotten as far as painting the walls a comforting butter-yellow, but the wall-to-wall carpet was the matted brown shag from the former owners. I crossed the room to the window that overlooked the backyard and closed the curtains. Next to the window, I'd placed a chaise lounge, a leftover from my single days at the Art Institute, which was now scattered with the butter-colored pillows I'd sewn. The side table wore a matching skirt, and I set the mug on the table, snuggled into the chaise and drew a wool afghan over my legs. The stomach cramps—very normal, my doctor husband had assured me—that had been bothering me all night seemed to be lessening somewhat, and I opened a decorating magazine I kept in a rack beside the chaise and relaxed into another world, a world of gleaming appliances and floral fabrics that I still dreamed of for our own home.

An hour later, the bedroom door opened and Cal walked in. He crossed the room and stood at the end of the chaise massaging the small of his back like he usually did after his long days.

"So what do you think, Zoe? What do you think of the kid?"

"Oh, Cal. He seems very nice."

He lowered himself to the edge of the chaise and perched beside me. He kissed me again lightly, and I breathed in the musky sweetness of his cologne. When he pulled away, his eyes and his smile were intimate and tender.

"Honey, look. I'm sorry he just showed up here. I got Seth's call and then right after Melissa had some things fall apart that she needed my help with."

"Cal," I laughed, "it's okay. Really. He seems like a nice young man, and I'm happy for you both."

I thought about the forty-five minute phone call to Mexico, but decided to keep it to myself. Why make things awkward? Seth would only be here for a few days. And as for the absurd moment when he leaned close and thanked me for using the phone—well, I was wildly hormonal, after all. He was simply trying to be nice.

Cal licked his lips and looked at the floor. He fiddled with the fringe on the pillow near my elbow. "This whole deal at work is getting so intense. It's very exciting and it's very scary at the same time. I mean, on one hand, I want to be with home with you more, and now especially with Seth here. But on the other hand, this thing with Mechin is so incredible. I'm more excited about this than I have been about anything in my life. And then when Seth called, I guess I pushed it out of my mind. I just don't need anything else crowding my life right now."

I reached up and cupped his chin in my palm. "Family doesn't crowd lives, Cal. That's why you're working these long hours, right? To provide for our family?"

He looked away from me. "Well, yes, that's part of it."

I knew what the other part was: his relentless ambition. But I didn't want to say that now. We'd traveled that road before and always reached the same destination: His work was his life.

He shifted his eyes back to me and grinned his teasing grin. "When my next son calls, I promise I won't forget to tell you."

He wrapped me in a crushing hug.

"Okay," I said. "But just out of curiosity, do you have any long lost daughters that may show up?"

He held up his hand like he was swearing on a Bible. "No. I promise."

He kissed me again, and I felt the old magic begin to work. He could do that to me. After a delicious moment, he pulled away.

He gave me a peck on the nose, stood and faced me. "I thought I'd knock off work tomorrow early and the two of us would drive up to the Dells for an overnight."

The Dells was an area in Wisconsin used both summer and winter as an outdoor playground: skiing, snowmobiling, snowshoe trekking. Before he shifted his career, when we still had money for extravagances, Cal had purchased the latest high-tech winter camping gear. He'd used it only once in the last two winters, so it was virtually new.

An overnight in the Dells wasn't my idea of a fun get-away,

so it wasn't that I wanted to go with them, but my feelings rankled nonetheless.

"The Dells," I said. "He's been here for a few hours and you're taking a day off work to take him to the Dells? How nice."

"Come on, Zoe, don't be like that. We'll be gone only one night. I've been wanting to get back up there, and this will be a great way to get to know Seth. We both love the outdoors. He worked as a wilderness guide for two summers with a sporting goods store in Minneapolis."

"Yes, he mentioned something about that."

"Come on," he said. "Big deal. I'll take one lousy day off work."

The green-eyed monster growled inside me. For Cal to take a day off work was a big deal, and it was one day more than I got.

But I didn't want to be a jealous shrew. I wanted to be a bigger person, wanted to act like a wife who knew her husband loved her. Wanted to work both halves, like I'd promised myself.

"Okay," I said. "You're right. I'm glad for you. The Dells will be fun."

He relaxed his posture and smiled. "Seth wants to drive. He's got that fancy BMW he wants to show off."

"I wondered about that. With the clothes and the car, his parents must do very well."

"He said he bought the car with most of his father's life insurance policy. After that, there was evidently enough left over for some nice clothes and this diving school he's signed up for."

"And evidently enough for his mother to take a month-long cruise."

He shrugged.

"Has he said anything more about how his mother told him about you?"

Another shrug. "Like I said, he's pretty casual about it. If

43

he's shook up, he's not telling."

"Hm. Yes, he glossed over it when hew was talking to Hattie and me. Seems odd. If my mother told me that I'd been adopted by my father, I think I would have been pretty upset."

"Well, maybe he is and just doesn't want to talk about it. He's a guy, Zoe. Guys don't have to talk to death every little thing that happens to them."

"I suppose." I watched him take his pajamas from the drawer. "What time tomorrow are you going to head for the Dells?" I said.

"I hope I can cut loose by noon or so. That would put us up there in time to rent some snowmobiles and ride out to the lake Tom Eisler took me to. Remember? The Mom and Pop resort with the cabins? I'll call Eisler in the morning and get the number of those people. It's a great place to winter camp."

I nodded. "I won't be here when you leave. I have to go to the farm tomorrow. It's Dad's birthday." My stomach knotted with the thought of seeing my difficult father. I didn't want to go.

"Try to enjoy the day," Cal said. "I know it's hard, but try."

"I will. And I want to see Red Leaf again. I realized this morning that it's been six months since I've been home. I couldn't believe Dad wouldn't come here for Thanksgiving."

He rubbed the small of his back again as he walked to the closet. I shoved the worries of my father to the back of my mind. Tomorrow would be soon enough to deal with him.

"Is your back hurting?" I asked.

"Just a little stiff," he said, then disappeared inside the doorway.

I called to him loud enough for him to hear me through the wall.

"Want me to rub it?"

His muffled reply came back to me. "No. Don't worry about it."

"Cal," I said. His head appeared at the closet threshold. "Seth will probably leave on Friday or Saturday. Since we're not going to Bermuda, let's get away together for a couple of days. I've saved a little money aside, and Sabrina would look after Hattie. Let's get a hotel room downtown. Take in a play or a concert. Go to dinner at that little French restaurant we used to love. Remember? That one in the alley by the State Theatre."

"What restaurant? Oh, you mean Bernard's. I didn't like it there the last time we went."

"You didn't say anything about it."

"Well, I didn't."

Here I'd thought of Bernard's as a yummy romantic place, and he hadn't liked it. We were on different wavelengths. Again.

He ducked back into the closet for a moment and returned holding one of his gray pinstripe suits.

"This has been cleaned, right? There's no tag in the coat."

"You only wore it once. It's fine, I think."

He examined it, brushed the lapel and straightened it on the hanger.

"No, needs cleaning. Take it in for me tomorrow, would you?"

He hung it on the door.

"So what about getting away next weekend?" I said.

He kept his eyes on the ties and tossed me an answer. "Sure, honey. Sounds great."

He ducked back into the closet again.

Had he granted me this out of guilt? Did he feel like he could hardly turn me down after just telling me he was going to spend an overnight with Seth? Probably, but I didn't care. I'd start calling hotels tomorrow. Maybe I'd book a suite for us at the Drake. No, too expensive. Maybe the Sheraton. Still pricey, but I thought I could swing it.

"Jeez," he called through the wall, "I still can't believe Seth is here."

He walked out of the closet and tugged off the cashmere pants. He folded them carefully, opened the drawer and arranged them on top of the sweater.

He swiveled to face me. "Hey, what about Christmas? It seems heartless to have Seth spend it alone in LA when he could be here."

"You want to fly him back here from LA? The ticket will be incredibly expensive."

"You're right," Cal said. He frowned a moment, then his face lit with a new idea. "How about he just stays here?"

I struggled to keep my voice low and reasonable, but a nameless disquiet stirred in my chest. Seth's face flashed in my mind, how he had looked, how close he'd leaned into me.

"Christmas is over three weeks away," I said. "That's a long time for someone to stay here. Especially someone we don't even know."

He shrugged. "Long time or not, I'd like him here for Christmas. He's my son and now that he's shown up, I think it's great."

"I thought he was only planning to stay a few days. I assumed, I mean, I thought he talked about getting out to California and getting settled before his school started."

Cal shrugged. "So? He changes his plans. As long as he gets there in time for classes, it won't matter."

I felt ridiculous and bitchy-picky that in my mind I kept coming back to that international phone call and Seth's manner of thanking me, but my words came out even as I tried to push them back.

"We don't even know this young man, Cal. I know he's your son, but what about his character, his personality? I don't want to invite him to stay for almost a month, share Christmas with us, then be sorry about it."

"Why would we be sorry?"

"I don't know, but there could be any number of reasons. Maybe he stays up all night playing loud music. Maybe he rifles through other people's papers and personal effects. Maybe he's a chronic pot smoker. All I'm saying is we don't know."

"Okay, fine. God, you're suspicious."

"Cal, be fair. We don't know what kind of person Seth is. At least acknowledge that much."

He heaved a dramatic sigh and buttoned the top button of his pajama tops.

"Okay, then," he said. "But could we agree we'll see how it goes for a few days, then if he doesn't turn out to be a serial killer, we'll ask him to stay for Christmas?"

"Oh, quit it. I know he's not a serial killer."

"Well, would you agree to that?"

I went to him and put my arms around his waist. I wanted so much for everything to be all right between us. I wanted him to put his arms around me, murmur in my ear that it was okay, that he'd give me time to adjust, time to get to know Seth. But he didn't. He waited stiff and silent.

Exhaustion overwhelmed me again, and I gave in with a sigh.

"Let's see," I said, "how it goes with Seth for a few days."

He nodded, and a delighted smile opened his face. I started to turn away from him when he grabbed my arm.

"C'mere."

He circled his arms around me, pressed me into his chest and kissed the side of my neck. He murmured into my ear. "You've been so sweet about this. Thank you, honey."

He pecked my forehead and then, tender and long, he kissed me; I took his affection inside my thirsty heart. I'd missed him. I'd been afraid he'd been drifting away from me, drawn to his career, his importance, and now, his new-found son. I'd been afraid I'd been shuffled to the back of his life like a taken-for-granted prop. But now, his breathing increased with passion while his lips opened my own. I met his tongue and the grind of his erection with my own tingling sensations. He kept his mouth on mine and walked me backwards until the back of my knees hit the bed. I fell back to the mattress and we came apart and laughed together.

He leaned over me and rumbled in my ear. "Are you still one hot mama?"

Evidently, I was one of those women whose sexual desires increased with pregnancy, and I drew him down on top of me. He lowered my sweatpants and panties and ran his fingers inside my folds. I felt my own wetness and giggled.

"I'm either a hot mama or you're one major stud," I said.

He growled and nuzzled his face into my swollen breasts.

He undressed me, then himself and ran his hands over my body as only he knew how to do. I closed my eyes and let the waves carry me, then opened them and roamed over his body: his penis, the little valley directly above the slight bulge of his stomach, the line of black hair below his belly button that dropped into his pubic hair. He had a scar on his nipple from when he was nine and had fallen bare-chested out of the tree house he and his brother had built. I kissed it and then the mole directly under his armpit. My husband tasted wonderful to me.

We made love until he rolled off me and fell into a comatose sleep. I got up and padded into the bathroom, gave myself a quick wash and put on my flannel pajamas.

The hallway echoed the brush of my bare feet as I went past the guest room where Seth was; the door was closed and no light shone beneath it. Downstairs, I re-checked the locks as was my habit every night and stole a glimpse of Hattie sleeping in her room. When I returned to the bedroom, Cal was exactly like I'd left him.

After I'd turned out the light and crawled in beside him, I relived our loving session. How long had it been? Over two weeks? Too long. I snuggled into the covers and spooned against my husband's back.

Safe. Safe and warm and loved.

My eyes flew open.

My father.

Oh Lord. Tomorrow I had to see my father.

While I fell into sleep, self-pity perched on my shoulder and whispered her condolences into my ear.

CHAPTER FOUR

The next morning, I awoke with a start, panicked, consumed by some anonymous fear. What was wrong? What had happened? A thin light of dawn outlined the window blind on the other side of the room. No creepy crawlies in the black night. No faceless visitor sneaking down the hallway to my room. But I could feel the tenderness in my jaw; I'd clenched my teeth while asleep. My breath still came in shallow gasps and my heart was pounding like I'd just finished a race.

I stayed rigid, waiting for an awful thing, whatever it was, but nothing pounced. The panic lessened and I deliberately took a few deep breaths, relaxed my muscles and spread my fingers across my stomach. The baby was fine. Maybe a nightmare that had evaporated when my eyelids opened? Something about Cal?

I smoothed my palm across the cold sheet beside me. He was gone already. He'd be home at noon to for his trip with Seth to go to the Dells.

And I was glad for them, I really was; I felt the genuineness of my feelings. Cal would enjoy the trip, and then next weekend, it would be our turn to get away. I'd call the Sheraton hotel from my cell on the way to the farm. Optimism and good will ballooned inside me.

Throwing off the covers, I scurried to the bathroom and flipped on the light, further banishing the shadowy threat of my dreams and turned on the shower. It was my father's birthday, and as I felt the water stream for temperature, I made myself a promise: I'd enjoy him today. I'd enjoy being at Red Leaf. My spirits spiked.

I dressed in my black wool pants, thankfully with elastic on the sides of the waistband, a scarlet cable sweater and my fleece-lined black boots. I surveyed myself in the full mirror on the closet door as I pulled my hair into a scrunchy. Thick, straight and black, Indian hair, my mother had said, from my father's side, the Truebloods, who had a distant Cherokee ancestor. Turning to survey my stomach in the mirror, I decided I liked the sweater; it didn't make me look fat.

Shutting the bedroom door behind me, the heels of my boots clacked on the bare boards of the hall floor. I stopped in front of the closed guestroom door. No sound from inside, and the bathroom next to it was dark and empty. Seth was a late sleeper, but then again, he was probably tired after the reunion last night with Cal. I probably wouldn't see him until they returned from the Dells tomorrow.

In the kitchen, Hattie puttered at the counter. She'd already made the coffee and let Goldie out, now she was busy buttering a piece of rye toast for me. I wrapped an arm around her shoulders and kissed her good morning on the soft folds of her cheek. I inhaled her rose-scented soap. I loved that smell.

She'd come to live with us a year ago, when Cal's own father, Hattie's son, couldn't persuade his young new wife to have an eighty-eight year old mother-in-law interrupt her retired Miami lifestyle. After Hattie's knee replacement operation, they'd placed her in an assisted living facility—not one of the luxury "active retirement" communities that dotted the east Florida coast like priceless diamonds thrown from the hand of a wealthy society, but a dirty four-bedroom home in a decaying neighborhood in St. Petersburg, Florida. When Cal and I walked through the front door, I literally gasped at the sight of the stained terrazzo floors and a kitchen where a caretaker, a harried middle-aged woman, prepared meals for the six residents while palmetto roaches scurried over crusted counter tops. Within twenty minutes, we'd packed Hattie's meager belongings and started back to Chicago.

"So what do you think of your great-grandson?" I said.

She kept her eyes on the butter she was spreading on the toast.

"I'm happy Cal has him here."

"That's not exactly an answer to my question."

I smiled at her, squeezing her shoulders to make sure she knew I wasn't criticizing.

"I'm just curious what you thought of him," I said. "But I guess you really didn't get a chance to talk to him alone. He and Cal will be leaving today around noon. They're going to go camping in the Dells."

"Camping in the freezing cold? Has Cal done that?"

"Once. They'll be fine. Cal has all the best gear. They'll stay in a cabin on a lake Cal's visited before. No electricity and an outhouse. Not my idea of a good time." I grinned at her.

"Nor mine," she said. "How long will they stay?"

"They'll be home tomorrow night. Maybe you'll get to spend some time with Seth then."

Her thin shoulders lifted in a shrug. "Such an urban young man has no time for an old woman."

"What makes you say that?"

She shrugged again. "Just an impression. I don't know him, but that's my feeling."

I started to give her assurance that as Seth's great-grandmother, she held a special place in Seth's life, that of course he would want to spend time with her, get to know her—but I stopped myself from offering what might have been empty platitudes. How did I know? Seth may not be interested in her at all.

I pecked another kiss on her cheek.

I thought again about my conversation with Cal last night and how he wanted Seth to stay here for several weeks. I didn't like the idea, not because of Seth personally, but because of the exact reason Hattie had just stated and what I'd told Cal last night: we did not know this person.

"Where are you off to today?" Hattie said.

"Red Leaf. It's my father's birthday."

"I remember the farm. It was beautiful."

Cal had flown Hattie down from her home in Philadelphia for our wedding at Red Leaf. Cal's grandmother had always been an important part of his life, and when Hattie was more or less abandoned by Cal's father and his wife, Cal remained devoted and loyal—a quality that, in my opinion, bathed him in a beam of pure goodness. So despite the fact that our wedding was rushed—we'd only known each other for six weeks—Cal arranged for Hattie to be with us. When I met her, I immediately sensed what Cal loved about her: Hattie was a fully conscious, fully realized human being, a true woman of substance.

"Why don't you come with me today," I said, "to Red Leaf?"

The words were out of my mouth without thought, but now that I'd said them, I liked the idea. Hattie would help buffer some of the negativity I knew I'd encounter with my father. I'd love to have her calming presence for the drive home, when my emotions would be as raw as a winter day.

But she smiled and shook her head. "Thank you, darling, but no." She patted my arm. "You go. You go to see your father on his birthday."

I hadn't shared with her the dark nooks and crannies of my relationship with my dad, but she knew it was strained. She'd remarked about the odd fact that my father had never been to his only child's home, and that we never shared holidays with him. But she didn't pry. That wasn't Hattie's style.

I dumped kibble into Goldie's bowl, checked her water and let her out. When she was finished, she scampered up the steps, anxious to return to the kitchen and her pallet by the heat register in the floor. A door slammed upstairs and a moment later, Seth pounded down the steps and barreled into the kitchen.

He stopped in the threshold and grinned at us. His hair was mussed, his beard was heavy and he held a bundle of wadded clothes tucked under one arm. Swollen muscles defined his chest and a six pack sculpted his stomach. He was barefoot, and I realized with a pop of shock, only had on his underwear. His thong was black with white skulls, fit tight, cradling his genitals. The skull on the front sported a red tongue, extended and shaped like a penis at the tip.

"Hey everyone," he said. "Got a load here." He motioned the wad of clothes. "Are the washer and dryer down in the basement?"

I blinked rapidly, trying to look away and at the same time, unable to do it.

"Uh, no," I said. "Actually, they're upstairs. Behind that set of louvered door in the hallway across from your bedroom. Everything's there, just help yourself."

"Oh, okay." He shrugged and grinned again. "Didn't need to come down here at all, I guess."

And with that, he turned and walked out of the room. I stared after his bare behind; the thong's black bow jiggled above his crack.

"Good gracious," Hattie said.

I turned to her, embarrassed and angry. "Can you believe he actually came down here like that? I mean—" I fumbled for words. "Who does that? What kind of person walks around in front of strangers only wearing thong underwear with skulls on them?"

Hattie shook her head, but a smile danced on her mouth.

"I'm glad you can see something funny in it," I said, "because I can't."

"Oh, Zoe. He's young. Young men and stupidity go hand in hand, I'm afraid. Don't let it bother you, dear."

I took a deep breath. She was right. He was young and good-looking and full of himself. I should dismiss it, but as I gathered the items I wanted to take to Red Leaf—a snack bar for the road and my coffee travel cup—I couldn't shake off the image of Seth's expression in his eyes when he looked at me; an expression that was intimate and teasing; the expression of a man coming on to me.

"Zoe," Hattie said. "Let it go. It was nothing."

She'd come beside me, circled her arm around my waist.

I looked down at her and planted a kiss on her forehead.

"You're right," I said. "I'm being silly."

I grabbed the paper grocery bag filled with the food I'd prepared for my father: homemade soup and rolls from Linderman's bakery. With a kiss to Hattie's heaven-scented cheek, I said good-bye.

The frosty air chilled the inside of my nose and sobered my over-active imagination. I trotted down the back steps and crossed the yard to the garage. Despite the frigid day, my Volvo responded immediately when I turned the key, and the heater roared to life. The CD player blared with the last disk I'd been playing when I'd driven to the grocery store yesterday: Jann Arden's soul-filled voice and no-frills songs. I backed out of the driveway onto Universe and headed to the ramp for I-88 West, toward the heart of Illinois. Singing along, I let my emotions weave into the music. After I'd gotten on the interstate, I stopped Jann long enough to call information and then the Sheraton for our reservations. Two hours later, I reached the Dixon exit.

Turning off the freeway, I felt like I'd finally cut the urban umbilical cord that tethered me to Chicago. The vista opened: brown fallow prairie pressed flat under the gray ceiling of clouds. I blew out a sigh that released some of the knots in my shoulders. My fingers found the scrunchy at the base of my ponytail and I yanked it free. Shaking my head, I smoothed my hands through the black strips. Better now. Better at least for a while.

My sense of release lasted for about fifteen minutes, until I crossed the river and reached the Penrose town limits. On the other side of Penrose, and another fifteen miles northwest on the blacktop, and then I'd be home.

My stomach knotted.

I'd asked Dad to spend Thanksgiving with us last week, but as I expected, he'd declined; he'd made plans to go to our neighbors, the Ingrams, for dinner. Today, I'd ask him to spend part of the Christmas holidays with us. I predicted he wouldn't accept that invitation either. Were we doomed forever to play this awkward game? I didn't want to, but he seemed determined to keep this wall between us that he'd built since Mom's death. It hurt. And more than once in the last three years I'd been tempted to reduce our relationship to a Christmas card and a couple of phone calls a year. I had several friends who'd shared with me about their minimal family contact: a few times a year, for a few minutes, and the obligation of blood ties was fulfilled.

I didn't want to resort to that. Our relationship would never be what it once was, but I wanted to make it better than it was now. My father claimed a unique place in my life; other than two distant aunts and uncles, he was my only living family member. Today would be an effort—a monumental grind to look past the blame he held in his eyes and talk past the awkwardness between us.

But I'd try. For Mom's sake, I'd try.

Even though she had been dead for three years, I felt the pulse of grief for my mother inside my chest—always. But each time I visited, the old farmhouse seemed to have the power to lessen rather than magnify my loss. On my first visit home after Mom died, I was terrified. What if the sight of Mom's belongings, the smells of home overpowered me, forced me to the floor, doubled over with grief? What a welcome surprise to instead feel my mother's presence like a loving stoke across my fevered forehead. I was relieved and comforted. If it wasn't for Dad, I'd have gone home every weekend.

The sign on the county highway told me to slow to 45 and I passed another marker, a square board painted white with black lettering, much of it chipped and faded: Fellsburg, Illinois, population 576, established 1878. A few miles more and I turned down the dirt road to my right.

The fields of our farm, Red Leaf, surrounded me, fields that Dad now leased to a tenant. The house, the barn and sheds sat on three acres at the end of the road. A white wooden sign with black letters was mounted on double poles: Red Leaf Farm, Harwood and Rella Trueblood, owners. I pulled into the drive in front of the two story farm house that had belonged to my mother's parents and turned off the ignition. Two emotions fought for dominance: quiet pleasure at the sight of my mother's house and bitter dread at the thought of seeing my father. I steeled myself to go inside.

The screen door slammed behind me, my boots echoed across the wooden porch, and I knocked on the front door. I twisted the knob and leaned in.

"Dad?"

He answered from a distance. "In the kitchen."

I shut the door behind me and walked across the dining room, its ancient boards groaning beneath my steps. I entered the kitchen and found him standing at the stove, stirring a pot of something.

He wore an old flannel shirt, soft and faded with age. His glasses had slid down his nose and rested on its bulbous end. I knew when he looked at me the frown lines in his face would be deep and unmovable and would stay that way even when he smiled. The wrinkles and creases spoke of a face who'd seen a lot in life: war, death, torture. He'd been in a North Vietnamese prison camp for over a year, an experience he never referred to, ever. Over the years, I'd formed the opinion that the imprisonment had etched the lines in his face, told the world life was serious business; none of this finding of self, searching for meaning.

He looked at me, but kept stirring as I sat the grocery bag on the kitchen table.

"What you got there?" He spoke in the slow gravel I'd always known, untouched by his seventy-six years.

"Some homemade soup. Frozen. I made it last week. And some rolls from Linderman's."

"I wish I would have known. I'm heating canned soup now. But you never were one for communicating all that much." He looked down into the pot.

I restrained a sigh. There was nothing new in an accusation like that, offhand and hurtful. Let it go, I told myself.

"What kind of soup are you heating?" I said.

"Tomato. Want some?"

"Sure. Sounds good. I'll put this other in the freezer."

I shrugged off my jacket and hung it on the back of the kitchen chair.

"Hang that out on the coat rack, will you Zoe? I know clutter doesn't bother you, but it does me."

A needle of hurt pierced my stomach, but I took up the coat and walked back out to the dining room to the coat rack. Don't take it personally, I thought. What was the big deal if he wants his house a particular way?

I walked back into the kitchen and started unloading the grocery sack. "The traffic coming out of Chicago was awful."

"Well, I guess that's what you get for wanting to move there in the first place."

I placed the rolls and butter on the table. Silently.

"Soup's ready," he said. "Get the bowls down, would you?"

We sat across from each other at the old speckled Formica table and ate the soup. Dad finished his by tipping his bowl up to drink from the rim, and I smiled. Small remembered habits.

I split the last roll, buttered it and stuffed it into my mouth.

Behind thick lenses, Dad watched me. He finally spoke after I'd swallowed.

"Too bad we don't have some of your mom's pickles. Those hot sweet ones. They go good with tomato soup."

"They went well with about anything. I should make those for us, Dad. I know the recipe. Matter of fact, I have it at home. I'll make some and bring them down the next time."

He sat silent for a moment, staring at the freckles in the Formica, then he cleared his throat, leaned back in his seat and stiffened his arms in front of him resting his palms on the table: Facts laid out, hard and fast.

"I may not be here the next time."

If Cal or Mom had said something like that, I would have joked and teased: "Where will you be? Taking the Grand Tour of Europe? Riding with a tribe of Bedouin warriors? Having tea at the Ritz?"

But with Dad, the age spots and protruding veins on the tops of his hands became my silent focus. Finally, I met his level blue eyes.

"I'm selling the farm, Zoe. Already made the deal. Angus Lohan's taking it, all of it and for a damn fine price."

I relaxed my tight shoulders. This was expected. I thought he might wait until the spring to sell, but I knew he was seriously considering it. He'd mentioned it several times since Mom's death. A thousand acre farm was something a man of seventy-six couldn't manage like he did when he was forty. Handling the leases was bad enough, much less the taxes, government compliance, all the intricacies of running a medium-sized company.

I nodded at him. "Well I'm not surprised, Dad. I figured you'd sell one of these days, although I hate to see it. But Cal and I have no desire to go into the farming business, so I knew it'd come."

He took a deep breath and blew it out letting his eyes drift away from mine.

"Don't blame you. Only a gambling fool who loves bureaucrats would take up farming now days."

"So this is good, Dad. You'll have enough money to live here just fine. Maybe you'd even travel a little. See Europe. You and Mom had always wanted to do that."

"Oh, I don't know." He got his eyes back to mine again, as solid and steady and card-laying as before. He crossed his arms across his chest. "Something else. I'm selling the house, too."

The air left my lungs for a minute, but then I thought maybe I hadn't understood. "You don't mean selling this house?"

He snorted a laugh. "What other house you think I own?"

"But—why? Why would you sell the house? With the sale of the land, you won't need the money."

"Got nothing to do with money. Got everything to do with getting out of this part of the country."

"I don't understand."

He stood up, stretched his shoulders back for a moment, took up his bowl and glass then lumbered to the sink. The dishes clattered when he set them down, and he turned toward me.

The light caught his glasses turning his eyes to opaque glistening circles.

"Don't want to live here anymore. Movin' to Arizona. Get a place down there. Relax and enjoy life."

The volume of this statement dared me to challenge it, but I kept my tone neutral.

"That's good, Dad. I knew you were looking into that, although I didn't think you were that serious about doing it this soon. But it's good. And you don't need to sell the house to buy a place in Arizona. Like I said, with what you get for the land, you'll have plenty of money."

He started to pace. "Don't you understand? I got to get out of here." He stopped at the kitchen window and looked at the black bare limbs of the oak. "Got to get away from the place where it happened."

Where it happened. Where Mom had died. Where I'd done what I'd done.

I closed my eyes and the memory formed inside me, a frozen vision of Mom lying in her bed, dying.

I turned my gaze away from him. The hot water pipe groaned, and I heard the clink of dishes as my father washed them in the porcelain sink.

And I remembered my mother . . .

She had assumed at first that she was growing weak with age, an absence of the right kind of exercise. So she enrolled in a senior fitness class at the Y in Dixon and lifted her legs and held her arms out at her side and circled them forward and backward and three times a week broke into a mild sweat from exercise. But then baking pans started clattering to the floor as she lifted them from the cupboard. Dishes broke in the soapy sink, rapped against the porcelain with a spasm of her hand. One evening when I'd come to visit for the weekend, she staggered through the hallway and fell face-first onto the living room rug. My mother, who never drank alcohol except for a thimble of sherry at Christmas dinner, reeled like a drunk. When I went to help her stand again, I saw tears cascading down her cheeks. The amyotrophic lateral sclerosis had staked its claim: my mother's body.

"Oh Lord, honey," she'd said. "I didn't want you to see that. Lord, I didn't."

I helped her to the sofa, sat beside her holding her close while my mother told me she was dying. The muscles in her body were dissolving—losing themselves, changing from solid matter into, into what? Vapor? Water? The doctors didn't know. Mom and Dad had even traveled to Chicago to see specialists, then on to Rochester to Mayo Clinic, and had never told me.

We cried together, then she paused. "I know you've got your career, Zoe," Mom said, "but you have no one to take care of you." My mouth opened to protest, but she cut me off. "I know, I know. You don't need anyone to take care of you. You're a great strong liberated woman who can care for herself. But, oh honey, if I could wish one thing for my girl, I'd wish you'd be married with a family. I could die happy if I knew you'd be married with a family."

"Mom, you're not going to die. You're not. We'll go to New York, Boston, anywhere. We'll find the best doctors. We'll get you well."

But Mom was already shaking her head, resigned. "I'd just like to see you settled, Zoe. Settled and loved."

The months went on, and my mother's disease ripped through our lives. I gave up most of my clients and moved back home to take care of her. And before her muscles ebbed from existence, I granted her wish.

Five days after Cal and I were married, she died—with my help. I'd done the right thing, I knew, but I desperately missed her. I sobbed for days until it hit me one morning while splashing cold water on my swollen eyes, that Rella Trueblood had died happy. I was married. Settled. Cared for. Loved. Two months later, I got pregnant, a few weeks after that, I miscarried.

Dad watched me, his expression detached and aloof.

"I already made the decision, Zoe."

I stood and leaned on the back of the chair. "I wish you would have talked to me first. I assumed the house would come to me. Mom wanted me to have it."

"Who's gonna care for it? I'm leaving, I tell ya."

"Fine. Leave. But I can care for this house. I want it. It's been in Mom's family for three generations. I only live a couple of hours away, Dad. It's not like I wouldn't ever come here. And it's all I have left of Mom."

He spoke, and the creases in his face turned as hard as the bedrock beneath my mother's house. "Rella's dead. You know that better than anybody. She's dead and the house should be dead too."

"Maybe for you. But not for me. I just wish you wouldn't have sold it, Dad. Can we undo it? I'll buy the house. Cal and I will."

"No! Goddamn it. It's done." He threw down the dishtowel he'd been using and strode from the kitchen. His work boots clomped away from me; I bolted after him and caught his arm.

"It can be undone, Dad. I want the house."

"It can't be undone. Lohan wants the house and property. It's part of the deal."

"Well then we'll renegotiate. We'll talk to him. He has the reputation of being a fair man. We'll—"

"Zoe. There isn't going to be any renegotiating. It's done."

"Why are you doing this? Why won't you let me have it?"

But he just stared at me.

63

I trembled with rage.

"It's done." He turned and strode from the room.

I glared at his retreating back and muttered under my breath. "Happy birthday, Dad."

I grabbed my coat and purse and fled my mother's house.

Chapter Five

The classic refrain of injustice raged through me: How could my father do this to me?

His selling the house was aimed directly at me, no question. There was no logic to his decision; he didn't need the money. After the sale of the farm, he'd be set for life. If he didn't want the house, why not just leave it to crumble to the ground in neglect? Why would he care if I had it? I knew the answer. He wanted to punish me—punish me for what he thought of as killing his wife.

That night at home, while Cal and Seth were camping in the Dells, I grappled with my bedcovers and my nightmares. I finally slept, but woke with my emotions sharp and sensitive, like they'd been filed to a rough edge. The view from my window revealed another pewter sky refusing to release its snow.

I made the bed then showered. Rubbing the towel through my hair, I leaned closer to the vanity mirror. A damp cloud of hair feathered around my face; I smoothed down the middle with my palms creating a part on the top of my head. Shifting to let the light shine on my scalp, I searched.

Good. Still only the few gray threads at the crown. Between the tumultuous visit with my father yesterday, Cal's ego-ridden son plunking down into the middle of our lives, plus my ever-expanding middle, I was surprised I hadn't sprouted silver tufts the size of rooster tails.

I dried my hair and gathered it into a ponytail at the base of my skull, being careful to brush the hair over my crown and the gray filament that lived there. A velvet scrunchie corralled the shiny mass. I pulled on elastic-waist jeans and wrestled an unattractively bulky but warm cable-knit sweater over my head. Red Christmas socks, thick and wooly, warmed my feet. Slipping into my clogs, I headed downstairs.

From her pallet in the corner, Goldie flopped her tail a couple of times. I bent to stroke the gold satin of her head, and she met my smile with adoring maple-sugar eyes. Dear Hattie had taken care of her; a few remaining kibbles dotted the bottom of her bowl and her water was clear and fresh.

Hattie sat at the table with her arms folded across the morning paper. A mug of coffee rested in front of her, its steam creating ghostly fingers that meandered to the ceiling. After pouring my own cup of the morning's brew and adding a plop of cream, I sat down across from her. She looked up from her reading, and after studying my face for a moment, a thin crease appeared between her gray eyebrows.

"I would say good morning to you, but it obviously is not," she said. "So what is it? Can you tell me?"

I took a deep breath and dived in.

"My father is selling my mother's house. And I don't want him to."

"Your farm? Red Leaf?"

I nodded.

She watched me for a moment, non-committal, waiting for me to go on. I pushed myself to tell her more, even though I didn't want to talk about it. I just wanted it to go away.

"He doesn't need the money. There's no reason in the world why I shouldn't have that house. He's doing it because . . ." I thought for a second about how much I wanted to tell her. "He's doing it because he holds me responsible for my mother's death."

She nodded and a knowing expression came to her face. "Yes. Of course. Responsibility."

I took another deep breath. "See, when Mom got sick—"

Her palm rose up to my face; the skin on it reminded me of onionskin paper I'd used in art school for pen and ink drawings.

"No more. You loved your mother, and her death changed the course of your life. It led to ill feelings between your father and yourself. This is all I need to know. Except for what you intend to do about it."

I laughed a little. "That's my frustration. There's not much I can do."

"Ah," she said. "A victim then."

"Well, no. I don't feel like a victim really, but—"

I stopped with a slap of realization: Hattie had pinpointed my sentiments.

Her insights had always speared to the heart of the matter, but until now, she'd helped me only with small things: a vexing client or a stubborn watercolor for the baby's room that wouldn't come to life. Whenever I'd expressed my frustration or folded into myself in pouting silence, she'd zeroed in on my feelings like a laser to its target.

Hattie either had this sixth sense about her, or she was extremely observant of nuances in people's non-verbal behavior. I'd watched her do it, admired it and tried to polish my own people-reading ability. When I'd asked her about it, she said she'd always had the skill to some degree, but had honed it during World War Two when she'd lived in Romania.

"When you live in terror," she'd said, "you miss nothing about people."

During the year she'd lived with us, she'd never explained her history, other than a comment now and then about details of her girlhood. I didn't press her. I figured she'd open to me when she wanted to.

She patted my arm with her own knotted hand, and I looked into eyes that I figured had seen the jagged bottom of deeper pits than I'd ever dreamed of.

"Now that I think about it," I said, "I guess I do feel like I'm a victim. I feel like Dad has me under his thumb and there's nothing I can do about it."

"And is that true? That there's nothing you can do about it?"

"Short of buying the house myself from Angus Lohan, that's the man Dad's sold the property to, there's nothing I can do."

"And of course that would be impossible, yes?"

I watched the crinkles deepen around her eyes; I felt a smile start in my chest and spread to my lips.

"I suppose," I said, "there's really no reason why I couldn't do that. If Cal would agree, and I think he would."

She beamed, pressing her face into a web of wrinkles.

A black thought marched through me. "Dad is doing this to me on purpose, though. That's what kills me. And even buying back the house wouldn't change that."

"But your father's heart and your ownership of the house are two different things, are they not? If your father decided today to give the house to you, would you expect that his feelings had changed?"

"I'd hope they had," I murmured.

"That is your hope. But what would you expect?"

I sighed. "No, I wouldn't expect him to change."

"Then if you are powerless to change his feelings, the only thing you can do is take care of yourself. Yes?"

I smiled. "Yes." My emotions swirled and swayed from hope-less anger to buoyant optimism. "I'll talk to Cal, but I'm sure he'll be fine with it." The knot in my throat had disappeared.

I called Angus Lohan immediately and told him that pending my husband's agreement, I'd like to buy my mother's house from him after he bought it from Dad. He agreed to keep my request confidential. His lack of surprise left me feeling as if I was the last one in the county to know about my father's plans to sell the farm. He promised to meet with me the following week, after he'd returned from a business trip.

I spent the day tapping away on the computer in my office finishing the ad copy on a brochure for a day spa located downtown, a small account, but one I hoped to grow. I'd redesigned their logo, updating the family-named business with bolder colors and newer graphics. Two weeks ago, I'd spent an indulgent afternoon being pampered with a free facial treatment, a sumptuous experience, so I could familiarize myself with their services. The brochure reflected my enthusiasm and I was happy with the work.

I stopped working around five to fix Hattie and myself the homemade soup and a sandwich for dinner. After we'd eaten in front of the fire on tray tables in the living room, Hattie retreated to her room to listen to the radio and to add to the luscious afghan she was knitting for the baby. I tidied the kitchen then headed back to the office loft to finish the last section of the brochure. About seven, from the transom window across from the loft, I saw the headlights turn into our drive. I raced downstairs, flung open the back door and propelled myself into my husband's arms.

He was home. I inhaled the frigid air he'd brought inside with him, a mixture of the outdoors and Cal who needed a shower; I realized I'd missed him intensely. Now, I thought, I'd get him to myself. At the thought of our own planned get-away to the city, giddy anticipation ricocheted inside my stomach.

Goldie panted and wagged her greeting while Cal clung to me as fiercely as I grasped him. Seth grinned his hello and scooted past us lugging his duffle bag upstairs to his room. My husband kissed me hard, then grinned.

"Wow. That's some welcome. And I've only been gone one night," he said.

His face shifted expressions, but only for an instant. Was his back hurting again? Certainly lying in a sleeping bag on a wooden bunk in a primitive cabin would do it no good. Wrapping my arms around his waist, I kneaded my fingers into the muscles just above that perfect rear end of his.

"Good thing you weren't gone longer," I said. I laughed and nuzzled my face in his neck. "I'd have to hunt you down and tie you up like I used to do with Biff."

I'd told him about the wandering Australian Shepherd I'd had when I was growing up. Biff had been famous all over the county. We'd get calls in the middle of the afternoon from the neighboring farm telling us they'd found Biff in their barn, once actually in the hay loft—accessed by only a rickety ladder. Once he got up there, he started howling to get down. Dad and I drove over, camera in hand, and after taking photos for proof, rescued Biff. Cal always laughed whenever I repeated the story, although I don't think he actually believed me until I found the picture that had been buried in the back of one of my mother's many family albums: proof that Biff had indeed climbed a ladder.

Cal laughed again, but the shadow I'd seen a moment ago returned.

"What's the matter?" I said. "Is it your back?" I kept my arms around him and massaged the muscles.

"No. No, it's okay." He pulled away from me. "I need to unload Seth's car," he said. "I want to re-fold the bed rolls. We packed in a hurry."

"Okay, but did you have a good time?"

He chuckled. "Oh yeah."

Whatever I'd seen in his expression was gone now. He

brushed my lips with a kiss, then turned and went out the back door. As it closed behind him, Hattie scurried into the kitchen.

"I heard Cal, didn't I?"

"Yes. He'll be back in a minute. He went to unpack the car. Let's make some popcorn and hot chocolate. I'll tell Seth to come on down and they can regale us with their adventures."

Thirty minutes later, the four of us huddled around the kitchen table with hot chocolate and a bowl of popcorn. Hattie and I laughed at their tales of sputtering campfires and attacks by phantom bears. To hear them speak of it, they endured nothing short of the traumas straight from one of Seth's favorite movies, *The Edge*. Seth would start telling an episode, then Cal would finish it, and visa versa; repeating their adventure bonded them as much as living it had.

During the course of the entertainment, I rested back in my chair and watched my husband's animated face. It'd been years, a lifetime, since I'd seen him like that. I couldn't wait for our private time together, for our trip to the city.

He threw back his head and guffawed with his mouth open. His throat, strong and masculine and shadowed by his day-old stubble, was exposed to me. A tender piece of my heart, born when he'd accepted my proposal of marriage, throbbed again.

Cal and I had met during one of my weekends in Chicago. My friend Sabrina had dragged me to a party hoping to divert my attention for forty-eight hours from my mother's perennial onslaught from ALS. I'd met the amazing Dr. Sterling, and we'd made one of those quick connections of people who recognized that out of everyone in the room, they were the two who should to be together. We'd escaped from the pulsing music and slurring guests and ended up walking along Lake Shore until the sunrise lit the sky with daring orange. That dawn foretold our relationship: unexpected and bold.

We'd been dating for about three weeks, and I was back at

Red Leaf with Mom when she went through several bad days in a row—days that slid quivering blades of dread through my stomach. Her ability to swallow had drastically diminished, and for the first time since her diagnosis, I witnessed the full scope of the horrid disease. My boyfriend, Dr. Cal Sterling, drove down to the farm for one evening, held my hands in his and told me she was dying and nothing would stop it.

The following weekend, Mom had stabilized somewhat. Dad was with her, and he certainly could care for her, so I traveled back to Chicago to escape the specter of my mother's death for a couple of days. Cal and I ate dinner in the restaurant at the top of the Hancock Building and then settled in for a drink in the Signature Lounge. We'd found a loveseat tucked away in a corner. The lights of Chicago acted as the backdrop, the music was soft, the décor plush. I figured it was the perfect moment.

He'd taken one sip of his after-dinner brandy when I did what until that moment I'd only toyed about doing: I popped the question. After he stopped choking, he placed the snifter on the glass and brass table in front of us and stared at me. But he surprised me: Instead of leaning forward to grasp my hands in his own and gaze at me with adoring dark eyes, he laughed.

"Poor Zoe," he teased. "You need a man to marry, and I'm the only one in target range."

We'd been dating only four weeks, less than thirty days. I giggled.

"Stop," I punched him in the arm. "You know I love you. You know we'll be married anyway. Why not make it now?"

His eyes brimmed with affection and, if I'd been honest with myself, a flicker of pity. He knew why I was pushing things: my mother was dying. If I wasn't married soon, she'd never live to see her hope for me fulfilled.

"I suppose," he said, "if I'm going to ever get married again, now's the time."

He'd already told me about his fleeting relationship with Seth's mother, and he'd also told me he'd tried marriage at thirty. It had lasted for three childless years.

"I love you," he said. "You know that. And I hate that you have to watch your mom go through this. If getting married now will make things better, let's do it."

A warning tingled in my chest.

"I don't want you to marry me because you feel sorry for me. I just thought that since we know this is it, why not do it now?"

And we did know this was "it." Beginning on our second date, we'd talked about other people who we'd known or heard of that whirled through courtships, married quickly and stayed married for decades. I wanted it to be like that with us. I didn't want pity to be a part of it. Before I could reiterate what I meant, he said something that would later come to define our lives.

"I'm not marrying you because I feel sorry for you," he'd said. "But—and this is a big 'but'—you must know how important my work is. My ex-wife couldn't take my career. She couldn't take the long hours." His eyes leveled with mine. "Can you understand about my career, Zoe? If you can hack it, then great. But I want you to be very honest with yourself."

I kissed him in response. I'm not sure I really took his words inside of me, let them drill their way into my thoughts. I wasn't focused on my brain; I was thinking with my heart.

I knew he loved me. I knew I loved him. I knew we were strong and could work out anything we wanted to work out.

I got to get married in front of my mother, her sick tears streaming through the hollows of her cheeks, granting her one wish for my happiness. And Cal got a wife to attend functions with and maintain a home for him to retreat to after his long hours. And of course, there was love.

But that was three years ago. And in those years I'd learned I had to fight for position in my husband's life. I knew when I married him I might take second place—although, I now admitted to myself while sitting at the kitchen table with him and Seth and Hattie, I didn't think it would be this distant a second place. I thought it might be more of a photo finish.

With my sides aching from laughter, I cleared the dishes. Hattie had returned to her room and Seth had gone upstairs to take a shower. Cal lingered at the table for a moment. His fingers drummed as he watched me wipe out the wooden bowl we used for popcorn and stow it in the cabinet above the oven.

"I'm going to take a shower in a minute," he said. "You're not going to bed for awhile yet, are you?"

"No." I glanced at the clock on the stove. "It's only nine-thirty. Why? Did you want to go out for a wild night on the town?"

I grinned and moved to stand in front of his chair. He rested one hand on my hip and leaned his head back to look at me. I smiled down on him and my fingers combed through his loose short waves. He gave his head a shake to push my hand away.

"Sorry," I said. My feelings were hurt at his gentle rebuff.

He grabbed my hand and looked up at me again.

"Naw," he said. "It's me. I'm just all grungy and nasty. You don't want to get your hands in that." He grinned at me. "I'll go upstairs and shower, then let's talk for awhile, okay?"

Some kind of warning ruffled inside me, and I examined the expression on his face. Innocent dark eyes looked back at me, but his open expression did nothing to quell the unease. For Cal to ask for time alone to talk was unusual. Matter of fact, I couldn't immediately recall when he'd done that before. I studied him again.

Maybe I'd imagined the nip of foreboding. My hormones on the rampage again, no doubt.

"Sure," I said. "I'll finish up here and let Goldie out then meet you in the living room."

He stood and pushed his chair into place. With a brief smile and a light kiss on my lips, he headed out of the kitchen.

Goldie rushed back inside and I closed the door behind her sealing out the raw dark night. The tags on her collar jingled as she shook out the cold; she plopped herself on her pallet and curled into her own warmth. Booted footsteps sounded in the hallway and Seth strutted into the kitchen.

"I'm out of here," he said.

I asked him if he needed any directions or help.

"No, thanks," he said. He slung his jacket around his shoulders and pushed his arms through the sleeves. "I'm cool. Guy I used to know in high school lives over in Wheaton. We're going to meet and have a couple of drinks. He told me how to get there, place called the Ninth Hour, and I'll call him if I get lost." He held up his cell phone for me to see. "See ya."

"Wait," I called.

I was interested in hearing more about his friend—I wondered what a friend of Seth's would be like—but he was obviously in a hurry to leave. The hand he'd placed on the door knob stopped its turn.

"What time will you get home?" I said. "I mean, I'm not trying to keep tabs on you or anything, I just don't like leaving the door unlocked after we go to bed. Maybe I should loan you a key."

He patted his jeans pocket. "Already got one. Cal had a copy made for me on our way up to the Dells. Told me I wouldn't have to worry about bothering you with my comings and goings."

Cal hadn't said anything to me about it. I thought back to our conversation after Seth came, about how Cal wanted him to stay here for several weeks and then over Christmas. He must be planning on my saying yes to his idea. It rankled me a little, the assumption he could persuade me to do things his way, but I didn't want to address that with Seth. I'd talk to Cal about it later.

"Is that all right?" Seth said. "Me having a key?"

My consternation must have shown on my face.

"Sure, fine," I said. "I guess you're set then. See you tomorrow."

He grinned and stuffed the cell phone into his jeans pocket. His slick good looks would open the doors of Chicago nightlife for him. Freshly showered, with his disheveled curls, the dark stubble coating his jaw, the blink of a diamond stud in his left ear—he would have no trouble attracting women. He lifted his hand in a wave, opened the back door admitting a cold gust, then went out into the night.

I crossed to the back door, turned the bolt and flipped on the porch light. That would help him to at least find the keyhole.

Chapter Six

Cal's stocking-muffled footsteps thudded down the staircase. He crossed the living room to where I sat waiting on the sofa. I lifted my head and he set a soft kiss on my lips. The scent of his soap, crisp and clean, drifted around him, and I patted the place next to me. He settled in with a sigh; my fingers caressed the damp edges of his hair, and I arranged dark curls on the nape of his neck.

He let me do that for a moment, then turned to watch my face. The fire in the grate cheerfully snapped, but between us, an ominous silence had descended like a fog blown in from a bleak sea. I dropped my hand. His manner—the slump of his shoulders and the way his mouth dipped down on the right corner—told me to get ready. Dread bubbled up from my stomach.

"When Seth and I were driving back from the Dells," Cal said, "I got a call from the Mechin people. I have to go to Uganda, Zoe, and I have to go Monday. In three days."

"But I thought you weren't going until the spring."

"Things changed. It has to be now."

"But for how long?"

"I don't know. I'll come back home for the holidays, stay here for a few weeks before . . ." His eyes moved away for a beat, then back to mine.

"Before what?" I said.

"Before I go back. They want me to direct the clinics personally," he said. "Hands on direction."

"Hands on? What does that mean?"

"It means that they want me there all the time. To live there and manage the clinics."

Live there? Move to Uganda?

He said something, but I missed it. I fumbled for words. "What did you say?"

Impatience flicked across his face. "You're not making this any easier, you know." He took a deep breath then blew out. "I said the Mechin people were very excited about me making the move. They asked me to go over there as soon as I could. They think under my direction, the clinics will avoid a lot of start-up problems."

"What did you tell them?"

His incredulous expression told me the answer even before he spoke. "I told them yes, of course."

A shard of anger slipped into my chest and twisted. "You told them yes? You told them you'd move to Uganda? Africa? Just like that? Without discussing it with me?"

"Karl Mechin called me personally. You know how he is: he expects one hundred percent commitment. Zoe, I couldn't just tell him that I had to ask my wife. I mean, I'm the one who's spearheaded the whole project. Of course I'd take the opportunity to see it through. I mean . . ." He snorted an incredulous laugh. "There's no question."

I swallowed, but it didn't help. My voice came in a choked whisper. "But what are they talking about? I mean, how long do they think this will take?"

"Year, maybe two."

"A year or two. In Africa." I shook my head. "I can't believe this. You should have discussed it with me, Cal."

He watched me in silence until a burning log shifted and flared in the grate sending a cascade of sparks up the chimney. I stared at the smoke as images I'd in seen photographs reeled through my mind: tribal people huddled together in the refugee camps, their stomachs swollen with hunger, flies crawling across the dark faces of children. A mother's desperate look into the camera.

Stop it, I scolded myself. Those images were not the reality for many parts of the continent. There were cities and businesses and theatres and art galleries and people raising their families like they do anywhere in the world.

But to live there. To have my baby in a hospital in Uganda. To raise my child in Africa.

I turned toward Cal; he was studying the floor, his expression inscrutable. The few feet that separated us felt as wide as the Atlantic Ocean. His eyes scooted to mine for a moment then away, and his jaw tightened in determination.

"It's important work, Zoe. Important work I need to do."

"I know that, Cal." I sighed, exhausted by the task that loomed before me. "But it's a huge move. And we haven't even talked about Hattie. How all that will work." I shook my head again, trying to get my thoughts in order. "I just can't envision how we'll live, where we'll live."

He blinked at me, and I shifted my gaze to the area rug under the coffee table. Would we live in Kampala? But Cal's commute to the remote clinics scattered in the countryside would be difficult. He'd be in and out of our home, probably several days on the road, then back for only a brief time. A vision flashed through my mind of him walking through a doorway, kissing me lightly on the cheek, then leaving again.

"Actually," I said, "the position is probably more suited to a single man than one who will come home every weekend to a wife and child."

"Come home every weekend? I can't come home every weekend. I'll be on the other side of the world."

"What?" I said.

He shook his head and smiled at me as if I was a poor dense child. "Zoe, honey, you can't come with me."

My thoughts braked for an instant, then a gush of comprehension. Ah, yes. Of course. I was not included. The baby was not included. He was talking about a separation. For at least a year, maybe two.

Blood swished in my ears in time with my heartbeat. Like flailing for a lifesaver tossed over the side of a retreating ship, I clutched for the words to persuade him to see reason.

"What are you saying?" I said. "You're talking about living apart. You're talking about me and the baby being here and you being half way across the world. I don't want to do that."

"I don't like it either, sweetheart, but that's the way it has to be. Uganda is no place for you and the baby."

"Of course it's a place for me and the baby. There are women and babies all over the world."

One side of his mouth tilted up in a smirk, and his frown line creased his brow.

"Don't be ridiculous," he said.

"Why is that ridiculous? From what I've read, what you showed me when this all started, Kampala is a beautiful cosmopolitan city, very Westernized. Or there's Entebbe and Jinja. I'm sure there are a lot of people who'd be like me, living in the cities and seeing their husbands and wives on the weekends, or whenever they can find time."

"Zoe—"

"I mean, if not that, just what did you envision for us? For me and the baby?" My voice sounded hoarse and pitched with panic, and a gush of nausea ripped through me again. I pressed my hand to my stomach.

"Zoe, I don't know where you've gotten this fantasy, but it is a fantasy. And even if you lived there, I wouldn't be coming home on weekends, as you put it. I'm the director of the clinics. They're hundreds of miles apart. I'll be traveling in a private plane most of the time, and it won't be in first class. We have a cargo plane to haul medical supplies and equipment, one pilot and one doctor. There's even some talk of me getting my pilot's license so the foundation wouldn't have to employ a pilot. The point is, this is a lifestyle, not a new job that I've been offered where we can sell the house, pack up and move so you can find a junior league to join."

My queasiness hardened to anger and galvanized me to my feet. "How dare you. How dare you patronize me like that. I know full well the importance and the impact of your work and as you well know, I don't have any desire to join a junior league. That was insulting, Cal."

"All right, all right. I'm sorry. But you know how I feel about this. I've always told you my career comes first. And now it's come to the test, and you want to pretend like you didn't know that priority."

"I knew there would be sacrifices yes, and I was prepared, am still prepared for that. But I am not prepared to live apart from my husband for a year or two of our married life. I'm not prepared for our child to have a father who lives on another continent. If I'd married a career military man, I would have expected it, but not a doctor."

"It's not the money I'm after, Zoe, although the pay is great. It's the important work."

Acid was in my eyes, burned in my throat. "And the glory."

I muttered it under my breath, but he heard me. His jaw worked, chewed on the words he'd like to say. In the end, he swallowed them. Maybe because he knew I was right: he'd like the money, he'd like establishing the clinics, but most of all, he'd revel in the glory and recognition from the medical community.

Ego. It was all about ego and he knew I knew it.

"I told you this before we got married." Anger had hardened his voice. "I told you then that I wasn't sure that marriage and my career could mutually survive. I don't know why this is such a big surprise. You said then that you knew the sacrifice of my career, but you could live with it, as long as we got married. You were in such an all-fired hurry to get married before your mother . . ."

He stopped, and I stared at him numb and silent. Finally, I slumped back onto the sofa, closed my eyes hoping the whole thing would just go away.

Mom, oh Mom. Help me. What should I do? Please, I silently begged the cosmos, the angels, God and my mother's spirit: Help me.

I turned my eyes to the black window behind the sofa. The wooden slats of the blinds were still open; I'd been so pre-occupied with Cal coming home from the Dells, I'd forgotten to close them. It seemed like a century ago. I stood now and staggered to the side of the window. A couple of lights from some of the neighbor's houses showed beyond the dark panes. All those people, with their lives going on, their own lives and their own problems, but families that lived together, maybe not every minute, but at least in the same country.

I closed the blinds with a clack, shutting out the world, and sudden bitter loneliness seared my throat. I scanned the living room, the room I had so many plans for, a room that should make me feel cozy and warm and safe, but that now, despite the fire cracking in the fireplace, felt like an empty cavern.

I sat down again in my original place, folded my hands in my lap and repeated the question I'd asked a moment before.

"So what did you envision for us? For our family?"

He stood, walked around the end of the coffee table and stopped in front of the fireplace. Turning his back to the heat, he shoved his hands into his jeans pockets and watched me. The slumped shoulders were gone; his body was square and straight, the posture of a man on a mission.

"I envisioned that you'd stay here with the baby. The pay is good, you can either work after the baby's born or not. You'll be fine."

He sounded so matter-of-fact, so oblivious to how his decision would impact us.

My own anger surged upward from my center. "Cal," I said. "I don't know how someone as smart as you can be so goddamn stupid."

He blinked at me a few times and his mouth sagged open with his shock. I seldom used such strong language. His amazement spurred me on, and I bolted to my feet.

"You announce, without any consultation with me at all, that you've decided to make this huge career move and then have the nerve to tell me that you expect me to stay here in Chicago, raise the baby by myself, and oh gee, Zoe dear, you'll be just fine and dandy."

My hands balled into fists at my side and I marched around the coffee table to stand in front of him. I shoved my nose an inch from his face and let him hear my raw disgust.

"What the hell are you thinking?"

He shook his head a little and found his speech.

"I'm thinking of my career."

"And only of your career. But what about us, Cal? What about our relationship?"

"Like I said, I figured you and the baby would stay here and—"

"You're talking about logistics, not our relationship. What about what we have together? Do you honestly think a marriage can survive like that?"

"Well, you mentioned military people. Their marriages obviously survive."

"Yes, but there's a major difference: those people make a careful decision, as a couple, Cal, to endure the rigors of military separation. As I said, living away from my husband was not a program I signed on for."

Sudden tears welled in my eyes and I whirled from him to hide them. Finally, I turned to him again.

"Can't you see that if you do this, Cal, if you just up and decide that we're going to live apart it will mean our entire relationship will change? Can't you see a decision like that might very well sacrifice our marriage? And what about our child?" I clutched my stomach. "Have you completely forgotten about the baby?"

His face shifted patterns from confusion to anger and then consternation. I pressed on. "You look like this is the first time that's dawned on you."

He gave a shrug and a self-deprecating snort then looked away from me. He was mulling something over. Something I'd said had gotten to him.

"Cal, I knew how you felt about your career when we married. But I believed, I mean I assumed, you'd give equal effort to making our marriage work, being a father to the baby, as you do your career. I didn't think one would have to be sacrificed for the other. Is that what it will have to be?"

He looked at the floor, then pulled his hands from his pockets and began to twist his wedding band. Even though he wasn't watching me, I extended my arms out, appealing for his understanding.

"Is that right, Cal? Does our marriage and family have to be sacrificed so your career can survive?"

He kept his eyes on the ring and after a moment murmured his answer. "No."

"Look at me, Cal. Talk to me. You're acting like—I don't

know what. I mean, are you really that shocked I'd be so upset about this?"

Finally, he dropped his hands to his sides and met my eyes with a blank unblinking stare. "No," he said. "I'm not surprised you're upset. I guess I . . . I guess I hoped it would be easier than this."

I laughed. "You're kidding, right?"

He snorted again. "No, I'm not kidding." He shook his head. "Pretty dumb, huh?"

I hurried to him and laid my palm on his cheek. "Darling, think. I know your career is important to you, it's important to me too. But think. Please."

He turned away from me jamming his hands into his pockets again. Finally, he blew out a breath, coming to a decision. "Okay," he said. He faced me and there was a look on his face of weary resignation. "Okay. How about I go over there on Monday and while I'm there, take a look at things. Let me ask Eunice Sherson, my contact at the American Embassy, if she knows who I could contact to find out about other westerners living in Uganda. Let me find out how it is over there to live— and especially about having the baby over there—and then we'll talk about it when I come home for Christmas."

Relief swelled through me. "Yes. Yes, that would be great, Cal. And meanwhile, I'll do some research on the web. I'm sure there's all kinds of resources. We just have to find them."

I crossed to him and put my arms around his neck. I kissed him softly on his lips and he watched me. "That's all I want, Cal. For us to work this out together, not to be handed an edict."

I kissed him again. His kiss back to me was perfunctory, but when I began to pull away, he wrapped his arms around me and nuzzled his mouth into my ear.

"I don't want to let you go."

He choked through his words, and I knew my husband well enough to know it wasn't an act. I turned to face him and he bent to kiss me.

It was a hard kiss, and I clutched at it. Eventually, he pulled away and watched me with moist eyes. His face twisted as he grappled with his own emotions, fighting his own internal war: his love for me, and his demon—the snake-haired siren of ambition.

"This has been my dream for years, Zoe, you know it has. It's something I—I have to do. I can't let it pass."

Searching his face, I knew the truth of his answer. He did have to do this. Like a drug addict, he was a victim of his own obsession.

"I don't want you to let the opportunity pass, Cal. But I can be a part of it with you, the baby and I can."

He stared at me a moment then looked away. "I just had something else pictured, I guess."

"Something else? That the baby and I would be waiting for you here while you were off being brilliant?"

He shrugged and shook his head—a gesture I took to mean he was shaking off his foolishness.

He moved away from me. "I know Seth will be disappointed that I have to leave on Monday," he said. "He just got here. But, that's the price, I guess."

"Yes," I mumbled, "that's the price."

"He'll go on to California, but I'd like to fly him back here for Christmas," he said, "It'll mean a lot to me. To us."

Yes, for the holidays, he would have it all: a dream job waiting for him in Uganda and a family to tend to him at home.

Now that I knew he wouldn't leave me behind, I became aware of a raw anger festering in my stomach: He'd made one of the most important decisions in our lives without me. I was angry, but at the same time I wanted his closeness. I needed the assurance he loved me and wanted me with him. I leaned my head back and started to kiss him, to reach out for a measure of comfort, but I saw the distant expression in his eyes.

Was he thinking of the famous pilot-doctor, the world-renowned physician who healed and saved, whose fawning public held him high above their heads, their eyes raised in adoration?

The rancid skepticism of my thought told me my anger had won out. I pulled away and exhaustion again washed over me.

"I'm tired," I said. "I've got to go to bed."

He watched me for a moment, maybe measuring something, taking stock of the crossroads where we were standing.

"That's a good idea. Let's leave it for tonight," he said. "I've got a meeting at seven tomorrow morning with Dr. Hamati and Melissa, meetings all day and a dinner meeting tomorrow night."

Melissa Delany. A pebble of discomfort caught in my throat, and I cleared it, concentrated on making my voice casual. "How much is Melissa Delany involved with this project?"

He laughed. "She's the only one who knows as much about this as I do. She's up to her eyebrows."

Yes, I thought. Up to those lovely arched eyebrows.

"Will she be going to Uganda on Monday?" I said.

"No."

I tried not to exhale with relief. That would be at least one positive outcome of this move. With Cal in Uganda and Melissa in Chicago, I could close the door on a shadow, either real or a figment of my hormonal imagination, that might divide Cal and me.

Later, as I changed into my pajamas and crawled into bed beside my already-snoring husband, my determined optimism ebbed from me and my stomach rumbled with the disquiet of my intuition. He'd been so oblivious to my possible reactions, like he'd been blinded by the glare of the vision of his career

87

and everything and everyone else had sizzled into mist. He hadn't even mentioned Hattie. Or Goldie. Only the great Doctor Sterling.

I tumbled into ragged dreams.

CHAPTER SEVEN

Early the next morning, the bed jostled when Cal got up; I tucked myself back under the covers and drifted in and out of sleep. After a while, I came fully awake but kept my eyes closed and listened to him opening and closing dresser drawers. He rummaged through the closet, and his footsteps changed from the brush of carpet to the click of his shoes on the bathroom tile. I followed his routine with my ears and nose: the hiss of hairspray, the light taps on his cheeks when he applied his spicy cologne. I wasn't ignoring him like a pouting child. I would not resort to snits and cold shoulders or the silent treatment, although I remembered my mother being a master of all those techniques. I wasn't snubbing him, but the hurt I'd felt last night when he'd pronounced his decision tightened my chest again. For now, it was best if I didn't say anything to him.

Finally, after the bedroom door closed and his footsteps echoed down the hallway, I opened my eyes.

He was gone, thank God.

I dressed, and, on my way downstairs, I passed Seth's open door and glanced inside the empty room. The bedspread lay rumpled in the same manner as it had before they'd left for the Dells. The rest of the room was in the same condition it had been since his arrival: his ready laptop on the desk, shoes and boots scattered across the closet floor. His closed duffle bag took a space beside the closet, undoubtedly where he'd dropped it after he and Cal had come home from their outing. No wonder I hadn't heard him come in last night; he'd obviously spent the night out. I would check to see if his car was in the driveway when I got downstairs.

In the kitchen, Goldie rested contentedly on her pallet. I knelt down beside her and gave her a pat; she smiled in return, and I noted her food and water were taken care of. Hattie again, maybe Cal, but I didn't think so. He had bigger things on his mind than caring for his dog. Goldie had been his for the seven years before we'd been married, but now I was her main caretaker.

Hattie sat at her usual place at the kitchen table in front of the window which showed another hard sky. A surge of affection for her welled up inside me and closed my throat.

Dear Hattie. Like Goldie, I'd inherited her from Cal, but I loved her like my own. I thought again of Cal's omission of his grandmother last night while talking about his glorious plans. In my chest, anger renewed its rumble.

I kissed Hattie's cheek, wished her a good morning, and gave her a tight squeeze around her shoulders. She smiled up at me and patted my hand, returning my extra affection with her own.

I fixed my coffee then sat in the chair opposite her, my back to the room, facing the dull light in the window.

"Cal's leaving for Uganda," I said, "on Monday. This Monday, three days from now. He'll be home for Christmas, but then—well, then we have some decisions to make. The Mechin people want him to live there. Probably for a year or two. To run the clinics."

Her creased lids dropped over the ancient eyes that missed nothing, then opened to reveal some expression I couldn't read.

"Did you know about it?" I asked.

She shook her head. "Why do you ask that?"

I shrugged. "I thought maybe you did. Something in your expression, I guess." I shrugged again. "I misread it."

"It is of no concern. And maybe what you saw was unsurprise." Her eyes examined my face for a minute and she tilted her head to one side. "You smile because I use that word?"

I nodded. It occasionally happened with Hattie, that she couldn't find the right word in English that would express what she wanted to say.

"And are you?" I said. "Unsurprised?"

She pressed her mouth together and looked out the window for a moment then turned back to me.

"I love my grandson. He has given me a home in the last years of my life. But I have not known him like a mother knows her child; we have the distance of many decades between us. He's been spoiled. My son and his wife made sure Cal and Ethan both never wanted for anything. But especially Cal. Ethan was the plodder, steady and predictable. It was their younger son who sparkled with charm."

I'd never met Cal's brother. He was a teacher living in Japan, married to a Japanese woman. They were a childless couple who enjoyed traveling. I'd spoken to him a few times; he called every year to wish Cal Merry Christmas, and when Hattie moved in with us, he called to lend his moral support for the decision. Now, to hear Hattie talk about the differences between the boys and the parents who obviously favored Cal, it came as no surprise that Cal and his brother weren't close.

Hattie continued. "Cal is the most driven man I've ever seen," she said. "And unfortunately he knows nothing of understanding what is truly important. He is driven by his need to be the best."

I gave a wry chuckle. "I was just talking to him the other night about that, about setting priorities. And you're right. He simply can't do it."

Hattie was silent for a moment, then patted my arm and smiled. "Will you go with him to Uganda, or wait until after the

91

baby is born?"

"That's what the decisions will be about: how and when I'm to go to Uganda."

She nodded. "Good. It will be an adventure for you. And, it is unwise for a man to be on his own, away too long from his wife and child. Men have an ego that craves attention. If a man's wife is not there to give it to him, he will seek it elsewhere. I know this from my own husband."

"Cal's grandfather?"

"Yes. I gave my attention to raising Cal's father and my other child, Edwin, before he died."

"I didn't know you lost a child. How did it happen?"

"By drowning. In our bathtub when he was only a year old."

I clasped my hand across my open mouth. "I'm so sorry, Hattie," I whispered. "I didn't know."

Her eyes clouded for a moment but other than that her face didn't change expression. "I left him there, in the water, while I went to take a simmering pot off the stove. I never forgave myself. After that, I devoted all my energy to being a good mother and I neglected my husband. He had many lovers over the years."

I collapsed back into the chair.

With a half smile, she examined my face. "You are surprised I confess this to you?"

"No. No, I'm just so sorry is all."

"When I learned of my husband's first infidelity, I was as appalled as you look now. It cut me to my core of being."

"But, you stayed with him."

"Oh, yes. In those days, a woman had few choices. I could stay with him and be cared for, along with my son, or I could leave and scrape by somehow."

"But could you ever get over it? His cheating?"

"Let me put it this way: I could get over it because years

before, he'd saved me and that was something I could never repay. But after Edwin's death, I withdrew from him. I was filled with hardness in those years. Hardness against myself and against one other person—not him, someone else. I deserved what I got."

I was on the verge of asking her more when a car's engine revved then stopped at the side of the house. I tore my eyes away from Hattie's face and craned to look out the window. I'd forgotten to check if Seth's car had been in the driveway, and I saw now it wasn't, but a white car, small and nondescript, had pulled to where he usually parked. The driver's door opened and Seth climbed out. He trotted up the walkway to the house, clumped up the steps and threw open the door. Sharp cold blasted through the threshold then the door shut with a rattle behind him. Goldie stood to sniff him, then waited at the door. I opened it again to let her out.

"Christ," he said, "that's cold out there."

He shrugged off his jacket and hung it on a hook beside the door.

"Good morning, Seth," Hattie said. "You must have been out early."

"Yeah," he said.

He tramped over to the coffee pot and filled a mug that he took from the cabinet above the counter. While he was adding copious amounts of sugar and cream, I let Goldie back inside. Through the kitchen window, I examined the car sitting in our driveway.

"Whose car is that?" I said.

He glanced behind his shoulder to look at me, then turned back to his stirring.

"It's a loaner. I had to leave mine at the garage."

He placed the spoon in the bottom of the stainless sink and ambled toward the table, being careful not to spill the hot contents of his cup. He stood in front of me, lifted the mug to his lips, blew, then slurped.

"Why did you have to leave your car at the garage?" I said.

He slurped again. "Aw. I wrecked mine last night. Had to have it towed."

"Wr-Wrecked it?" I sputtered. "How? Are you all right?"

He shifted his weight a little and his mouth lifted up on one side in a grimace of disgust.

"Yeah, I'm fine. It was just bullsh—"

He caught himself and looked at Hattie who watched him with her usual calm acceptance of events.

"Sorry," he said. "It was just such a bad deal. See, Jason and I had just left this place, Outrage, it was called, and this guy just plows into my right front fender."

"Jason's your high school friend you told me about?" I said.

He nodded.

"I thought you were going to someplace called the Ninth Hour," I said.

"Yeah, we did. This was after that. And I was pulling out onto Hubbard, you know, north of the river?"

I'd been there, but wasn't very familiar with the area. I nodded.

"Yeah, so, I pulled out and this guy just rams me. Big time. Jason was behind me. He saw the whole thing. I told the cop that too, but he didn't even want to talk to Jason. Just had his own sweet-ass mind made up and slapped me with a ticket. Gave me a breathalyzer, but I passed." He snorted a laugh. "Ruined his night, I'm sure."

"Well that's good, at least," I said. "But a ticket. That's a shame, Seth. That'll be expensive."

He shrugged. "Jason says he knows this lawyer that for a couple of hundred can get me off. I might go talk to the guy. But the whole deal is just a pain in the butt."

"So where did they tow your car?"

"To the BMW dealership on Grand. I spent the night with Jason and he dropped me by there about six this morning on his way to the airport. He's got to go to New York for his job for a week." He shook his head. "Man, it looked even worse than it did last night. Jesus. And with the deductible and all, it's going to set me back."

Hattie spoke from her place at the table. "How long will they need to repair your vehicle?"

"Aw, they're saying two or three weeks, but I'm gonna call down there later this morning and talk to the service manager. I can't believe it'd take that long."

I stared at him a moment.

"Two or three weeks?" I said.

I knew I sounded like an idiot, but the phrase whirled in my mind: two or three weeks, two or three weeks. Would he assume he'd stay here? For two or three weeks?

"Like I say," he said, "I can't believe it will take that long. But the guy who looked at it this morning said there'd be a ton of body work and they have a bunch of the mechanics taking vacations now, around the holidays and all, so they can't get to it right away. He said it's close to being totaled."

He sighed. "Geez, I just bought it." He looked down into his coffee. "With some of the money I got from Dad's life insurance." He glanced back and forth to Hattie and me. "My adopted dad, I mean."

"The car has sentimental value to you," Hattie said.

He shrugged and nodded.

Fumbling back to my chair, I sank down, deflated and suddenly exhausted. I lifted my mug to my lips, but the coffee had cooled. I thought about tossing it out and pouring myself a fresh cup, but it didn't seem that important.

"Seth," I said. "I have something to tell you. Cal is leaving on

Monday for Uganda. He won't be home until Christmas, and then only for a few days."

I had assumed Cal would tell Seth about his plans tonight. I'd also assumed that tomorrow or the next day, Seth would pack up and head out to California knowing Cal would fly him back here to share the holidays with us.

"Yeah," Seth said, "I know about the Uganda thing. We were driving back yesterday from the Dells when he got the call, remember? He told me you'd be pretty pissed about it. Are you?"

I'd forgotten Cal had gotten the call in the car with Seth. And how dare he; how dare my husband discuss my possible re-action with Seth. I was furious at his audacity.

Seth must have seen something in my expression that told him he'd crossed a line, because after mumbling an excuse that he had to check his email, he rushed from the room so fast he slopped a dollop of coffee on the floor. I stayed silent and watched him stoop to mop it up with a paper towel, throw it in the trash, then scurry his way through the back hall and up the stairs.

I turned to Hattie. "I can't believe Cal told Seth I'd be upset about the job in Uganda."

"Is that so bad? The call came in front of Seth. I think it would be natural for Cal to tell Seth you'd be upset about it."

I stopped myself from saying a defensive reply and instead stared out the window to the pewter sky. She was right. And I knew a comment from Cal to Seth was not the thing bothering me.

"I'm not upset because of that. It's just that Cal didn't even consult me on this." I slapped my palm on the table; the anger, fresh and raw, rose to my throat. "He just accepted the job."

"Oh," she murmured. "I assumed you'd been discussing this possibility all along."

I shook my head no, and she looked away from me.

I pushed myself from my place at the table and strode to the kitchen desk. The telephone tones sounded in my ear as I punched in Cal's number. He answered on the second ring.

"Cal, I need to talk with you. Do you have a minute?"

"Yes, but just barely. What is it?"

Impatience clipped his words, and in the background, muted conversation drifted through the connection. He was busy.

"It's Seth," I said. "He was in an accident last night."

"Is he all right?"

"Yes," and I told him Seth's story.

"He has a loaner car," I said, "so he won't need one of ours. But his car won't be fixed for two to three weeks. That's what the dealership is telling him."

"The damage must have been pretty extensive for it to take that long."

"But Cal, what about Seth? I mean, now that you're leaving for Uganda on Monday . . ."

"Let's don't talk about this now, okay honey? Please? Let's put everything on hold until tonight. Okay?"

I took a deep breath and kept silent.

Cal was right. Why was I so jumpy? Why was I acting like the Mad Bitch of Chicago? The bubble in the carpenter's level had slid off the scale; these hormones were killing me.

"Zoe?" Cal said. "You still there?"

"Yes. I'm here."

"I have to come home to change for the dinner tonight. A bunch of the Germans flew in so I'll need my black suit. We'll talk about all this then. I'll call Seth and tell him to hang around until I get there. Okay, babe?"

His voice had taken on the tone I loved: sweet, giving, low with the hint of intimacy, but he was only trying to diffuse my anger. I took a deep breath to calm myself and gave in.

"Okay, Cal," I said. "I'll see you tonight."

"Great, honey. We'll work it out, you'll see."

We said good-bye and I disconnected the call.

Replacing the receiver in its cradle, I sneaked a glance at Hattie. She was in profile, her head was bowed forward like she was still reading the paper, but from this vantage point, given the angle of the dull light from the window beside her, I could see one lone tear shimmering on her withered cheek.

CHAPTER EIGHT

I dressed for the day, distracted and uncaring how I looked. The trip to the grocery store took an inordinate amount of time; I couldn't seem to remember what I needed and had to backtrack through the aisles a few times. By the time I got home and pulled into the garage, the sky had lowered and turned an ominous charcoal gray. Hustling around to the rear of the car, I gathered my coat collar around my neck and with my free hand and punched the button to pop the hatchback. Behind me, footsteps sounded on the gravel of my driveway and I turned around to see Neva Reckart hurrying toward me.

"Wait, Zoe," she called.

She jiggled toward me wearing her Burger Barn hat, a kind of red nurse's hat with the famous smiling hamburger logo that perched over her forehead. Her dingy fake-fur coat was unbuttoned and flew out like wings at her ample hips. The red and white stripes of her uniform pants stretched over the hamlike thighs and stopped mid-calf. Red socks scrunched down around the top of her tennis shoes, and the exposed shins and ankles dazzled as she walked. She looked like a walking circus tent that hadn't unfurled to the ground. I felt my mouth purse toward a smile, but worked to keep it at bay.

"Hi, Neva. What's up?"

Panting for breath, she stopped in front of me. "Oh shit," she said.

I was a little taken aback by her cussing, but I wasn't sure

99

she'd heard herself so I didn't react.

She took a couple of deep breaths and pressed her hand to her chest. "I saw you drive in and I was like, 'Oh thank you.' Could you give me a ride to work? My mom had to go in early to work and she took the car without telling me and I missed the bus. Could you?"

"Sure," I said. "Just let me take in a couple of the bags here. I have some ice cream in one of them."

"Oh great. Thanks. Wow. I was so afraid I couldn't get to work."

I lifted the bag with the ice cream and closed the hatchback.

"Want to come in the house for a minute while I put this away?" I said.

Her mouth circled into a small 'o' of consternation, then she shook her head a little.

"No. I better not."

"It's okay, Neva. Really. You're welcome to come into the house. Are you in a hurry? Do you have time to sit and have a cup of coffee?"

She shook her head again, the cap bobbing with her movement. "I don't drink coffee."

"Okay. You can have something else if you like." I stepped toward the house. "But if you have time, I'd love to have you."

She shook her head again.

I'd met Neva while unloading boxes in our driveway the day Cal and I moved in. She pointed out her bedroom window to me, second story about twelve feet across the air from our own upstairs guest room. She and her mother, who I'd only seen a few times as she drove past, lived alone in a house that desperately needed paint and carpentry. Judging from the rusted car they shared, Neva's clothes, and the night-shifts they both worked, I judged them to be struggling with money.

Neva and I had talked a fair amount during the warm summer evenings about inconsequential things: the brilliance of my impatiens that bloomed beside our garage, the hawk we'd occasionally see gliding between the houses, her boredom with her job at Burger Barn. But despite my invitations, she'd never come inside the house. She suffered, I felt sure, not necessarily because of her size, because I'd seen many large girls happy with full lives, but with a desperation to please, a hungering for any kind of attention.

After storing the ice cream and calling to Hattie that I'd be back in a few minutes, we got in the car and backed out of the driveway. I headed down Universe toward Chicago Avenue and Neva watched me drive.

"I like to drive," she said. "I'm saving up for my own car."

I smiled at her. "Good for you. How much longer do you think until you can get one?"

She shrugged. "I don't know. It's hard to save the money. I keep putting twenty dollars aside, but then something always comes up."

"The bills do tend to demand attention, don't they?"

"But I really want a car. I never can go out when I want to. My mom always needs it for something; then we get in a big fight."

"Maybe you should open one of those accounts at the bank where you can't touch the money before a certain time. You know, like a Christmas club account? That way you wouldn't be so tempted to spend it when you got a little saved."

Her eyebrows came together and she thought about that for a minute.

"No. I don't think that would work. I always need the money, you know, for going out and stuff."

I laughed. "That's the way it is."

I remembered my recent discussions with Cal about setting priorities, but I kept my mouth shut. I hadn't gotten through to

Cal, and I was sure the last thing that an eighteen-year-old girl needed was a lecture from an adult.

I dropped her off at the Burger Barn, and she assured me she could get the regular bus home at the end of her shift. I drove back home, unloaded the rest of the groceries, then balancing a cup of hot tea, made myself go up to my office.

Six hours later, I took stock of my accomplishments for the day: The flyers for the Griffen account still needed editing. I wasn't happy with the logo design for their spring convention, and I needed to revamp the artwork for it. And my friend Sabrina Owens, who worked there and managed my contract, was waiting for a draft of the flyer to show her boss. To top it off, the article I'd written for their newsletter read stilted and dull.

So what was I doing playing my twelfth game of computer solitaire?

Five o'clock in the afternoon, and all I had to show for my day were twelve solitaire losses and a website history a mile long. I closed down the game and leaned back in my chair examining the photo on my desktop: Mom and me on our front porch at Red Leaf. I was eighteen and I'd graduated high school a few hours before Dad had snapped the picture. My mother's smile was soft and proud, mine was dizzy with the excitement of starting school at Chicago Art Institute in the fall.

For the millionth time, I scrutinized my mother's face. We had our arms around each other's waists, I was as tall as she was and thinner. I was grinning at the camera, Mom's face was turned full front, but her eyes had cut to me at the moment of the camera's click. I hadn't noticed that until after she'd died. As a matter of fact, it wasn't until after she died that the old photos of her and I together shifted in status from treasured mementos to nearly sacred images. There were only a few, and this one was my favorite.

I clicked off the monitor plunging my office loft into near

darkness. I looked across the half wall in front of my desk and through the transom window set above the front door opposite me. Dusk had set in, and I hadn't yet turned on any of the lights downstairs, picked up the mail or even thought about dinner for Hattie and me. Cal said a dinner meeting, and Seth would undoubtedly go out also. I wanted to catch him before he left to make sure he'd be here when Cal said for him to be here.

Seth's wrecked car, Cal's decision to take a job in Uganda, my father selling the house—could anything else go wrong?

With a frustrated sigh, I got up from my desk and crossed the room. The pale evening light gave enough illumination for me to see my way to the stair landing outside my office. I stepped down the first couple of steps when I heard a series of clinking sounds from the living room, like ice rattling in a glass. Seth or Hattie? That was odd, I thought.

More clinking, and I stepped down two more steps and leaned forward to peer under the living room ceiling into the room. Through the dusky light of the front window, I saw Cal sitting in the chair next to the fireplace holding a crystal tumbler of what was undoubtedly his favorite scotch. He still wore his overcoat, although it was unbuttoned and fell open on either side of his crossed knees. He twirled the glass in his hands rattling the ice again, then tipped it into his mouth. After setting it on the table beside him, he folded his hands in his lap and stared at the cold fireplace. He was obviously lost in thought, and for a chilling moment I felt as if I were watching a stranger, a man who had nothing to do with me or the child I carried inside me. Shadows hid the details of his expression, but from the way he lifted a finger and held it to his chin, I knew he was brooding over something. The sense of being a stranger suddenly became too much for me, and more than anything, I wanted to be a part of the scene in my living room.

I stepped down to the next riser. "Cal?" I said.

He evidently didn't hear me because he kept his eyes on the fireplace and began rubbing his chin in contemplation.

"Cal?" I spoke louder and his head jerked up.

A shocked gasp caught in my throat. I'd never before seen the look on his face—morose, tortured, and weighted with worry—and on the verge of tears.

But he recovered quickly, arranged his face into a neutral but pleasant expression and stood to face me.

"Zoe. I didn't hear you."

I continued down the stairs into the foyer and through the living room. My heart pounded like a piston. "Why didn't you let me know you were home? I was up in the office. I didn't hear you come in."

He shifted his weight from side to side and swiped his sleeve across his eyes. "Yeah, I saw the light from the computer screen when I looked up there. I, uh, I didn't want to bother you. I figured you were working."

I crept toward him softly, like I would a wounded animal. He shoved his hands in his coat pockets and watched me.

"Yes, I was working," I said. "But I can do that anytime, you know that. I would have much rather talked to you." A frigid lump congealed in my stomach. "Is something wrong? You just looked so, I don't know, so unhappy sitting there in the dark all by yourself."

He stared at me a moment like he was trying to make sense of something. "I, uh, just had a quick drink here."

He gestured behind him to the table with his glass of melting ice.

"Oh," I said. "Well. I wish I'd known. I would have at least sat with you while you had your drink."

He shrugged and gave me a half smile. The mellow tick-tock of the wall clock in the foyer was our only background noise.

I moved closer and rested my hand on his chest. "Is everything okay, honey?"

He stared at me.

"Cal? What is it? What's the matter?"

He broke the spell with a shake of his head. "Nothing. Nothing, just thinking."

We stood like that for a moment—close, but disconnected: me, in the clutch of nameless fear, he, in an isolated world of his own making. Gradually, I became aware of the sound of the shower running in the upstairs bathroom that Seth used. In that second, the pipes squawked once as he turned off the water.

"I guess Seth is getting ready to go out," he said.

I glanced up at the ceiling where the guest bathroom was above us. "Yes."

I waited a silent moment, then turned toward the floor lamp that stood beside my chair near the fireplace. His voice stopped my hand before I switched it on.

"Leave it, okay?"

I lowered my hand and faced him. "What is it?"

He glanced to the ground then back at me. "I, uh, I've been doing some thinking. About this whole Uganda thing."

"Yes?"

"I'm just not sure what will work out, you know? I mean, with you coming over there after Christmas. I don't know."

"What do you mean?"

"I mean I don't know." Exasperation. "There's going to be so much to do. I don't see how I'll have time to get you settled and find a place to live and set up the initial clinic . . . all that. It's a complicated situation."

"Complicated," I said.

"Well, yes. It's a lot to take on at once." His tone had sharpened.

I moved toward him and again placed a hand on his lapel.

He let me, but I had the feeling he wanted to move away. "I don't want you to worry. Let's don't think too far in advance, okay?"

"That's what I'm trying to tell you. I'm the one who has to think in advance, and I'm feeling pretty overwhelmed right now, okay?"

He reached up and patted his hair.

"I don't want you to feel overwhelmed," I said. "I'll do all the research. And I won't be ready to join you in January anyway. I have a lot to arrange before I could make a move like that. I want to be sure that having the baby in Kampala is the right thing to do. And with Hattie and all, it's not something I can be ready for in three weeks."

He sighed. "Okay, look. Just, uh, just do whatever. I have to concentrate on this project. I can't figure out what to do about a pregnant wife right now, okay? Just do what you want."

The churning in my stomach intensified. He was avoiding something.

"Is there something else bothering you?" I said.

I held my breath, waiting for an answer like I was waiting for the roof to fall in. "Something else bothering me?" he said. "Isn't moving to Uganda enough?"

Relief eased through me. "We're not going to rush into this, Cal. We'll take our time. All I wanted last night was to be a part of the decision, not just to have you dictate to me what would happen. That's all. We don't have to rush into a huge move like this."

I reached my arms around his shoulders. He relaxed and wrapped his arms around me. He stroked my hair, which was loose around my shoulders, and buried his face in it.

I held the back of his head. "It's okay, Cal. It's okay. We'll work it out."

Every man, no matter how manly, needs mothering now and

again, at least according to my mother. I believed her at that moment. He was engulfed with worry, much more so than I realized. I should have been more sensitive. He needed to know I'd be there as his partner, not as a stone around his neck.

We stood like that for a minute until the guestroom door closed upstairs, and Seth's footfalls pounded down the staircase. I watched him over Cal's shoulder while he stepped into the back hall and looked both ways, to the kitchen to his right and the living room on his left. He smiled when he saw us and hustled into the room.

"Hey, everybody," he said. "Why no lights?"

He reached under the shade of the table lamp, the same table where Cal had set his drink, and switched on the light. I blinked from the sudden brightness and Cal did the same. He dropped his arms from around me and stepped away.

Seth's hair was still wet around the edges and his cologne bordered on over-kill. He wore gashed jeans and boots and the blue cashmere sweater I'd seen on the first evening he'd arrived. The edge of a white tee shirt showed at the neckline of the crew neck, and the lobe of his left ear glinted with his diamond stud.

"Hi." He grinned at Cal. "What's happening?"

Cal's obvious delight at seeing his son transformed him. The man who sat drinking alone in the twilight had vanished. Now, he grinned at Seth, shrugged off his coat and tossed it on the sofa. "You getting ready to go out for another crazy night on the town?" Cal said.

"Yeah, but I think I'll do it without the car accident tonight." They laughed together. "Unless you're going to be home tonight after all?"

"No," Cal said. "Just stopped by to change clothes. Sit down. I want to talk to you."

I'd wanted to talk to Cal about Seth's situation privately. But it was too late now, because Seth perched on the edge of the hassock I kept in front of my fireplace chair, elbows resting on his knees, leaning forward, ready to hear his father. Cal sat in the chair across from him.

"Did you talk to your insurance company?" Cal said.

"Yeah," Seth said. "They said no dice."

"What?" I said.

Cal turned to me. "I called Seth today, after I'd spoken with you, and told him about your idea to fly him to California now, then back here in a few weeks to pick up his car and spend Christmas with us."

Irritation nipped at me. The way he'd put it made it sound like I was making all the decisions. Why couldn't he have supported me on this? Since he hadn't talked to me about this privately, he should have worded it like we'd made the decision together.

"The thing is," Seth said, "if I fly out to LA, I gotta rent a car. Because I can't get by without one. And it'd be for almost three weeks. So I called the insurance company and asked since they're paying for a rental car here, would they pay for one in LA. But they said they wouldn't do that because I didn't live in LA yet and for all they knew, I could be going down there to take a vacation and they weren't in the habit of paying for people to rent cars for their vacations."

He'd sat up straight to explain this to me, using his hands in back and forth motions to indicate the cities he was talking about. The careful and deliberate delivery made me wonder if he thought my mental capacity wasn't quite up to understanding this detailed scenario. I controlled the defensiveness that pinched inside my chest and tried to keep my face neutral.

Cal focused on me. "So basically, Seth is stuck here. That is, unless we want to not only pay for the plane ticket, but pay several hundreds of dollars for him to rent a car in LA."

"We pay for it?" I said. "We didn't wreck his car."

It was a snotty thing to say, I knew it the minute I heard my own words. Cal fixed me with a look that asked me why the hell I'd say something like that. My excuse rushed out.

"I didn't mean anything nasty, Seth. Sorry." I glanced to Cal. "I just thought Cal and I would discuss this alone before we talked to you."

"Oh, sure," Seth said. He waved a hand in the air to dismiss any offense. "No problem. I get what you mean. And I'm sorry I'll be stuck here just waiting for the car. I don't want to put you out. I want to pay you something. No, no, I insist. Just a few bucks to cover food and stuff, but I really don't have enough money to rent a car for three weeks in LA."

"Of course you don't, Seth," Cal said. "And I don't want you to have to be short of money." He looked at me. "I'd loan him my own car to drive out there, but the lease miles are almost maxed out as it is. We'd have to pay additional mileage. A round trip to California would end up being just as expensive as renting him a car in the first place. No, the best thing is for Seth to stay here, wait for his car to be repaired and stay for Christmas. He'll be company for you and Hattie while I'm gone." He smiled at Seth. "And it's nice that you'd offer to pay a little, but you don't need to."

Seth made a back and forth refusal motion with his hands. "No, I insist. Really. A couple of hundred dollars isn't going to hurt me, and it's only fair."

I sat on the sofa in a kind of trance, observing this duet. They obviously had done the male-bonding thing, and done it in a major way. Their voice tone, their body movements, how one would insist, the other refuse, reminded me of a well-choreographed dance.

"So," Cal said. He looked between Seth and me. "It's settled then. I'll try to get back for more than a week at Christmas. We could have some real family time."

He grinned, and my stomach flipped.

Was I nervous about Seth? Did he intimidate me? Or was it that the whole scenario seemed so . . . I searched for the word. Bizarre? Planned? Staged?

No, I decided, wanted. The whole thing was so wanted by both of them. And, once again, I'd had no say in the decision.

CHAPTER NINE

"So let me understand this," Sabrina said. "Cal decided, all by himself no less, to move to another continent so he can perform medical miracles, and you're staying here for three weeks while you're two months pregnant and taking care of his grandmother and son. Do I have that right?"

I'd asked Sabrina to meet me on Saturday morning under the gateway in Portage Park, an equal fifteen minute drive for both of us. I'd left Cal and Seth sitting at the kitchen table planning an excursion to the hockey game that night, their last outing together before Cal left for Africa on Monday. I needed to get away from Cal, from Seth, from Universe Street. And I needed to talk to a friend, someone who'd known me before I'd become Mrs. Cal Sterling.

A jogger breezed past us exhaling frosty clouds, a stocking cap pulled over his ears, the muscles of his thighs like rounded rock. The pewter clouds and the threat of snow had vanished, but despite the brilliant crystal of the sky and sunlight that seemed to be enhanced by an invisible magnifier, it was cold. Goldie trotted along beside me, grinning at her opportunity to take her person for a walk.

Sabrina and I hooked arms, compressing the padded sleeves of our heavy coats. The concrete path meandered through bare elm and maple groves. Around us, brown wrens dabbed at miniscule crumbs and squirrels thick with fur scurried from one buried treasure to another. The world was progressing as it was supposed to, and I breathed a sigh of momentary contentment.

I glanced at my friend's face, burnished by the cold to a deep copper, surrounded by the white fur of her hood like a brown egg nestled in white feathers.

"You make it sound like I'm left holding the bag," I said.

"And you aren't?"

I looked to the toes of my leather boots and watched the concrete pass beneath my steps. Finally, I met her eyes.

"I'll join him eventually. He wants a family, Reena, he really does. It's just that he's so driven by his career."

"He may want a family, but he certainly doesn't act like he wants a wife. I mean really, Zoe, what kind of guy makes a huge decision like that without even consulting his wife?"

"He was offered the position and he took it, that's all. Like I said, I'll join him later. We have a lot to do first: find out about hospitals and apartments. And we have Hattie. And Goldie. It'll be a huge move."

"A move he decided on his own."

"They called and needed an immediate answer."

"Hmmm."

I told myself to quit white-washing my words. As much as I tried to justify Cal's actions to Sabrina, I was just as unsettled by them as she was.

I stopped beside a wooden bench and we sat. A fat squirrel scurried in front of us, reared up on his hind legs to see if we had an offering, blinked in disappointment then darted across the concrete walk into the open meadow. We watched as he ran up a tree and ducked out of sight.

"How's Mitch and Devon?" I asked.

"They're both good. I may kill Devon before the end of the month, but they're good."

"Mitch spends a lot of time with him, though."

"I know. Especially for a step-father."

Fourteen years ago, Sabrina bore her son on her own. The day she'd announced her pregnancy to her lover was the day he left for parts unknown. We'd both been shocked. James was in art school with us, one of the most promising in our group. But when Sabrina told him he was to become a proud papa, he packed up his small apartment under the El and left school. She raised her son by herself until he was ten, then she met her husband, Mitch. Mitchell the Marvelous we'd nicknamed him.

"I'm lucky," Sabrina said. "I found a guy who's willing to put out the energy to be a good parent." She cut her eyes to me.

"And you're thinking Cal won't be very good?"

"I'm just mad at him, I guess. Mad at him for doing this. For making this huge decision without talking to you about it."

I reached across and squeezed her gloved hand. "Me too," I said. "But the fact is, I really don't feel like I have much of a choice now. He's made the decision. I mean, what am I supposed to do? Demand that he call Mechin back and refuse the offer?"

"What would he do if you did?"

I snorted. "Laugh."

She watched me. "In other words, he'd choose his career over you."

"That's nothing new, Reena." I'd answered her quickly, like I'd long ago accepted that, but hurt welled into my throat.

With a sudden gust of wind, I shifted my eyes to an eddy of dry leaves twirling past us; we huddled against each other for warmth until it passed.

"I think," I said, "well, okay, I hope—once Cal gets over there and starts the clinics and then Hattie and I go over—well, everything will be fine. It'll be a wonderful opportunity for us."

"Hmmm. I just don't trust him," she said. "He's been working this incredible schedule now for, what, over a year?"

"Eighteen months."

"He's always so consumed by this work of his. He's just so ruthless about it."

"Ruthless?"

"I'd call putting your career over your marriage ruthless, wouldn't you?" She shook her head. "I don't know. I hope he doesn't throw you over when you need him most."

I cringed at her bluntness, but I'd heard her opinions about Cal before. She'd labeled him as patronizing and arrogant. I'd seen him as confident. And, I reminded myself, Cal hadn't cared for Sabrina either. He called her secretive and sneaky. She wasn't, but I knew what Cal had sensed. Sabrina was a woman's woman, so to speak. Her motto was: "Men may come and men may go, but we will survive." It wasn't so much that Cal thought she was overly independent, because he liked independent women, but Sabrina's dismissal of his place in my life bewildered him. My best friend and my husband had taken an almost instant dislike to each other.

We stood and ambled along for a silent moment, and she got a far away look on her face. Shaking her head at her memory, she laughed.

"What?" I said.

"You remember Jeff Peyton?"

I looked to the heavens. "I can't believe you brought him up."

"Why not? Here was another Mr. Wonderful who you thought would stick by you till the bitter end. Until I proved you wrong, that is."

"Yeah, thank you world-famous Detective Sabrina."

When I first started dating Jeff, Sabrina had become suspicious of his motives and his eligibility. She hatched a scheme to save me from my own blind devotion. Even though I could have sworn I was the one and only love of his life, Sabrina was convinced he was two-timing, and maybe even three-timing me.

We planned to sneak into his apartment: me to prove he would be sleeping alone, Sabrina to prove he'd have a girl in bed with him.

"You remember how cold it was that night, and we were out there in those bushes for hours?" she said.

"We were not out there for hours. It only took you ten minutes to get the bright idea to actually break into his apartment."

"We did not break in. The slider was unlocked."

"Oh, now we've moved from Detective Sabrina to world-famous Attorney Sabrina who would have saved our frozen asses from getting busted."

"Well, we didn't get caught so we didn't need saving. Thanks to my brilliant scheme."

I rolled my eyes at her. "Sure. Brilliant."

We'd slid the door open and stepped in to the darkened living room. Crouching low, we tiptoed through the back hall to his bedroom, a route I knew quite well, I'm embarrassed to say. We crept to his bedroom door and hit the light switch. He bolted upright and stumbled around his bed, obviously confused by the explosion of light.

I was right, he was alone—wearing a black lace negligee, black stockings and a garter belt with red bows.

"The only thing I regret," Sabrina said, "is we didn't get the name of the shade of lipstick he was wearing. I'd kill for that color. All I can say is that it was a good thing I did for you. No telling how long you would have hung on to him if I hadn't discovered the truth."

"Yes," I said, "but you suspected him of infidelity, not of being a cross-dresser."

"That's true. He just wanted to be one of the girls all along. Too bad he dropped out of school after that. Did you ever hear from him?"

"Once. About three years later. A wedding announcement."

We both laughed, and then settled on another bench. The frigid breeze held steady for a moment and allowed the warmth of the sun to penetrate our coats. We lifted our faces to it, and I closed my eyes.

Sabrina's voice broke my reverie. "But what about the stepson? Seth? Why is he staying while Cal's gone? I don't get it."

"He had an accident. His car was almost totaled. No one was hurt, thank God, but his car will be in the shop for at least two weeks, maybe three. After that, it's only another week or so until Christmas, and it seems cruel to send him on to California to have Christmas out there. I mean his adopted father is dead, and his mom is on this cruise, and . . ."

"And you figure if Seth is there, Cal will be sure to come home as soon as he can for the holidays."

I hadn't admitted that to myself, but when I heard it, I knew it was true. She knew me too well.

Goldie whined and tugged on her leash. We stood, and I took my sunglasses out of my pocket and put them on, and we started back to the parking lot.

Sabrina jammed her hands in her coat pockets and looked at the sidewalk as we strolled. After a minute, she spoke again, low and intimate, as only best friends can talk to each other.

"And what else?" she said.

"What do you mean 'what else?' "

"What else is going on with you?"

I sighed. We'd known each other for a long time. Sabrina never let me get away with only talking about the crust of my feelings. She knew how to dig into the soft center of my desires. And my fears.

My throat tightened. I stopped again and this time Goldie sat beside me, leaning against my leg. "There's something else that's bothering me," I said, "and I can't put my finger on it."

"About the move? Or his decision?"

"I don't know. It's not that Seth intimidates me or anything."

"Intimidates you? How?"

I shrugged. "Nothing. Just kid stuff. Talking on the phone long distance for a long time. Walking into the kitchen with nothing on but his thong underwear."

Sabrina's laugh echoed in the near-empty park. "No. Tell me he did not do that."

I laughed. It was funny, just as Hattie said. And now Sabrina. "Yes," I said. "A black thong with white skulls. I swear."

"Oh, heaven help us."

We laughed together and I shared the entire encounter. After we'd settled, she asked me again what was bothering me.

"It's Cal," I said. "He's been so focused on this Mechin project I've almost forgotten what he was like before it started, when we first got married. Last night I found him sitting alone in the dark having a drink. And the look on his face . . . It was so unlike Cal. It's like I'm married to a different man."

"The wrong man?"

A stab of panic hit me in the stomach. "No," I insisted.

"Are you sure?"

I stopped and looked at her. "Reena, Cal is not the wrong man. He's all caught up in his career now, but he'll come back to his old self. He will. He'll be the man who I've loved and who my mother adored."

"Your mother?"

"You remember how she loved Cal on sight."

"Yeah, but what does that have to do with these funny feelings you've been getting?"

I shrugged. "That's probably all hormones. Pregnant stuff. You remember." I grinned at her.

We walked for a moment longer and then she spoke. "Let me

ask you something. Would you have married Cal when you did if your mother had been healthy?"

I became aware of my heart beating.

"Well, yes. I mean, no, not necessarily. I . . . of course I'd want to marry Cal. Even if it weren't for Mom's hopes for me, I'd have married him."

"That's not what I asked."

I stopped, took off my sunglasses and stared at her. I made myself listen.

"Did you rush into marriage because your mother was dying?" she said.

Finally, I spoke. "Maybe. But that doesn't mean I love Cal any less."

"I know. I just wondered. I mean, your mom wanted for you to be married so bad. Maybe that's kind of weighing on you, you know?"

"How?"

"Maybe kind of like you'll do anything to keep your marriage together. Especially—"

"Go on," I said.

"I was just going to say especially given the role you played in her death."

"That has nothing to do with it." There was a snap to my voice I hadn't intended, and she flinched a little. "Sorry," I said.

"It's okay. But I'm telling you the way I see it."

I smiled at her and kept my voice tone light.

"Well, thank you Doctor Sabrina, world famous psychiatrist. I'll certainly take your diagnosis under consideration."

"No, I mean it. It makes sense. Because you're not a doormat, never have been, but you can be stubborn about some things."

I grinned and gave her a playful shove against her shoulder. "Like I keep hanging around with you even though you're a worthless cause?"

We laughed again.

"But you know what I'm saying?" she said. "I know you. You'll hang on to something until it's pried out of your fingers. You can be stupid like that."

Even though I knew Reena's intentions were sincere, I thought she might be projecting her own life onto mine. She'd been saddled with a goddess of a sister, and a mother who was overtly partial to her. All her life, Sabrina had tried to win her mother's approval. And now, even though she was successful and stable with a wonderful husband and son, and her sister had gone through dozens of men, Sabrina still felt like she was the unwanted child. I wondered if she'd stick with a man just to please her mother. Maybe she would, but that wasn't the case for me. I'd never felt like I had to fight for my mother's love and approval. She'd only wanted the best for me.

"I think that may be stretching it a bit."

And she gave me a look with brimming eyes that told me she loved me.

I smiled back and squeezed her arm. "I appreciate what you're saying. Really. But we're going to move to Uganda and make the most of this opportunity. Like I said, it'll be an adventure. For myself and Hattie and the baby."

She looked at me a moment and her expression was one of patient compassion. She hugged me, and I wondered if she was thinking that I needed all the hugs I could get for the hard road ahead.

CHAPTER TEN

During the final forty-eight hours before Cal left for Africa, my emotions careened like a driverless racecar. I alternated between living in a black hell and a brilliant cloudless heaven. We didn't make love either night, and I found myself on the verge of tears several times, but swallowed them back. I told myself if military spouses could be strong and positive even when sending their loved ones into danger, I could certainly do that while Cal worked in Uganda for a couple of weeks to help sick people. And in my good moments, I had hopes that once he got there and experienced a few weeks without me in a foreign country, he'd come back at Christmas and beg me to move overseas with him. Of course, the thought of doing that pushed me into another round of emotional crises: thinking about raising our child in Africa, leaving my clients and our house on Universe Street.

On the day before Cal left, Angus Lohan called and told me he'd be able to meet with me anytime about the sale of my mother's house. I was glad of the diversion for my battered emotions. On Monday morning, I took Cal to the airport, we said quick good-byes and I headed west from Chicago.

During the two-hour drive, as I sped through the small towns I knew so well and dipped into the solace of the open prairie, the tight knot in my chest begin to loosen and I caught myself taking several deep breaths, almost like purging myself. A weight began to lift from me, and for the first time in a week, I could breathe. I enjoyed the scenery. And when I turned off the county road onto the Anderson-McComb road, the familiar scenery evoked the nostalgic feelings of coming home. Even though I hadn't been in this area for years, I knew it well. The Anderson family had three kids; the middle boy was in my class through school. The McComb family had a girl a year younger than me. Revisiting where I'd traipsed around during my girlhood helped me to center myself again. I took a couple more deep breaths and blew them out hard.

I whizzed past the Anderson place, manicured and ordered, and about two minutes later, the McComb farm came into view. Two miles further, and the Lohan turnoff appeared on my left.

A grove of oak and cottonwoods must have shaded his lane during spring and summer, but now bare branches snarled into the gray sky. I pulled to the side of the road, overcome for a moment with the memories of my sweet childhood and my mother. I pushed the window button and smoke-tinged air drifted into the car. I took a deep breath and watched a V of geese honk and flap across the flat clouds overlaying the stubbed fields. One straggler beat double-time to try to catch up to the formation so he wouldn't be separated from his family. I hoped he'd make it. I knew how it felt to work as hard as you could to be a part of something only to have it drift away from you.

I pulled from the side of the road, drove about a half mile and stopped in front of the farmhouse.

Angus Lohan, like most long-time farmers in this part of the country, had inherited his acreage and a farmhouse from his family. The Red Leaf farmhouse, my mother's, had belonged to my grandparents and their parents before them, since before the Civil War. I didn't know how long ago the Lohan family had started farming this area, but probably as long ago as my own. However, Lohan had torn down the original farmhouse and built a new one on the site. I'd seen it before, a number of years ago, but now I surveyed the area with renewed appreciation. Even without the frame of full trees and lush hedges, it was magnificent.

The house swept across the top of a rise, long and low and the same colors as the earth. I'd heard Angus Lohan had designed and overseen most of the building himself, even though he had no formal training. Large gray stones, almost California-looking in their regularity, surrounded the base of the structure and also made up the columns surrounding the door and the porch that ran the length of the front. Deeply carved double doors provided the entry.

The house itself was of stained wood, a deep red-brown, with large plate windows that looked past the drive where I'd parked and onto the open prairie beyond. A barn stood apart from the house, its boards stained the same red-brown. Two silos stood in a distance, along with several sheds and outbuildings, but far enough away from the house and barn so that the impact of the house was preserved. It was the picture of a prosperous sophisticated homestead. Long steps made of the same stones as the house formed the walkway, and I got out of my car and climbed to the porch. I rang the bell and behind the leaded glass in the door, the light changed as someone moved inside. The door opened and Angus Lohan stood framed by the light behind him.

I hadn't seen him in over ten years; our paths hadn't crossed and his two daughters were several years younger than I, now in their late twenties, and had moved away from rural Illinois, so there was no connection to bring us in contact. My first thought was that he looked younger than I'd expected. His jeans and flannel shirt outlined defined muscles and his brown hair, slightly receding but still thick and heavy, showed only a tint of gray at the sideburns. I guessed him to be early to mid fifties, and still arresting with a defined jaw and a cleft in the middle of his chin. He smiled, and the lines beside his mouth spread wide in welcome. His hazel eyes were frank and unsuspicious.

"Hi, Zoe. Come on in. Sorry it's taken us a week to get together."

"Thanks. And it's no problem, Mr. Lohan."

"Good. And please, call me Gus."

He opened the door to let me enter. I stepped up into the foyer, stood beside him and realized he was taller than I first thought. My artist's eye roamed the entry and a warm admiration settled inside me.

The light from the foyer was given from a skylight above us, and even though the clouds covered the sun, the honey-colored paneling glowed with warmth. The wall on my right separated the foyer from the living room, and I smiled with delight when I realized it had been created from shards of colored glass and small stones, then mortared together with cement. The effect was like a rock wall with fragments of brilliant glass punctuating the surface. I traced it with my fingertips.

"This is so cool. I love this."

"Thank you. I used mostly local stones, but of course I had to send away for the glass."

"You made it?"

He nodded and smiled, obviously proud of his accomplishment.

"I'm impressed. I'm an artist too, so I know what it took to design that."

"I know you are. I remember. Come on in."

Large windows, gleaming wood floors, and more of the paneling dominated the living room. In the mammoth stone fireplace on the far wall, a fire burned between two andirons crowned with brass knobs. The opening was large enough for me to stand in. Unnecessary, but impressive. Around it were grouped two dark leather sofas, some easy chairs and an white alpaca rug; its fur ruffled against the sleek floor and provided a contrast I loved. The chairs and sofas held pillows made from different tapestries; some Navajo looking weaves, others mid-Eastern rustic and textured.

"I'm impressed again," I said.

He laughed and led the way over to one of the sofas. "I guess you didn't know Sybil and Celeste well enough to come here before, right?"

"No, they were behind me in school."

He took my coat and tossed it over the arm of one of the easy chairs, then sat on one end of the sofa that faced the fireplace. I sat on the other end in front of a coffee table carved from a giant tree trunk. An irregular shaped dish, kind of a flat bowl, took most of the top and I studied it. Wild and vibrant daisies decorated its surface; a lovely piece of art, hand-thrown and glazed.

"Are you a potter as well?" I gestured toward the dish.

"No, although I'd like to learn some day." The green eyes surveyed me, and I wondered if he was using this time to appraise my business sense for our transaction. He would find me to be a soft negotiator, I thought. I wanted my mother's house.

"I'm not either, but I took a couple of courses in art school. I love this piece. Daisies are my favorite flowers. They remind me of the prairie."

"I like it, too," he said.

I waited for him to give a polite follow-up, but he didn't. He obviously wanted to get down to the reason for our meeting.

"Thanks for seeing me," I said. "I really appreciate you being open about the Red Leaf house."

He settled into the corner of the sofa and stretched his arm across the back. Despite the interesting hole in his chin, he had an arrogant look to him that irritated me, like he knew something I didn't.

"I thought you'd show up sooner or later," he said.

"Why?"

"When your father sold me the farmhouse, I figured you weren't in on it, but I thought you'd want to be."

"Why did you figure I wasn't in on it?"

"Just something he said during negotiations, something about his daughter having severed her ties to the farmhouse."

"Severed her ties? What did he mean by that?"

I said it more to myself than to get an answer from Lohan, but he answered me anyway.

"I asked him what he meant, because I knew you still came around here, but your father just shrugged and said not to worry about it. He said he owned the farm, and I didn't need to know any more in order to close the sale."

I shook my head. "That sounds like him."

Gus kept silent, and I fidgeted at the thought of my father and I being the topic of conversation for most of the county. A land sale, especially one as large and as established as Red Leaf, was always news. And in most instances, the homestead was kept within the family, so I was sure most of the county residents were surprised when Harwood Trueblood had announced he was selling every part and parcel of Red Leaf Farm.

"The house was my mother's. I knew Dad would eventually sell the farm, what with me in Chicago and married to the most non-farming man in the world. But . . ."

I let my sentence trail off. I didn't really want to share all of our dirty family laundry with Gus Lohan. I didn't want to confess the reason my father wanted to sell the house had nothing to do with money and everything to do with retribution. And Dad was right about one thing: Lohan only needed to know so much to conduct business.

I started again. "Let me put it like this: I'd like to buy my mother's house back from you. I want the house and the yard. I think it's about an acre. The barn would be nice, but I don't have to have that. And none of the outbuildings. Would you be willing to consider that?"

He smiled, relaxed and maybe a little amused. "Well, you certainly don't let any grass grow under your wheels, do you?"

"What do you mean?"

He laughed out loud. "I mean you get right down to business. Don't get all defensive about it. Your father and I have a contract for the farm, but I have no desire to unearth the family skeletons. If you and your dad have ill feelings, it's really none of my affair."

"You're right. It's not," I said.

He watched me a minute, the smile still working around his mouth, and I felt a hot flush begin on my chest and wash over my face. I smiled at him and shrugged.

"Sorry," I said. "I just—I guess I'm a bottom line lady."

He gave me a polite smile, but kept silent.

"So would you?" I said.

"Sell you the house?"

I nodded.

He examined my face a minute before he spoke. "I might. But first, how are you? How's Chicago?"

I caught myself and blinked a few times. "Oh. Well. It's fine. My husband is busy. But we have a nice house and I'm expecting a baby in the spring."

He smiled again. "Congratulations. And your husband is a doctor, right?"

"He's a doctor turned administrator. He's set up a group of clinics using a business model he invented, so now he's really only doing that. As a matter of fact, he'll be setting up the same kind of thing in Africa. Uganda."

I forced a smile.

"Wow. High powered stuff. When will that be happening?"

"Actually he left this morning for three weeks. He'll be home for Christmas, then go back." I thought for a moment, then added, "We're not sure yet, with the baby and all, when I'll join him."

Below the rush of words I felt the squeeze of embarrassment, but I tried to keep my face neutral.

"Well, that's a big move," he said. "Takes awhile to figure out the logistics."

"Yes, well, we're not sure how long he'll be there and everything. I mean, we're only in the beginning stages."

I felt like I was tripping over myself. I hated when I over-explained like some teenager caught in a lie. But if Lohan thought my rambling was odd, he didn't show it.

"Would you like a cup of coffee or something?" he said.

"No, thanks." I looked around. "I really should be going soon. I just wanted to see if you'd think about selling the house to me. If you'd consider it."

He crossed his arms over his chest. "Depends on if it works to my advantage." He examined my face. "This is a major purchase on my part. There's no room for sentiment."

I could be as hard-nosed as he could. I waited a beat then made my voice deeper and firm. "Maybe not for you, but senti-ment is why I want the house. You must know that. I'll pay you a fair price for it, but I won't be taken advantage of." I silently gulped at that last statement. I hoped he didn't guess I'd pay almost anything for my mother's house.

He watched me a moment with a hard glint in his eyes. "One of the wells is in the backyard. I'd need that."

"I know. And I think we could work that out."

"Will your husband be part of this? I mean, will he have some input into the negotiations?"

"No. No, it's all me. I mean, I guess technically it's his money, because I don't have enough of my own to buy the house outright, but it would be in my name."

He watched me a moment more, uncrossed his arms and seemed to relax through the shoulders. "You know, if you wanted, I'd work out payments with you so that you could buy the house without touching his money."

Did Cal and I really sound as estranged as all that? Even after I'd been so careful to tell Lohan that I'd be joining Cal at some point in the future? I must not have sounded that convincing. Despite my best efforts, I suspected Gus Lohan knew that my husband had made a life-altering decision without my wholehearted approval. Or maybe I was just oversensitive and poised to read too much into a simple business transaction.

He must have seen something change in my expression because he rushed to reassure me.

"I've just found," he said, "that most people like to personally own something that means a great deal to them. My daughters tell me that even applies to women."

He grinned.

There was probably some tax advantage for him to hold the papers that I wasn't aware of, and he was smart enough to put his offer on the table without explaining it, but it was an offer that would work for me, too. With that arrangement, I'd have the ability to own the house by myself. I was certain I could make the payments; I had every intention of keeping up my client list after the baby came.

"I'll take you up on the offer."

"I didn't know what I would have done with the house, frankly. I'd hate to tear it down, but I didn't want the upkeep. And I'd like to see it stay in the family of the original owners. Let me think about it and get back to you with a price."

"That's great. Thanks, Mr. Lohan." I smiled and shrugged. "Gus."

Pleasure warmed my chest. This was good. Suddenly, Cal and Seth seemed like worries belonging to another world. Sitting here in these beautiful surroundings, knowing I'd be able to have my mother's house—for the first time in days, I relaxed into the current of emotion flowing through me: peace of mind.

"I don't want to say anything about this to my father," I said. "Not yet, anyway. I hope that won't be a problem."

"This is a transaction between you and me. I won't say anything to anyone."

"Thanks. It's just awkward and—"

He held a hand up to stop my nervous rambling. "You don't have to explain. I'm sure you have very good reasons for doing this the way you want to."

I was grateful to him for that, for saving me the embarrassment of stumbling all over myself. I stood up to leave, and once again surveyed the room.

"What other art do you do? Besides the glass?"

"Carvings mostly. Woodwork. The glass is usually a part of that. I have a lot more in my studio out back, if you'd like to see it some time. As an artist, it might interest you."

"I'd love to. Do you sell your work?"

"Oh, yeah. All over. I just got a website up six months ago and business is booming. Matter of fact, I wondered about buying your father's acreage. I'm getting busy enough with commissions that farming is squeezing me pretty tight. I'm going to have to think about how I want to balance all that. But when I found out your father wanted to sell, I just couldn't pass it up. He's got a couple of very prime sections."

"I know. Well, I'm glad it'll work out for you. I'm glad that you'll be the one buying the land."

"I am too. He could have gotten more from a corporation, but he decided to go with me. And believe me, he won't starve off of this sale."

I laughed and gathered my purse and coat. "I'm sure he won't."

I stuck out my hand to shake and his fingers wrapped it in a firm grip. The thought crossed my mind: a hard businessman, but a man to be trusted.

"Thanks, Gus. We'll be in touch."

"You bet," he said. "And keep well, now."

We said our good-byes and after walking through the glow of that foyer, I left, carrying a warm contentment with me.

CHAPTER ELEVEN

Two days after Cal left, my rollicking emotions were replaced by a kind of mellow cozy feeling. At odd moments, I found myself thinking of my mother and the holiday preparations we'd made each year, watching out the window for snow flurries that would bring a white Christmas, playing a Christmas CD in my office as I worked.

Cal had called when he landed in Kampala, and we'd spoken briefly once again after that. I was glad to hear from him, but I'd been at the computer working both times, and I'd wanted to get back to my task before I lost my train of thought. The poor timing of his contact nipped at me, and after I'd hung up, I wondered if he'd detected the impatience in my voice. But not even that worry was enough to ripple my cheery well-being. I didn't stop to analyze my feelings; instead, I vowed to enjoy this time, the Christmas of my pregnancy.

On the third morning after Cal had left, Hattie returned to her room after breakfast for her usual activities, knitting and listening to the classical music hour on one of the local radio stations. Seth was still sleeping; he'd gone out the night before and sometime in the wee hours had used his key to get in the house.

I decided to make some cookies to take to the Griffen Uniform people. Every table in the break room would be mounded with Christmas goodies, but as one of their independent contractors, I needed to make sure my offering was in the mix. Besides, it was a perfect gray morning to fill the house with the homey aroma of fresh-baked cookies.

Humming "Jingle Bells," I assembled bowls, the ingredients and the recipe on the counter. As a precautionary measure of a novice cookie maker, I dug out a full apron from one of the drawers and looped it over my head. Tying the apron string around my ever-expanding waistline, I glanced out the kitchen window to the sky. The clouds were hoarding snow in an iron grip, but hopefully they'd release it soon. I hummed and danced my way to the pantry, fished into the candy jar, and at the end of the song, dropped a chocolate into my mouth. Closing my eyes, I stood still for a moment to experience my senses to the fullest. Heaven.

The Reckarts' back gate squealed on its hinges and slammed shut. A second later, Neva Reckart crossed in front of the window. She'd mushroomed in size with the addition of a white fake-fur coat, and she carried a plate covered in foil and topped by a red bow. Her knock sounded, and I hurried to open the back door.

"Hi, Neva. I saw you from the window. Come in."

I felt a sincere smile widen my face; she'd come to the back door rather than sneaking around between the houses.

She stepped inside the kitchen and looked around for a moment, a tentative shy expression on her face. She offered me the plate.

"I brought over cookies for you."

She smiled at me, showing tiny crooked teeth that should have had braces. Her eyes dipped to the floor. I took the plate and placed my hand on her arm nudging her further into my warm home.

"I was just getting ready to make cookies myself. This is so nice of you, and now we can trade. Would you like to stay and help?"

"You're going to make cookies, like with flour and stuff?"

I nodded.

"Oh. I bought mine at Shop-Rite."

"And that was very thoughtful of you. Can you stay for a while and help me?"

Cold-chafed fingers grasped the edges of her coat together and she leaned sideways to search the room. I studied her face. I'd never seen her wear make-up, even when going to or coming home from work, but now her cheeks were inflamed not only by the cold, but by an abundance of blush. Dark liner squiggled around her eyes, and neon pink lipstick transformed her lips to those of a carnival novelty doll offered as a prize in a shooting booth. Gold chandelier earrings twisted in her hair.

"It would be just the two of us," I said, "and I'd love to have some company. Cal's not home and Hattie, Cal's grandmother, is in her room. Please stay."

I wanted to reassure her we'd be alone. I believed that by coming over this morning, she was attempting to reach out, poking her head out of what I guessed was the lonely shell of her life.

She brought an iridescent blue thumbnail to her mouth and began to chew.

"No one will bother us," I said. "How about it?"

"I, uh, I just wondered if that guy was here. I've seen him a couple of times going in and out of your house. Is that his new car in the driveway?"

"Oh, you mean Seth, Cal's son. He's still upstairs, but he won't bother us. And that's not his new car. It's a rental."

Her eyebrows lifted in a hopeful look. "Does he live with you now?"

"No. He's from Minneapolis, but he's headed to California after Christmas."

"Oh."

She continued surveying the room for a few more seconds and met my eyes with a resigned look.

"Speaking of cars," I said, "how's the savings going for your own?"

The brilliant lips parted in a grin. "I saved a hundred dollars."

"Good for you, Neva. That's great."

"Yeah. I got a raise."

"Super! Did you get a promotion?"

"No. Just my raise that I was supposed to get. They give them to everyone after two years there."

"But that's still good. And the extra money will help you save more."

She shuffled in place for a moment, maybe a little embarrassed, then smiled.

"Hey, could I see the baby's room?"

"Sure. Want to take off your coat?"

She shook her head, tangling the earrings into the web of her hair, and tugged the coat lapels tighter together, determined to hang on to the drab garment. I'd seen her wearing it during the three winters we'd lived next door; I assumed it was her only coat. She obviously wanted to keep it clutched to her chest, like an insecure child clasps a tattered blanket. I set her plate of cookies on the counter and led her down the hall to the nursery.

Inside the room, I opened the shutters and clicked on the giraffe lamp on the dresser. Neva stood in the threshold, a smile expanding her garish pink lips.

She didn't look at me when she spoke, but instead addressed the room.

"I knew it would be like this."

Her tone was soft and filled with magic. She stepped further into the room and began to stroll around the perimeter. The refurbished old floorboards creaked under her weighty steps until she stopped beside the wicker bassinet I'd so carefully decorated.

"Was this yours when you were a baby?" she asked.

"No. But I found it in an antique shop in Rockville. It probably belonged to some farm family; the owner of the shop couldn't remember where she'd gotten it. It looks old doesn't it?"

She nodded, trancelike.

"I like to think of all the babies who slept there," I said. "I think it'll be the perfect first bed for my baby."

She nodded again. "Your baby will be a lucky little baby," she said, "with you for a mother."

She looked to the floor then, embarrassed, I think, but because of the layer of crimson powder, I couldn't tell if the hue of her cheeks had changed.

"Thank you, Neva. That's such a nice compliment."

"Everything is so special here. Like you really want your baby."

"Yes, that's the best way to bring a child into the world."

A faraway look came over her face, and she shrugged. Meandering to the rocking chair that stood in the corner, she placed her hand on its arm and began to move it back and forth.

"This is the way I'd want it, too," she said, "if I was having a baby."

"Well," I said, "when you're a little older, you'll hopefully find the right man and have a family."

It was an inane remark, I knew it as I said it, but she seemed so forlorn that I wanted to comfort her. She reminded me of a lost poor child with her nose pressed against a windowpane, staring inside a happy home. A tingle of guilt worked on me. I was so fortunate, and I took my fortune for granted most of the time. I just wanted to help Neva, help her somehow to feel happy. A naive sentiment, tantamount to a kid saying that when she grows up, she wants to save all the animals in the world, but there was something about Neva that brought out the protector in me. Or was it pity?

"I'll be a good mother, too," she said. "Not like . . ."

Her lips pressed together; obviously her own mother would be her negative role model.

"You can make your own life, Neva. You can make happen what you want to happen. You may need some help to achieve your goals, but other people have and you can too."

She smiled at me and resumed running her finger along the arm of the rocker. I watched her for a second. Should I say more about being the mistress of her life or let it drop? She broke into my self-debate.

"When your baby's born," she said, "maybe I could come over and help you with it. I could take care of it and hold it and kiss its little face . . ."

Her words trailed off and her eyes moved away from mine to roam the remainder of the room.

The thought of Neva kissing my baby's face sent a chill through me, but I squelched it in shame. She was a young woman who needed all the love and attention she could get. Who was I, blessed with a mother who'd built her life around me, to deny Neva some measure of acceptance?

"Of course," I said, "you'd be welcome any time."

But I placed a hand on my lower belly, the nervous impulse getting the better of me.

We spent a few more minutes in the room. I watched while Neva examined the pictures I'd painted, a series of three pandas juggling stars and rainbows, and the accessories I'd purchased over the last few years.

Finally, she faced me and smiled. "It's really pretty in here."

She was back to the innocent child, her face transfused with the wonder of a one-year-old seeing a balloon float up to the clouds. I turned out the lights and we left the room.

I led the way to the kitchen, speaking to her over my shoulder as she followed.

"So can you stay awhile and help me make cookies?" I said. "I'd love to have you and that way I could have you take some of them home with you."

"Oh . . ." She paused for a moment and shrugged. "I don't guess I better. I need to—"

Bare feet slapped down the hallway and we both turned to see Seth make his appearance.

He wore his usual morning attire, a stretched out gray sweatshirt with Ball U printed on the front in peeling black letters. Ball State University was in Indiana, I knew, and a good private school, but Seth had admitted the first night he was here that he thought college was a waste of time, so I knew that he wore the shirt for its insinuation rather than as a hopeful student. His sweatpants had slipped low on his hips and the string around the waist hung loosely to his crotch. With his matted hair, eyelids still heavy from sleep and the snuffling noises he made, I knew he'd literally just rolled out of bed.

He stopped in the threshold. "Hey. What's up?"

"Seth, this is Neva, our neighbor. Neva, Seth."

Seth gave her the same once over he'd given me at the front door when he'd first arrived, but in the next instant, unlike the appreciative reaction I'd received, his face settled into dismissive neutrality.

"Hey," he said. He paddled over to the coffee pot, scratching his head as he went.

"I was hoping to convince Neva to stay and make some cookies."

I looked to Neva, the first glance I'd given her since introducing her to Seth. The expression on her face conveyed one emotion: awe. Her eyes traced Seth's movements, and a dumb-founded grin inflated her vivid cheeks. The protective feeling welled inside of me. Seth was way out of Neva's league.

"I think I can stay after all," she said.

Still watching Seth as he added cream and several spoonfuls of sugar to his coffee, she opened her coat and shrugged it off. A shocked gasp caught in my throat.

A sweater, baby blue with a crew neck, molded to her ample flesh, several sizes too small. She hadn't worn a bra, and her nipples jutted like small knobs at the ends of her ponderous breasts. Body rolls at her sides stretched the fabric to the point of near-bursting, and her stomach protruded from the bottom of the sweater and jiggled over the waistband of her jeans. I took the coat and looked at her face, embarrassed that she might have seen my shock, but I needn't have worried: she only had eyes for Seth.

I hung her coat in the hall closet, and came back into the kitchen just in time to see her pull out the chair next to Seth and wedge herself in the seat. She rested her chin in her hand and wearing a simpering smile, gazed at the object of her adoration.

Seth's spoon clinked the mug as he stirred.

He looked at her and nodded. "How ya doin'?"

"Fine."

"So, uh, are you in school or what?" Seth asked.

"I graduated."

"Yeah? Where'd you go?"

"Oak Park."

"Is that a high school?"

"Uh-huh."

"Oh. I thought you meant you graduated from college."

"No, but I'm nineteen already. I was the oldest in my class."

She'd told me in last summer that she'd turned eighteen, and

I had no reason to doubt that her statement to me then was more truthful than this one to Seth. She obviously was doing everything possible to make herself appear sophisticated and worldly. I wanted to plead with her to give it up. My intuition told me Seth was far more experienced socially and sexually than most thirty-year-olds, much less an eighteen-year-old mis-fit.

Seth returned his gaze to the coffee swirling in his cup.

Neva leaned toward him and spoke. "My friend Regan is twenty-one. She goes to all the clubs."

"Yeah?"

"Uh-huh. I go with her. I could tell you where all the good clubs are." She covered her mouth with her hand, and I noted the stubs of chipped cobalt blue fingernails. Her giggle was a strident wheeze that made me cringe.

"Neva," I said, "you want to help me now?"

She snapped her head in my direction and gaped at me.

"Now?"

I nodded.

She turned her attention back to Seth. "I could show you some good clubs," she repeated.

Seth stood, scooted his chair back under the table and holding his coffee mug, crossed the room to the back hall.

"Uh, yeah. Sure. Thanks. I gotta go upstairs. See ya."

"Okay, Seth. See ya."

She watched him leave and turned to face me.

"I've had boyfriends before. Lots of times."

I harnessed my shock at this statement. Neva appeared to be lacking any kind of social life, and I wondered what she meant by having boyfriends. Daydreams about boys? Or more?

"I hope you're not thinking of Seth as a boyfriend. Remember, he's leaving in a few days for California."

She must have forgotten I'd told her that, or the information just now registered. Panic claimed her features.

"Why's he going to California?" she asked.

"He's going out there for school. He wants to be a dive instructor. He's only here visiting for a short while, Neva."

Crestfallen, she rose from her chair and moved her eyes around the room like she was asking herself how she'd gotten here.

I kept my voice soft. "How about we make those cookies now?"

She shook her head violently and the chandelier earrings slashed back and forth from her lobes.

"I don't feel like it. I just want to go home. Could I have my coat?"

"Sure. But I was hoping you'd stay."

She shook her head again and her chin quivered with a repressed sob. I hurried to the coat closet, retrieved her coat and handed it to her. She bunched it to her stomach, not even bothering to put it on, and ran out the back door into the dreary day. I called after her once, but she kept her back to me and loped through the gate and into her own backyard.

CHAPTER TWELVE

The next morning, I bundled up my cookies in plastic wrap, stuck on a bow and headed out for work errands. Eventually I'd wind up at Griffen Uniforms, although not until considerably later than I'd counted on. The meeting with the printers took three hours instead of the expected fifteen minute conference, but we finally found the perfect colors for the brochure I'd designed for the day spa. When I left there, I grabbed a fruit and protein smoothie to settle my queasy stomach. With my energy renewed, I made another stop at a client who owned a dry cleaners. He wanted a new logo and a promo package, and that conference took another two hours. It was getting late, past four, but I needed to stop by Griffen Uniform on my way home and pick up the latest revisions from Tom Twellman, the leader of their promotional launch. I pulled into the parking lot and parked in the visitor's space. I checked my lipstick, grabbed my briefcase and the plate of Christmas cookies and went inside.

Twellman's office door was open, lights were on and soft music played from a radio beside his computer monitor. Knowing him, he was off somewhere attempting to flatter an unsuspecting woman who had yet to learn of his insatiable ego. I threaded my way through a couple of rows of cubicles toward the break room. A few people recognized me as I passed and said hello, but most of the spaces were empty. It was after four and a lot of the staff worked flex hours to be home with their kids in the late afternoon.

The break room was deserted as well, so I left my offering on the table. As I suspected, it was burgeoning with sugar-laden temptations. My plate fit nicely in the middle, and I displayed the holiday card with my signature for all to see.

I left Sugar Central Station and turned to my right, heading for Sabrina's cubicle. After I'd woven through another few rows, I heard Twellman's voice along with Sabrina's, raised in a heated discussion.

Sabrina and I had been at the Art Institute together, eons ago, and despite our divergent backgrounds—she, a black girl from Chicago's south side, me, a country girl with Irish and Cherokee roots—we'd remained friends because we had similar views on people. Her opinion of Twellman matched my own; we'd shared many a commiserating cup of coffee, so when I approached their voices, I wasn't hesitant to shamelessly eavesdrop. I stopped several feet away in back of the head-high partition to her cubicle.

"The point is," Twellman said, "the company has budgeted a lot of money for this project. Now you're the one who's the liaison with her, you're the one who needs to account for how the money's spent."

I held my breath for a moment. I had no doubt the "her" Twellman referred to was me.

"Tom, we've been over this before," Sabrina said. "I said in the meeting this morning that in my opinion, the cost accounting didn't need to be broken down any further than it is. Rodriguez was sitting at the head of the table, and she didn't say a word. If she was bothered by that, she would have, you know her. If you wanted to address the situation, you should have said so then, in front of her."

Twellman's voice raised another notch. "I'm not going to sit in a meeting and tell my boss how to do her job. She should be checking the independent contractor guidelines, and if she's not, that's her problem."

I'd heard enough. I stepped around the partition corner and spoke.

"I gather I'm the topic of this discussion," I said.

Two heads jerked in my direction and two sets of astonished eyes widened. Sabrina's mahogany face deepened with a blush and she smiled. Twellman reddened, and his lips pressed into a penciled line.

"Damn," he said. "Nothing like sneaking around, Zoe."

His eyes narrowed in annoyance, and maybe something akin to a threat. His face hinted at savageness, with a brush-like gray beard that framed his pinched crimson lips.

As an independent contractor, I had to work with him if I wanted to keep Griffen for a client, but I'd vowed that Tom Twellman wouldn't intimidate me. I'd learned through business training that humans had a comfort zone of about eighteen inches from their bodies. If someone was outside of that, most people were comfortable and basically unthreatened. But step inside that invisible circle and people started to bristle, most of the time without knowing why; something registered on an unconscious level, animal instincts warning us danger might be close by—prepare for attack. As a woman, one of the best methods I'd found for being almost aggressive without being nasty was to step into that zone. My first few times doing it, I'd been uneasy, but the action had been effective enough that I'd continued in using the technique. It worked. It told others that I would not be forced into a lower status.

Now, I went inside the cubicle and crossed a few inches into Twellman's comfort barrier. I kept my voice low and even.

"I didn't sneak in here," I said. "Your voices were carrying several rows back."

Sabrina stepped toward me and turned her body just enough to give the signal that she and I were united. I appreciated that, and I cut my eyes to her and smiled.

"Well, then," she said, "then you know we're talking about your promotion materials."

"Yes," I nodded. "But Tom, you know how I feel about this. When I gave you the bid, I told you I hadn't built in time for filling out all the paperwork that Griffen requires for the bigger projects. You assured me then there was no problem. Now if that's changed, I'll be happy to do what's needed, but I'll need to file an addendum for my billing. What I'm charging you covers design fees only."

He glared at me, then at Sabrina. "Damn," he muttered.

Heat burned his cheeks and his mouth opened and closed a couple of times like he was preparing for a zinger of a retort, but he turned his shoulder to pass me and left the area.

Sabrina watched the doorway for a moment, then tiptoed around and leaned into the passageway to look for him. When she turned back to me, her white grin had transformed her into a mischievous brown elf.

She spoke in a whisper. "You never know about that guy. Nothing is beneath him, including listening right around the corner."

I spoke in my normal tone. "I really wasn't eavesdropping."

"I know. I know." Her hand flapped away my concern. "He's got his shorts all in a twist because he thinks Rodriquez is going climb all over him for not having you itemize your fees."

"He told me last spring he didn't need them itemized," I said.

"I know," Sabrina said with a shrug. "But now he's thinking he should have put a little more time into writing your contract. Exactly like, by the way, I advised him to do. Now, he's living in perpetual fear that Rodriguez is going to throw his sorry butt out of marketing and make him chief broom-pusher."

"Do you think Rodriquez will be upset about the accounting?"

"Who knows? But you have your contract, that's all you need to prove you only did what he outlined in the proposal."

"True," I said. "I know it's his own fault, but I hate to think his own slip-shod work is going to get him in trouble."

She rested one hand on her hip and gave me a sarcastic look. "Yeah, I feel real sorry for him. I'll cry in my pillow all night long just thinking about it."

Laughing, she sat at her desk and I took the chair across from her. She reached to the file cabinet directly behind her, lifted a cardboard mail cylinder from the top and set it in front of me.

"Here. I know you said you'd come in today to look at these specs, but I went by your house earlier to drop them off. I tried to way-lay you so you wouldn't have to see Tom-Tom the Terrorist. Where were you? I thought you said you'd be home this morning?"

"I thought I would too. A fifteen minute errand to the printers took three hours. Sorry you made the trip for nothing. I would have hung around if I knew you were coming by. Call me before you come next time."

She shrugged. "No biggie. I was out running around anyway. I had a couple of things to pick up for a training session I'm doing this afternoon. And I didn't call because, once again, my dearest son took my cell phone to school with him."

I laughed. "Don't you just love teenagers?"

"Oh, yes." A sarcastic snicker punctuated her remark. "Teenagers are just the best."

"Are you still against the idea of getting him his own phone?"

"Yes. I told him again the other night that he could get one for his sixteenth birthday and not a day before. He doesn't drive or ride with other kids. I take him to school and Mitch picks him up. We know where he is every friggin' second of the day. He doesn't need a cell phone."

I shook my head. "I don't know, Reena. All the kids want their own phones. Saying no is like trying to stop a tidal wave with a sandbag."

"I know. But I've got to put my foot down on some things. And he's already begging me for a tattoo." She sighed. "It's tough being a parent these days." She rested her elbow on the desk and shook a finger at me, but a grinned. "You just wait. You have so much to learn."

I laughed again.

"So anyway, as I was saying," she said. "I went by your house to drop off the specs. Your stepson answered the door and said you weren't home, but I didn't want to just leave them. There's a couple of things I wanted to show you." She raised her eyebrows and winked. "So that's Seth, huh?"

I nodded.

"And how long is he going to stay?"

"Through Christmas. He's headed out to California in January for a dive school out there. He wants to be a dive instructor at a resort in Mexico, but I suspect he's focused more on wine, women and song than he is on diving."

She grinned at me and leaned back in her chair.

"He's a real lady killer," she said.

"He is gorgeous, isn't he?"

"Yeah, and evidently a fast worker."

"What do you mean?"

"Well, with the two girls in the house there. I mean, he obviously made some girl friends pretty fast if he's only been here for a few days."

"What are you talking about? What two girls?"

"There were two girls in your living room. With your stepson. You didn't know?"

146

I shook my head.

"When I went to your house, he answered the door and I told him who I was. He said you weren't home and didn't know when to expect you. And right behind him, I could see them from the front door, two girls were sitting on the sofa."

"What'd they look like?"

"One was really heavy. I mean very heavy. The other looked like the goth thing. You know, the coal black hair and really made-up eyes and all in black clothes."

I thought the black-haired girl must be a friend of Neva's, maybe the twenty-one-year old who knew all the best clubs, as Neva had said. But the thought of Neva and her friend in the house when I wasn't there brought a queasy feeling to my stomach.

"What time was that?"

"Maybe twelve-thirty or so."

"Did you see Hattie?"

"No. I didn't see anyone but the two girls and the boy. Well, young man I guess."

That wouldn't be unusual. By twelve-thirty, Hattie would have eaten the sandwich I'd left in the fridge for her and retired to her room for a nap.

"Is everything okay?" Sabrina asked. "I just assumed you knew about it. Didn't he ask if it was okay?"

"No. He didn't. And to tell you the truth, I don't like it."

"Can't say as I blame you. But they weren't hurting anything as far as I could tell. And I didn't see any liquor bottles on the coffee table or smell any pot or anything."

She laughed and I joined with her, but the queasiness had hardened into a stone of disquiet.

I shook myself out of it. "I'm sure everything's fine," I said. "It just surprised me is all. I didn't expect Neva to be there. That's the heavy girl. She lives next door and met Seth yesterday. And she obviously has a friend and they obviously like Seth."

"Well, like I said, I didn't see that they were doing anything wrong. He probably just didn't think you'd mind."

"I suppose," I said. But the unease sat heavy inside me.

"Hey, you want to look at these specs?" she said. "There are a couple of areas I need to clarify with you."

We spent the next half hour going over the details of my artwork. I'd created a logo for the new spring launch which interwove with their traditional logo. A few color changes, and the old and the new worked together for an introduction to their new line of uniforms. I'd also designed the booth for their April trade show in Las Vegas that incorporated enough room for mannequins and live models, as well as a continuous video feed for the two screens mounted in the corners of the booth.

Opening my draft of one of the pamphlets, Sabrina grinned with approval.

"This is great, Zoe. I love it and I think Rodriguez will, too. Can I keep this copy?"

"Let me refine it a little more and I'll get one to you in a couple of days. I want Rodriguez to see it at its best. But you can show that to Twellman if you want."

She agreed and tucked it into her folder. Gathering my materials, we hugged good-bye and I finally left for home; impatience gnawed at me to talk to my stepson.

I stood in the threshold of the guestroom watching Seth's back as he tapped on his laptop keyboard. He sat at the desk in front of the window that looked across the side yard to Neva's window.

"Hi," I said.

Turning around to see me, he hung his arm over the back of the chair and smiled the smile that he and his father used to change the world.

"Hey. How ya doin'?"

"Tired," I said. "I'm going to rest a minute before dinner."

He smiled again. Welcoming, open, accepting of the interruption.

"Okay," he said. "Don't worry about me. I'll be heading out of here later. Hey, you know I've been meaning to tell you. I really appreciate you putting up with me all this time. I called the BMW dealership again today and they still think it's going to be at least two weeks. So, well, thanks. And Christmas here with you and Cal, and Hattie of course, will be cool."

He grinned, and genuine pleasure sparked in his eyes.

"We can do all kinds of things," I said. "Decorate the tree. Eat fattening Christmas goodies."

"That'd be great. I mean it. Mom and Dad and me had some great Christmases. And with Dad gone now, and Mom on her cruise, well, I wasn't looking forward to it too much."

I wondered what kind of mother would leave her son for the first Christmas after losing his father, but then again, I didn't know the whole story. Seth said his father's death had hit his mother hard. Maybe she'd had to get away to survive the holidays, and I doubted if Seth, being twenty-one with his own plans for his future, would be interested in cruising for a month with his mother and her friends.

The first Christmas without my mother had been horrible. Cal had insisted decorating a tree would be good for me, so I spent a good deal of time staring at a it with that dredged out feeling in my chest, fragile as one of my mother's glass ornaments nestled in the branches. If I hadn't been so happy to be pregnant with my first baby, I think I would've gone insane.

Poor Seth. The jealousy that prowled inside of me quieted its growl. I didn't want to be mean and selfish. He was my stepson, and I was glad now that Cal had insisted he would be here for the holidays.

149

"I'm glad we're here for you," I said.

I watched him a moment and wondered if he would broach the subject of Sabrina's visit today, but he only met my gaze with a passive, although friendly look. I carefully kept my voice tone casual.

"My friend Sabrina said she came by today and met you."

"Yeah, yeah. She had something for you but decided not to leave it."

"It worked out fine. I stopped by my client's office and picked up everything I needed."

I paused a moment, but I saw he had no intention of volunteering information about his guests. I wanted to give him the benefit of the doubt; he wasn't hiding the event as much as he just didn't think it was important enough to mention.

"Sabrina said you had some company here with you."

"Yeah. Neva and Regan."

"Neva, huh?"

"Yeah. Well see, I've been getting out to some clubs and stuff. Places that Jason took me to before he went to New York. Neva showed up at Willie's last night and told me she and Regan would come over today."

"Willie's?"

"That's a club I go to."

"You saw Neva at a club?"

"Yeah. She and her friend Regan." He grinned again.

"I know she said she went to clubs, but I thought it was all talk. How can Neva go to a club? She's not twenty-one."

The dark eyes rolled in disbelief. "Oh, please. Get real."

Even with cynicism etched into his face, he was still GQ-model handsome.

"Well, I know people can do that, but it's not smart, Seth. She could get into real trouble, legal and otherwise."

"Oh, I wouldn't worry about ol' Skeevy Neevy. She and

150

Regan know how to take care of themselves."

"Skeevy Neevy? That's not nice, Seth."

He shrugged, his expression bland and pleasant.

"It's not nice," I repeated, "and Neva is a very sad girl. The other day when you met her was the first time she's gotten up the nerve to come to the door. She usually sneaks around the house. She's afraid and insecure. I feel very sorry for her."

"Sorry for her? Are you kidding? She and Regan are major partiers."

"Partiers?"

"Uh-huh." He shook his head and grinned. "Major. Don't worry about her."

"Do you, I mean, you don't really hang out with her and this Regan, do you?"

The image of my ruggedly handsome stepson socializing with the misfit girl next door and her goth girlfriend just wouldn't mesh.

He shrugged, and I could have sworn a leer played across his mouth before he grinned again.

"Neevy's a no-holds-barred girl. The wilder, the better."

"Seth, I'm concerned about what you're telling me. She's not like most girls you knew in high school, I'm sure. I worry about her. Physically and mentally."

No troubling expression altered his features, and he gave no indication he was considering my judgment. He remained cool, collected and bland. He either had no empathy for what I was saying, or he hid his emotions.

I appealed to him again. "Seth, I mean it. I have to tell you, I don't like how this is sounding."

He made a gesture with his hand brushing away my concern. "Don't worry about it. Listen, I gotta get back to this stuff, okay?"

He pointed to the computer screen behind him.

I waited a moment, feeling indignation burrow into my chest.

"I didn't hear you come in last night," I said. "What time was it?"

He shrugged. "Maybe two. Two-thirty. So?"

"I just wondered."

"Since you didn't hear me, I must not have bothered you. Cal said to make myself at home, so I am. I figure until he comes back for Christmas, I'll do my own thing."

I cringed at this. In other words, Seth had a free place to live and the city of Chicago at his disposal. His words left a bad taste in my mouth, like I'd bitten into a moldy apple.

"What are you looking at me like that for?" he said. "I'm not doing anything wrong. Just hanging out."

He turned back to the screen.

I stared at his back for a moment until he glanced at me over his shoulder. "Okay? See you later?"

"Sure," I said.

I pushed myself away from the doorframe and stood a moment more, but he kept his eyes on the dancing screen in front of him.

CHAPTER THIRTEEN

My daily phone conversations with Cal were brief. He was har-ried. The first time I'd heard the exhausted tenor of his voice, a part of me silently cheered: he was tired and frazzled, he'd need his wife for comfort. Since he'd left, I'd done a little research on Uganda, and in particular, Kampala. It all looked intriguing and fascinating and incredibly foreign. But I didn't let the im-ages sink in; I didn't spend time imagining what it would be like to live there. My own work claimed my attention, and I let it.

I'd devoted long hours to the Griffen account, and the work was good. Finally, on the tenth morning after Cal had left, I completed the final draft for the promotional pamphlet I'd promised Sabrina. I clicked off the computer and stuffed a few pages of notes into a file folder.

I stepped out of the office loft but hesitated on the landing. I'd spoken to Cal every day about the same time. He'd call in another hour, but I had an appointment with the printer this morning, and I wouldn't answer my cell in the middle of design-ing layouts.

Should I call Cal now, before I left the house? No. My schedule was rushed today. I needed to get to the printer's before noon, run a few other errands, then get back in time to take Hattie to a three o'clock doctor's appointment. I might miss talking with him today, but I'd catch up tomorrow. And, I reluctantly admitted to myself, I wondered what we'd talk about. His existence was so alien to me that aside from the details of running the house, we simply didn't have that much to say to each other.

I hurried down the stairs and stepped into the foyer just as footsteps scurried across the front porch. Too early for the postman. I crossed the foyer and pulled the curtain aside from the narrow rectangle window beside the door just in time to see Neva Reckart's backside jiggling down the steps. I opened the door and leaned out into the snappy winter morning.

"Neva? Did you want something?"

She turned to me. Her eyes scoured the yard searching for escape. A gust of wind caught her hair and blew a tangle across her face, but she didn't brush it away. Plump hands, the stubby nails painted an iridescent blue, tugged her jean jacket across her breasts.

"Uh, no. It's okay. I just . . ."

She darted her eyes away, shifted her weight, pulled the jacket tighter around her and crossed her meaty arms to keep it in place.

"Would you like to come in for a minute?"

"Well I, no, that is, I really have to get back. I have to be at work at noon."

"Oh. All right then. But did you need anything?"

"I, uh, I just left something for Seth."

I followed her gaze to the corner of a white envelope peaking from under the mat. I withdrew it and held it up for her inspection.

"This is for Seth?"

"Yeah, I put his name on it."

Her chin came up, a little defiant, and I got the impression she was daring me to challenge her action. On the front of the envelope, "Seth" was written in full looping letters. In the top right corner where a stamp would've been, she'd drawn a heart with an arrow slanting through it.

If this had been anyone other than Neva, I would have smiled at the girlish gesture, but instead, a fist of discomfort pushed against my chest. I kept my voice as gentle as possible.

"He's not home now, but I'll be sure to give it to him, Neva."

"Okay. Thanks."

She turned from me and bounced across the front yard to her own front porch, clambered up the steps and went inside. I went back into the house and strolled to the kitchen, lightly slapping the envelope on my palm. At the kitchen desk, I examined the childish address again. The contents felt thick, like a stack of cards or pictures. I turned it over. The flap had been firmly sealed. Dare I? No. I slid it behind a perpetual stack of bills in the wire organizer.

My day unfolded as I'd hoped. My errands accomplished, I treated Hattie to a late lunch at the Ukrainian deli a few blocks from our house, then we went to her appointment. The doctor pronounced Hattie's knee fit and marveled at the eighty-eight-year-old woman who had such an amazing ability to heal. About 4:30, I pulled into the garage. I scampered across the backyard, Hattie hurrying behind me, and plunged through the backdoor. Goldie greeted us with licks, wags and a grin. I let her out quickly, she did her business then trotted up the steps and back into the warmth of the kitchen. I turned on some lights, re-set the thermostat for warm, warm, warm and rubbing my hands together for heat, walked back to Hattie's room.

"Come in," she called after my knock.

She'd made a cozy spot for herself, as always. The scent of roses from her soap, crèmes and sachets wove through the air along with the faint symphony which broadcasted from her radio. She'd snuggled into the warmth of her lounge chair in front of her window which was now hidden from the darkness by the cheerful poppy-print curtains, the same print we'd chosen together for her bed comforter and the shower curtain in her adjoining bathroom. A crimson Shetland wool throw with enormous fringe, last year's Christmas gift from Cal and me, draped over her legs. The floor lamp behind her streamed golden light across her face deepening her character lines. She'd already opened her book, but now marked it with a ribbon and closed it on her lap.

"It's cold outside," she said. "I wanted to get under my blanket quickly."

"It is absolutely freezing. I'm going to make us toasted cheese sandwiches for dinner and start a fire. We can eat in the living room."

"Sounds heavenly, dear."

"I'll come get you when supper's ready."

"Thank you, Zoe."

I left her and crossed the living room to the front door. Bracing myself for the cold, I opened it, snatched the mail from the box on the front porch, and quickly closed myself in. Meandering back to the kitchen, I sifted through the stack of catalogs and a few Christmas cards, mainly from Cal's business people. I set the mail on the desk and was about to turn away when I caught sight of the envelope Neva had left that morning. My fingers lifted it from behind the stack and traced the sealed flap. Snooping was wrong, but my motivation was pure: I was worried about Neva.

Sabrina had told me a few months ago she suspected her fourteen-year-old son of smoking pot, and she'd resorted to searching his room. She'd found the evidence, and Devon was furious with her, accused her of invading his privacy, spying on him. She'd confiscated the pot and punished him by denying him what he loved most, his computer. When she told me the story, her voice held the convictions of the rightness of her action; she would do whatever was necessary to protect her kid.

Even though Neva wasn't my kid, that's the way I felt. I wasn't sure what I could do to help her, or even if the contents of the envelope would be anything of consequence, but I knew it was the right thing to do. Seth's casual confession that he hung around with her at a club, plus Neva's hypnotized fascination with him on the day she brought over cookies reinforced my opinion: Neva had a thing for Seth, and Seth was way out of her league.

I tore open the flap and withdrew four Polaroid photographs.

At first, I was so taken aback, I could hardly decipher what I was looking at. Flesh. Wet flesh and black creases and dark red ridges. I shuffled to the next picture: the back of dimpled thighs, a woman bent over at the waist, the cheeks of her rear end spread and her sex open to the camera. The next picture was taken with the camera looking into a woman's vulva as she laid flat on her back. Her head angled back so far that except for a rounded chin with several creases, the face was obscured. An enormous belly protruded behind the crotch, like a soft mountain of dough. The last photo was much like the first. A close-up of the woman's vulva, only this time one stubbly finger probed her vagina; the rest of her fingers spread the flesh wide for the camera. The fingernails were bitten to the quick and painted iridescent blue.

The chair caught my fall as I collapsed into it. Breathe, I told myself, slow and deep.

Oh Lord. Had Seth taken those pictures? Dear God. Please no.

With shaking hands, I stuffed the pictures back into the envelope and fumbled to hide it in the stack of bills. No way he was getting those now. A glance at the clock told me it was just after five. The window beside the kitchen table was a black square, the panes reflecting my pallid features. If Seth kept to his usual schedule, he wouldn't be home until the wee hours.

I'd have to wait until tomorrow to talk to him.

My brain numb with twirling images, my fingers shaking and colder than when I'd been outside in the bitter winter air, I gathered cheese and butter from the refrigerator and set them on the counter. I needed to make sandwiches, but I'd lost my appetite. And damn it, I was tired.

The butter, hard from the fridge, wouldn't allow my knife through. I'd have to use the microwave to soften it enough to spread on the bread. Why couldn't anything ever be easy? Why did everything have to be such a hassle?

I slammed the knife onto the counter; my exhaustion had flipped into a slow twist of anger. Cal should be here. He should be here to talk to his son, to take care of this situation. But he'd left the country, without my full support, without my input into the decision, without me. And now, Seth and his tawdry little entertainments were left for me to deal with, and I was beginning to get royally pissed off about it. I wished Seth didn't have to stay here. I should have insisted Cal spend the money to send Seth on to California; God knows, now with his big-time job he could have afforded it. Maybe I should just buy the ticket myself. Charge it on the Visa and tell Cal too bad, we'll have to pay for it. Just tell Seth he's leaving and that's final and he's going to have to somehow get around without his car.

Damn Seth. And damn Cal for putting me in a position where Seth was using my house for some sleazy porno headquarters.

I marched over to the desk, snatched the phone from the cradle. The tones sounded as I punched in Cal's cell number. He answered on the third ring.

"Cal. Thank God I caught you. I was expecting your answering service."

"Hey, Zoe. Everything okay?"

I heard his sleepy hoarseness, and my stomach knotted. I'd forgotten about the time difference. I glanced at the digital clock on the desk that I'd set to Ugandan time:

Two-twelve AM.

"Oh, Cal. I'm sorry," I said.

The urgency that had gripped me a moment before flew away with the realization I'd awakened him. All of a sudden, I saw myself as he'd probably see me: silly and hormonal and wild, and incredibly inconsiderate of his need for sleep.

"Zoe? Are you there? Is everything okay?"

"Yes. Yes, I'm here, Cal. I, uh, oh gosh I'm sorry I woke you, honey. I just didn't think."

He yawned. "Yeah. Well, what's up?"

I took a deep breath. "It's Seth. I'm upset about Seth."

"Why? What'd he do?"

"Well, I . . . it's just that I intercepted some pictures of Neva that she'd sent over to him. Terrible pictures, Cal, of Neva."

"What? Pictures?"

"Pornographic pictures. Of Neva. Remember I told you a few days ago he said he'd hung out with her in a club? Well, now she left these pictures for him and I—I opened them. And it's just a bad situation, Cal."

I felt stupid. I'm sure I must have sounded insane.

He laughed; harsh, incredulous. "Jesus, Zoe. You wake me up at two in the morning to tell me the kid is getting a piece of action? Christ." He bit off that last word, the sure sign he was seriously angry.

"It's not just that. It's that Neva is so . . ." Words failed me. "She's a pathetic young woman and I feel like Seth is just using her. I just wish you were here to deal with this, Cal."

"Well I'm not. I'm thousands of miles away and it's in the middle of the night. Damn it, Zoe. Now look. I'll be home in a couple of weeks. Until then, do what you need to do. Talk to him. Tell him to get his shit together. I don't care what you say to him just take care of it, will you?"

Hot humiliation burned behind my eyes and I squeezed them shut. Why did I call him? Why hadn't I left it alone?

"You there?" he said.

"Yes." I cleared my throat and spoke louder. "Yes, I'm here."

"Now honey, I don't want you to be upset about this, but remember, you've got those baby hormones raging around, making you crazy. You said that yourself. Now take a deep breath and it'll be all right. Okay?"

"Yes. Yes, okay."

"All right then, Zoe. I'll call you tomorrow night. My night, over here. Your morning. But I've got to get some sleep. We're meeting with the Prime Minister tomorrow to finalize some of this stuff. We've been working solid for forty-eight hours and I'm beat. I don't think poor Melissa has slept since she got here."

A knife went through my stomach. "Melissa? Delany?"

"Well, sure. Who else?"

"I didn't realize . . . you said she wouldn't be going to Uganda."

The knife in my stomach wrenched during the beat that followed.

"We had a change of plans. I needed her to work on the visa process for an Indian doctor we hired. Listen, don't worry about this thing with Seth. I'll talk to you tomorrow, okay?"

I finally found my voice. "How long will she stay there?"

"I don't know. Jesus, Zoe. Until we get it all worked out, okay? I've got to get some sleep. I'll talk to you tomorrow."

I managed to choke out my answer. "Yes. Tomorrow. Goodnight, Cal."

He hung up without another word.

I went up to my room and allowed myself the luxury of breaking down in tears.

CHAPTER FOURTEEN

My dreams exploded with images of Melissa Delany and Cal together. But the next morning as I dressed in my blue wool hoody and elastic-waist pants, I vowed to stop thinking like a jealous seventeen-year-old who finds out her boyfriend has given another girl a ride home from school. Melissa was a talented doctor and lawyer. Of course she'd be on Cal's team in his most important venture. If I allowed myself to create these insidious fantasies, I wouldn't survive until Christmas. I'd cried myself out last night, and now I renewed my determination: Forget Melissa and banish this unwarranted jealousy. And handle Seth. Handle it.

My clogs tapped down the hallway as I passed Seth's room. The bed was unmade and a white sweatshirt lay wadded on the floor beside the closet. The bathroom door was shut, but there was the sound of water running. He'd wander downstairs in a minute in as usual, barefooted, wearing jeans and a sweatshirt.

At the sound of my footsteps across the kitchen floor, Hattie looked up from her place at the table.

"Good morning, Zoe." She smiled, and I sat in the chair close to her own.

"Morning, Hattie. Listen, Seth is on his way downstairs and I want to talk to him. I think it would be better if we were alone."

A bemused expression settled on her. "Is it such a delicate problem? One that an old woman should not hear?"

"No . . ." I shifted my eyes from her. "There's just been a

161

situation that's come up, and I need to talk to him about it."

She watched me, and I finally smiled and shook my head. This was a woman who could pinpoint a person's deepest motivation inside five minutes of conversation; she would not be put off by my avoidance tactics.

"You know the girl next door? Neva Reckart?"

"The one who helps you plant flowers?"

I nodded. "She's sent some pictures to Seth, pornographic pictures. I suspect he took them."

I spoke low, a conspirator confiding in an accomplice. She answered me in the same tone. "How did you find them?"

"I, uh, opened the envelope she left. I know it was wrong, but I had a feeling there was something going on between them, and I'm worried about it."

Hattie nodded, fully understanding the situation. "It seems odd that a handsome young man would attend to a young woman of the girl's caliber. I wonder why."

"I don't know," I said, "but I see it as detrimental to Neva. Do you think I'm off base here? Am I being silly?"

She answered at once. "No. You are being compassionate. Why do you think you might be silly?"

My hands clenched together on the table top; I watched my knuckles whiten. "I called Cal last night and told him about it. Of course, I did wake him up—" I looked up at her wanting her to understand. "I felt so horrible, Hattie. Here he is over there working so hard, and I wake him up to tell him this."

Despite my steely determination to banish the images from my dreams, a picture of a smiling, charming and alluring Melissa Delany popped into my head. My eyes and nose burned.

Hattie grasped my forearm. "What is it?"

I shook my head, but she tightened her grip. She wasn't going to let this slide.

"I'm only being moody," I said. "Baby hormones, you know?"

I shrugged a little and gave a weak smile. "He has another doctor there, a woman named Melissa Delany. He told me she wouldn't be going to Uganda to join him, but last night he told me they'd had a change of plans and he needed her there. She's beautiful, Hattie. Beautiful and single and brilliant."

I watched her, and in the back of my mind, waited for the platitudes of consolation that I wanted: You're beautiful, too. And he loves you. Don't worry. It's natural you should feel this way.

But she gave me none of that. Instead, she leaned back in her chair and stared at me for a long moment. Finally, something in her face shifted. She started to speak, but stopped at the sound of feet slapping the hardwood floor in the hallway.

"Hey, everybody." Seth sauntered through the door, hands jammed into his jeans pockets, wearing the Ball U sweatshirt I'd seen wadded on the floor a minute ago. His sleep-tangled hair jutted out, and he looked slow and lazy. His sense of entitlement irritated me; he wore the subtle message that the world owed him, a prince ready to be endowed with gifts and favors. He took a mug from the cabinet and poured his coffee.

Hattie rose from her seat and carried her mug to the sink. She rinsed it quickly and set it in the bottom.

"I'm going to go back to my room now. I wanted to finish the letter to my son and get it in the post this morning." She looked at me. "We'll talk later, Zoe. Seth, have a pleasant morning."

"Yeah, okay, Gram." He grinned and stirred in sugar and cream, clinking the spoon against the sides of the porcelain mug.

I felt the surprise spring to my expression, and saw it mirrored in Hattie's. I'd only heard Seth call Hattie by her name, and evidently she'd never heard anything but that either. Her eyes flitted back and forth from him to me for a second in stunned amazement, but then she smiled at him. She came to me, placed her hand on the back of my head and kissed my forehead. I looked up to see her calm smile. With one final stroke of my hair, she hurried from the room.

Seth pulled a chair to the table, spread the newspaper, folded his arms across the print, and with his mug of coffee steaming beside him, began to read.

A flat piece of slate sky showed through the window. The bare limbs of the mature oak that shaded the backyard in the summer bounced with the puff of raw wind. Goldie scratched one paw on the back door. I opened it to let her out and admitted a sliver of frigid air. I watched her squat and then canter back up the steps. I let her inside, poured my coffee and sat down next to Seth.

He glanced up, then resumed his reading.

"I wonder if I could talk to you, Seth."

"Sure."

The wooden chair creaked when he leaned back, relaxed, but with half-lidded eyes that bordered on arrogant. Be fair, I thought. He looked like he was ready to listen, what else did I want? He lifted the cup to his mouth and took a noisy sip.

"Something has come to my attention that I'm worried about."

He sipped again and looked at me over the rim of his cup.

"It's about Neva."

The laugh lines around his eyes deepened in amusement. He lowered the cup.

"What's she done now?" he said.

"She's posed for some very disturbing pictures, Seth."

"What pictures?"

The amusement still held around his eyes. I had the feeling he knew very well what pictures. He was toying with me.

"I won't be patronized, Seth."

The chair rocked back on two legs. "You're the one who

164

opened the envelope, not me. Yes, I know all about the pictures. Neva asked me last night at Willie's what I thought of them and I told her I never got them. We both figured then you must have opened my personal mail."

"I'm not going to justify my actions to you—"

"Good. Because you can't."

"Just please tell me you didn't take them."

He stared at me, then after a moment decided to answer. "No. I didn't take them."

His tone was heavy with a sneer and he drew out the word "no," but I believed him.

"Who did then?"

He tossed me a casual answer. "Her friend Regan."

"I've told you before," I said, "I'm concerned about Neva. I think she's a very sad girl, and I don't like you dating her."

His eyes stayed on me, and he burst a short laugh while shaking his head.

"I mean it, Seth. You're a good looking young man and you could get any girl you wanted to. That means to me that there's only one reason you're dating her. For sex, and I think that's awful of you."

The sneer from his voice had spread to his lips. He kept the chair tipped back, cocked his head to one side and twirled the coffee cup on the table.

"Well," he said, "did it ever occur to you that maybe I like her? That she has a nice personality?"

I stared at him a moment as a flush worked over my face. No, that had not occurred to me.

"Talk about judging someone," he said. He laughed again and shook his head.

"Well, are you?" I said.

"What?"

"Dating her because of her wonderful personality? Because if

165

that's true, let's have her over here, now. Let's invite her over for coffee and we can talk and I can get to know her a little better and understand the magnetism that draws you to her. Is that what I should do, Seth?" I pushed my palms down on the table and started to stand up. "Should I go ahead and phone over there right now and tell her I'm so happy that she and my stepson like each other enough to date?"

He looked at me a moment, then turned to stare out the window to the bleak day. He blew out a steam of air.

"Jesus." Under his breath.

"Don't bullshit me, Seth. Any fool can see exactly what's going on here. I think it's despicable. And your father will be very disappointed in you."

He swung his head back to me and his eyes wide with shock.

"You're not going to tell him, are you?"

I didn't want to tell Seth I'd already tried that and had gotten the brush off. Besides, this was between Seth and me. Cal had told me to handle it, and that's exactly what I intended to do—but now that I thought about it, using Cal's status with Seth might be effective.

I leaned back in the chair and tried to appear relaxed and confident.

"Don't you want me to tell Cal? Don't you want him to know you have a girlfriend who lives right next door?"

A deep frown line snapped between his eyebrows.

"All right, Jesus Christ. What do you want from me?"

"Are you having sex with her?"

"None of your damn business."

"Oh yes it is. It's my business and Cal's business what goes on under this roof."

He heaved another sigh.

"I want you to stop having sex with her and stop leading her on."

He shook his head and took another slurp of his coffee. The mug twirled in his hands and a slow moment passed. Finally, he met my eyes, angry still, but resigned.

"It was only once," he said. His low volume carried an intensity I hadn't heard from him. "And now, Christ, she won't leave it alone."

"That doesn't surprise me a bit. I'm sure she'd love to have you for a boyfriend. And she'll do anything to get you, including sending you pornographic pictures."

He stayed silent and looked out the window again. I let another minute or so pass.

"Yeah," he said, "and now she's all hung up on this thing she thinks is between Regan and me."

"That's the black-haired girl who was here when Sabrina came by the other day?"

He nodded. "Not like Neva, though. She's hot. Neva's her fat friend."

"I just don't want Neva hurt. I'm extremely worried about her. I'm going over there later and talk to her mother."

His eyes swerved to mine. "You're not going to tell her about the pictures, are you?"

"No. I wouldn't do that to Neva. I don't know what I'm going to say, but Neva needs help, and somehow I want to encourage her mother to get it for her."

"Have you ever met the mother?"

"No. I've only seen her from a distance coming and going to work. I just hope she's open and easy to talk to. Especially about her daughter."

He stood and pushed his chair under the table. "Well, you do what you want, but like my mom used to say, hens don't like other hens messing with their chicks."

That was an interesting observation from Seth's mother, but I didn't say anything. He rinsed out his mug in the sink then turned to face me.

"I didn't mean for it to get this way, Zoe. I really didn't."

Sincerity blanketed his face, and his voice held the tone of a child who'd discovered he'd stumbled into something beyond his ability to deal with, one part whining excuse and one part a plea for understanding.

His hand extended in an appeal. "I didn't think she'd get all weird about the whole thing, hanging around all the time and with the pictures and all. I thought she'd be cool about it."

"Seth, you have to understand. Neva probably hasn't dated much, even though she says she's had boyfriends. She's unsophisticated and almost like a child. She thinks you like her."

"Hey, listen," he said. "Let's get one thing straight. The part about her not having boyfriends is a joke. It wasn't like she was a virgin. From what Regan said, Neevy's been a very busy girl since she was thirteen. So don't be thinking I've corrupted some innocent, okay?"

With that, he turned his back to me and left. I heard him charge up the steps two at a time.

CHAPTER FIFTEEN

I wiped up Hattie's toast crumbs and rinsed the coffee pot. The only fitting activity for the remainder of the icy morning would a cup of hot tea beside a glowing fire and delving into a good book and another world: a world that didn't include husbands who put their careers first or stepsons who were spoiled and unthinking. I let the lure of the comfortable setting be my reward for the task ahead.

I didn't want to talk to Gladys Reckart, but leaving the situation alone bordered on immoral. I hated nosy neighbors, but I knew that lack of intervention, the fear that most people seemed to have that a near-stranger's life was not their business, sometimes allowed awful things to happen when they could have been prevented.

Two weeks before Cal and I had moved into our house, a man in a jealous rage had shot and killed his wife and two daughters. It happened six blocks from our new home, and after the shooting, the neighbors were quoted in the paper as saying how they knew something was wrong with the man, knew his actions were a couple of steps out of sync, but didn't intervene. But, because the tragic family kept to themselves, no doubt threatened into isolation by a controlling husband and father, no one befriended the wife. Vicious and loud arguments went unquestioned. Children running from the house in terror only served to propel the neighbors inside their own homes to watch the pathetic events from safety behind a slit in the curtain.

And that's not to say the tragedy would have been averted if someone had intervened, but an event like that always made me wonder. I liked to think that if I'd been neighbors with the family, I would have had the fortitude to make some attempt to step in, to listen as a friend to an obviously frightened woman, to offer my help in caring for the children or encouraging her to go to a women's shelter before things ended in tragedy. Now, with Neva, I had a chance to act on my convictions. If Gladys Reckart threw me out of her home into the cold, I could at least console myself that I'd tried to help her daughter.

Donning my coat, I headed to the front door, my courage stiffening my backbone, when the phone rang. A glance at the digital clock on the kitchen desk gave me a clue who might be calling.

"Hi, Zoe," Cal said. "Listen, I just have a minute. We're going to a dinner meeting soon. But I wanted to call you back. I felt bad about our last call. Are you feeling a little better now?"

Of course he'd phrase his question so that I, not his son, was troubled. But I was determined to be strong, and my determination bolstered my resolve. I decided I wouldn't give Cal the satisfaction of labeling me as his poor hormone-controlled wife back home.

I answered with a lilt in my voice. "I'm good, Cal. It's cold here again, and overcast, of course. I wish it'd go ahead and snow and get it over with."

"Yeah. So did you handle all the concerns you had about Seth last night?"

I gritted my teeth to keep from sending a firestorm of anger half-way across the world.

"Oh, don't worry about it, Cal." Breezy and casual. "Everything's fine here. Don't worry about a thing. I'll let you get to your meeting. I know you're pressed for time. I'll talk to you again tonight. My night. Your tomorrow morning."

"Okay, sure, honey. I, uh, I'm sorry about that phone call. I was in a dead sleep and reacted bad. I don't want you to worry about Seth or anything else. I love you. I really do."

His words, spoken low and velvety close even across thousands of miles, soothed the sharp edges of my angry worry. He loved me.

"I love you, too. And I'll take care of everything. I will." And I meant it.

"That's it, Zoe. Good girl. I'll talk to you later, honey."

I punched disconnect, but stared at the phone for a moment. Good girl?

I strode over to the pantry and opened the door to the spicy closet. I grabbed two chocolate drops from the candy jar, unwrapped one, popped it into my mouth and stuffed the other into the pocket of my hoody.

All the rage and frustration I felt last night resurfaced like a stubborn stain. I was not his good girl. I was an angry woman. Angry with him for not telling me Melissa Delany would be working over there, for flicking away my worries about Neva, and most of all, for taking the job in Uganda without my input.

Good girl, my ass. I'd show him good girl. I buttoned my quilted jacket and left my warm abode.

The wind had picked up, and the bare limbs of the maples and the furred pines hummed with its onslaught. I ducked my head and trotted across the yard. The steps of the Reckart house creaked in protest as I ran up to the porch. I pushed the door buzzer and hugged my jacket to my throat. The chipped paneled door swung opened to reveal Gladys Reckart in a tattered rose bathrobe, mussed hair and late-morning puffy eyes.

"Oh, Mrs. Reckart, I'm sorry. I should have called first. I wanted to talk to you for a minute, but I've obviously come too early."

She looked down at herself, then met my eyes with a kind of surprise, as if she'd forgotten how she was dressed.

"Oh. I was just lazin' around. I didn't get off work till one." Hinges squealed as she pushed the aluminum screen door open and held it for me to enter. I stepped through the threshold, and she shut the door behind me, sealing me inside the dusty living room.

Odors invaded my nose: overflowing cigarette ashtrays, a furnace that needed cleaning, and somewhere on the bottom of the miasma, cooked onions. In another room, canned laughter blared from the television. Through the gloom of light filtered by dingy drapes, I saw newspapers and tumblers half-full with a dark liquid, Coke maybe, littering the scarred coffee table. Worn brown tweed upholstered a sofa and a chair, and cotton stuffing protruded from the arms of each of the pieces. A wooden rocker with arms gouged and scarred with cigarette burns faced a small cold fireplace. Faded sprigs of Lilly of the Valley adorned the wall paper, yellowed in spots, and the yellow spread to irregular stains on the ceiling telling of numerous roof leaks. A few prints decorated the walls, prints someone would buy at some discount store. The entire room could use an intense cleaning and a coat of paint.

Gladys Reckart stood with her arms crossed over her chest. The set of the mouth and hooded eyes told me that she'd noted my perusal.

"Sorry if I caught you at a bad time." I looked around again. "I didn't realize what the layout of this house was. I know both of our houses were built by the same builder decades ago, but the people before us had torn down most of the interior walls. I didn't know the original entrance was this side of the living room."

Suspicion tattooed her expression. She wasn't about to believe I was noting architectural details, but she answered civilly enough. Sleep mucous matted one eye, and she rubbed it with her index finger.

"Yeah. All theses houses along here were like this. Big, but closed up and dark, like they used to build them in the Twenties."

Her voice was tight and hoarse, raspy as if the gravel of left over cigarettes and bourbon still lined her throat.

"How long have you lived here?" I asked.

She snorted a laugh. "Forever. This was my folks' home, and Stan and I moved here after we were married. After he left, I stayed on. Didn't seem any sense in trying to move at that point."

"Then you've seen a lot of changes to the neighborhood."

"Yeah, I've seen changes all right. Only good thing is if I wanted to sell, I could get some good money out of it."

"Are you thinking of selling?"

She shrugged, tired and resigned. "Ain't got no where else to go. That's the trouble. Can't afford to sell and can't afford to stay. Didn't used to be like this. Used to be a nice neighborhood. Although probably not good enough for you yuppies."

Her insult pressed at me like the hand of a bully, and I debated for a half-second whether to ignore it. But I didn't.

"Cal and I aren't yuppies, Mrs. Reckart. We like older homes. We simply fell in love with the neighborhood and our house."

The eyelids drooped to hoods again, and Gladys Reckart regarded me a moment, the suspicion of the invaded for the invader.

"What brings you out on this nasty day?" she said.

"I, uh, I just wanted to talk to you. About Neva."

"What's the matter?"

"Nothing. Everything's fine. I just wanted to ask you about her."

I stumbled through my thoughts trying to get the words out.

I had the feeling Gladys Reckart couldn't muster the concern to help herself, much less her daughter.

I kept my voice even and friendly. "What I mean is, I wanted to know if she was okay. I mean if she's happy."

She snorted again. "Happy?"

"Well, yes. I just—"

"Okay, look, Mrs. Sterling, just spit it out. Neva evidently did something that really pissed you off. I may not be no smart yuppie, but I can tell at least that much."

I felt myself flinch like she slapped me. The woman was rude. Rude and awful. From the disdain in her voice to the snarl on her lip, Gladys Reckart screamed low class, and it had nothing to do with yuppies or blue collar or anything in between. My impulse to blurt a smart comment pushed against my throat, but my determination to help Neva was stronger. I controlled myself.

She slipped her eyes from my face to my feet and back again and at the same time stuck her hand in the pocket of her robe. A crumpled pack of Camels made their appearance, and she fiddled with it and withdrew a wrinkled cigarette. She lit it from a frayed book of matches she fished from the same pocket. In that instant, I abandoned my initial strategy of asking her to help her daughter.

"Mrs. Reckart, what I was wondering is if Neva would be free to help me around the house a few days a week. Cleaning and things. I was hoping that would be all right with you."

Gripping the cigarette between her lips, she tilted her head to one side and narrowed her eyes at me. After a moment, she pulled the cigarette from her mouth, blew out a gust of gray smoke, and without taking her eyes from me, opened her mouth to display nicotine-stained teeth.

"Neva!" she yelled. "Get down here."

From upstairs, I heard a door slam and footfalls on the stairs.

Neva appeared, in the same state of undress as her mother. She stopped in her tracks and her eyes widened when she saw me.

"Hello, Neva," I said.

Gladys motioned with her head for Neva to get over there. Loose threads spurted from the faded print on Neva's robe; she grasped its edges and bunched the collar at her throat. A sliver of blood from a hangnail outlined the chewed blue thumbnail.

"She says she wants to hire you to do some work for her," Gladys said. She looked at me. "You did mean to pay, didn't you?"

"Of course," I said.

Neva kept her eyes on the floor. "What kind of work?"

"Housework. Cleaning and a few chores," I said.

She stood silent and stared at her bare toenails. Her mother poked her with an elbow. "So what do you say? Don't just stand there like a dummy."

She stayed silent with her eyes to the ground.

"I really could use the help," I said. "Maybe you could stop over in an hour or so, after you get dressed, and we could talk about it."

Neva's head snapped up, and she glared at me. "Why don't you just leave me alone. Just leave me alone."

She turned and ran up the stairs.

"Neva!" her mother called. "Neva!"

"It's okay," I said. "Really. Please just let it go. I'll catch her on a better day."

Gladys kept her eyes on the staircase as if she was still picturing her daughter's disobedience. When she faced me, her face had fallen into terrible exhaustion. "I don't know what's the matter with her," she mumbled.

"Actually, that's why I wanted to talk to you in the first place. I have the impression Neva isn't happy. I'd like to help, if I can. I thought—"

"You don't have kids, do you?" she said. The cigarette came to her lips and she took a long pull from the end.

"No." Neva evidently had not told her I was pregnant, and no way was I going to.

"Well, don't," she said. "They'll drive you crazy."

Would I say that about my own child one day? The child I carried inside me that I was so excited to be born? Gladys Reckart must have had hopes for her child when she was pregnant, hopes that had morphed into despair. I pitied her. She had her hands full with an unhappy daughter and a dead-end life.

"I'm going to leave now. Sorry to bother you, Mrs. Reckart. I'll catch Neva another time."

I turned and left. I couldn't get out of there fast enough.

CHAPTER SIXTEEN

While opening a can of chicken noodle soup for lunch, I consoled myself that at least I'd tried to help.

I plowed deep inside my conscience. Was it pity that was driving me to connect with Neva? Did I feel like I could save her and thereby get a gold star in heaven? I wasn't sure what was the well-spring of my actions, but I did know one thing: for me to turn away from Neva was unthinkable. I knew I had the power to somehow affect a positive influence on her life. As for the reason that was driving my decision, well, I'd leave that to the philosophers and psychologists.

I added water to the soup, set it on the stove and the burner clicked and whooshed to light. I glanced out the back window to the driveway. Seth was obviously still upstairs; his frosty rental car sat in the driveway. Hattie was no doubt in her room; I'd serve her lunch at her small café table. I'd crossed the kitchen to the hallway when the phone on the desk jangled. I answered, and my father's gravel-like voice sounded in my ear.

"If you want anything at the house, you better come get it. I'm building a mound of trash here."

I shook my head and closed my eyes in exasperation. My father, my father. What would I ever do with him?

"Hello to you too, Dad."

Silence.

"So you're starting to empty closets and everything? I thought you'd hire packers."

"I will, but I've got to go through everything first, don't I? I'm not taking all this junky stuff to Arizona with me. So if you want any of it, you better come get it before I haul it down to the Salvation Army."

I'd planned to do some work today, but saving any treasures that my father considered junk was more important, and, if I knew my impatient parent, urgent. I'd better get to Red Leaf if I was to rescue anything at all. After promising him I'd be there in a few hours, we hung up.

I dished up soup for Hattie and put some in a thermos for my drive west. I was ready to call upstairs to ask Seth if he wanted some when he thundered down the steps.

"I'm gone," he said.

He grabbed his coat off the hook beside the back door, swung it across his back and pulled open the door.

"I'm driving out to the farm," I said. "I guess I'll see you later tonight."

"Don't wait up on my account."

With a final thud, the door closed behind him.

I clenched my teeth. This was not a damn motel. Should I go ahead and buy a ticket to LA for him? Cal would be disappointed—and furious. I hated to resort to that. As long as Seth stayed clear of Neva, I didn't mind him being here. The fears I'd expressed to Cal, that Seth would play loud music, smoke pot or snoop through drawers had proven to be baseless. He was hardly ever in the house, and when he was, he quietly worked on his computer. Besides, I couldn't take time to do anything about it today. I had things on my mind other than Seth Pruitt.

I made ham sandwiches, wrapped my own to carry and stuck it along with five chocolate drops into a brown bag. After placing Hattie's soup and sandwich on a tray, I carried it to her room, knocked and entered. She closed her book and moved to the table in front of her window. We paused for a moment. Outside on the pole-mounted feeder, three lipstick-red cardinals perched at the holes pecking for seeds. Their bright plumage against the backdrop of the dingy sky and the putty-colored lawn looked like an artist had swished a paintbrush heavy with crimson paint across a gray canvas.

"Beauty happens at unexpected times, does it not, Zoe?"

I smiled my agreement.

"Sit down, please," she said.

I did, and folded my arms across on the table. The steam from the soup wafted between us giving Hattie a look like a spiritual medium about to make contact with the dead.

"How did your talk with Seth go?" she said.

"Oh," I sighed, "hard to say. I don't know if he'll stay away from Neva or not. He said he would."

"Then all you can do is take his promise."

"I know. But I have a feeling he's going to do exactly what he wants to do."

"You expect the worst from him?"

I laughed. "That's not very nice, is it? Expecting the worst from my own stepson? And I spoke to Neva's mother, too. Just a few minutes ago. I was hoping . . . I don't know what I was hoping. Maybe that her mother would be willing to listen or willing to help her daughter. But she wasn't. She's tired and poor. I feel sorry for them both."

She nodded and after a moment spoke again. "And Cal? Have you spoken to Cal about his son?"

I didn't want to hurt her. Cal was her grandson.

"He's preoccupied, Hattie. Setting up the clinics. He basically told me to handle the situation as I saw fit." My stomach gave a slight twist.

She waited. As I should have known she would. She waited with infinite patience for me to tell her the truth.

I looked away from her and out the window into the dull noonday mist. "Cal has got more important things on his mind than me and what I'm facing here. And it's hard to explain over the phone. I don't think he understands my concern. I think he sees Seth as a typical young man looking for a good time."

Her face sagged in disappointment. "That's unfortunate. Very unfortunate. And what of this other doctor? The one who you said has arrived in Uganda?"

I should have known Hattie would get to the crux of her concern. She'd not let that drop. I wanted to. I didn't want to think about it, but she waited.

"Oh, I was probably just overreacting. The baby hormones again." I knew I was deliberately making light of the situation, but I also knew if I allowed myself, my emotions would drive me into the arms of paranoia. I had to stay balanced and real. "There's no reason for me to feel threatened by Melissa Delany. If she was plain and married, I'd feel perfectly comfortable with her there. Now that I think about it, that was really unfair of me, to tell you how pretty she is and how I didn't like her being there. It was very prejudiced, and I shouldn't have said it."

"Whether you should have said it is not the point. It's your feelings that matter. And prejudiced or not, you are worried and uncomfortable about her being there. True?"

I blew out a breath and looked out the window again. I felt like I balanced on a teeter-totter. I could either wallow in my worries about Melissa Delany, or I could pronounce my marriage challenged, but strong.

"No. No, Hattie. I simply have to believe that my worries are only churned up from the stress of this whole situation of moving to Uganda. I can't let myself go on and on about this." I watched her face and a kind of sudden desperation gripped me. She had to believe me. I had to believe myself. "I can't let myself get carried away with my imaginings. Do you know what I mean? I have to stay strong."

Her hand gripped my forearm, and I looked at her again. Tears filmed her eyes, and she wrestled with a small quiver in her chin.

"You are strong, Zoe. You are."

I wondered if she was thinking of her own husband, of Cal's father, who'd cheated on her for years. I wondered if she was remembering the pain of that betrayal and projecting it onto me. I watched Hattie a moment more; she'd turned her profile to me to gaze out the window. She was an old woman. As dear as she was, she was old and saw the world through her own prism. Cal and I would be fine. He'd come home for Christmas, we'd make a time-table for my move to Uganda, Seth would go on to California and Hattie and I would prepare for the move. I'd have my baby, either here or in Uganda, depending on what my research turned up. I repeated to myself what I'd told Sabrina before Cal had left: this would be a wonderful opportunity for us.

"Thank you, Hattie." I squeezed her hand. "But I'm okay about it."

She tilted her head and squinted at me with doubt.

"I think I was blowing the situation out of proportion. He'll be home in fifteen days." I kissed her cheek. "I'm okay. Thank you, but I'm okay."

She nodded, but the doubtful look hung on her face. I said good-bye and left the room, convinced that I'd told her the truth. I was okay.

I refilled Goldie's water bowl, let her out and back in again, grabbed my lunch and scurried to my car. I arrived at Red Leaf in record time.

I entered the dining room through the back door and halted mid-stride. Thank heavens I'd pushed my speed in I-88 and risked getting a ticket. My father had wasted no time.

Just as he described, packed boxes and bags littered the floor. The walls had been stripped of the cheap prints my parents had accumulated, probably tossed now, but my own paintings that Mom had hung were stacked on top of the dining room table. I lifted the top one and studied it for a moment.

One of my first forays into oils, and I'd used the old wash house in the backyard for my subject. I tilted my head to give it some critical examination. Not bad for a seventeen-year-old with a couple of years of art classes at the township school. I'd captured the sunlight behind the maple on the side and the knotty shadows the leaves made on the whitewashed boards. I'd done it in the summer, so Mom's pink and white impatiens lined the bottom of the little structure. When I'd presented it to her, she smiled that soft smile of hers that told me again that I was the love of her life. I set it aside, the first in my stack to keep. I shuffled through the rest of the stack, maybe twenty in all. Some were very good, others were horrid. At least my father hadn't tossed them out without consulting me.

"Found those pictures, huh?"

He stood behind me and looked at the stack of pictures over my shoulder.

"Some of them aren't bad," I said. "I think I'll keep them."

"Well, your mother liked them."

He turned and lumbered back into the kitchen. I started to follow him, then took a moment to survey the rest of the dining room. The bare walls were sadly in need of paint. Standing in one corner, a packing box displayed a casual mound of my mother's glass knick-knacks and her one silver-plated candelabra, souvenirs of the formal table she'd set for holidays a few times a year.

My father's stony voice cut through my memories. "You going to stay out there forever?"

Shaking off my visions, I strolled into the kitchen. Boxes and paper shopping bags mounded with tea towels, a hand mixer and cooking utensils concealed most of the floor, and next to the old dry sink a tipsy stack of canned goods balanced in the corner. Some of the cupboard doors were open and I could see that all but a few items had been cleared away.

I pointed to the boxes. "What are you going to do with all that?"

"That's what I told you. I'm trashing whatever you don't want. Well, giving it away to Salvation Army. I won't need any kitchen things. My condo is fully furnished."

"I remember you told me that. But you aren't leaving for two weeks. What are you going to eat in the meantime?"

"I've saved some stuff aside." He pointed to the items on top of the kitchen table. "I figured you might want Rella's rooster salt and pepper shakers. And that set of embroidered tea towels from her grandmother."

I began stacking the items inside one of the empty boxes sitting on the floor under the table.

"Do you have anymore boxes?" I said. "This won't be large enough and I didn't bring any with me."

"On the back porch. Help yourself."

With that he turned away from me and went back to the cabinet filled with old casserole dishes and chipped mixing bowls. I walked to the porch, grabbed a couple of boxes and crossed back through the kitchen.

"I'm going to Mom's room, okay?"

He didn't look up from wrapping a casserole dish in newspaper. "Take what you want."

"Did you get everything you wanted to keep of hers?"

He looked at me hard, the prison-camp survivor alive in his eyes.

"Got what I wanted three years ago. Her wedding ring and the memories."

I knew we were teetering on the edge of the slope that would hurtle us into a black pit. I left.

A year before Mom died, Dad had moved into one of the upstairs rooms; Mom became so sick they couldn't sleep together. I slept on the living room fold-out sofa, rather than my old bedroom, to be near her in case she needed something. We did that for two years. The original master bedroom was hers, at least in my mind.

Now, I opened the door and entered the cold gloom.

I pulled the cord on the flowered-print curtains to expose a dull day, then turned from the view of the farmland and focused on the room where my mother had lived and died. The flowered coverlet that matched the curtains blanketed the double bed. On her bedside table, a lamp rested on a crocheted doily, along with her tiny brass clock and the blue china dish where each night before going to bed, she'd place her watch and her wedding rings. The drawer to the table was closed now. A picture flashed in my mind of me kneeling beside the bed, fishing through that top drawer retrieving the instrument of my mother's death. I blinked the picture away. Not now. I couldn't stand it now.

Arranged on the top of her dresser were pictures of me at all ages, and some of Dad, her parents and her brother Chet, who'd died in Vietnam. I wrapped them in paper and placed them in the box I'd brought from the porch. I opened the dresser drawers. Even though I'd emptied them after she'd died, I wanted to double check. The bottom drawer stuck a little as I pulled and would open only a few inches. It was empty anyway, I was sure, so I closed it and went on to her closet.

All of her clothes were gone, but a few boxes perched on the shelf. I knew their contents: a special shawl she liked, my grandmother's embroidered bed jacket, a dried bouquet of flowers, more pictures—the stuff of her life. I pulled down the boxes one by one and opened them to once again look at the contents. While I was resealing the flaps, Dad came into the room.

"You gonna take all of this?"

He swept his arm to indicate the three boxes on the bed.

In another month, thanks to Gus Lohan, I'd own this house. I'd bring these same boxes right back here and put them into this very room. Pretending I'd never step foot in this house again was dishonest. Dad would find out about the sale; the legalese of the transaction would be public record, and I had no doubt my father's friend Harold Ingram would call Dad in Arizona to impart the morsel of gossip. Dad would feel mocked and furious when he thought back on today's box-packing.

But no sense in worrying about my charade; his feelings of being duped wouldn't change anything between us. Since Mom's death, his anger and bitterness toward me had blossomed and then festered like a piece of spoiled meat. In his mind, I was beyond redemption.

The sour taste of anger rose in the back of my throat. He really had no right to sell Mom's house in the first place, no moral right. Mom had wanted me to have it, and he knew it. He deserved the sense of betrayal he'd feel when he found out I had repurchased it.

He watched me, his eyebrows raised in question.

"What?" I said. "Sorry. I was thinking of something else."

"I said you gonna take all of this with you?"

"Yes, I thought I would. I can put it in the carriage house or the basement. I have tons of room to store it."

He stayed while I opened the last box from the closet and pawed through the contents.

"Dad, have you seen that small jewelry box of Mom's, the one with the little cameo in the lid?"

He frowned for a moment in concentration and shook his head slowly. "No, can't say as I have."

"She kept her gold heart locket in it. You know, the one that opened and had my picture and a lock of my hair."

"I remember Zozo, but I haven't seen it."

I looked at him sharply, but he avoided my eyes, meandered to the dresser and began fingering the doily I'd left there. He hadn't called me Zozo in a long time, not since Mom had died, or as I'm sure he thought of it, since I'd killed her. The blurted pet name had caught him as much by surprise as it had me. It left us both in one of those awkward awful moments that I didn't know how to end, but would do anything to make it stop.

I closed the box flaps and lifted it in my arms. "I'll just put this in the car," I said and hurried from the room.

CHAPTER SEVENTEEN

Cal and I were married in the living room of my mother's house. Seeing her tender with peace, her dream fulfilled that she could see me married before she died, made the day more beautiful than any church wedding I could have imagined.

After the ceremony, we traveled to Chicago, spent our honeymoon night at the Drake, and then after three days, we moved into our house at Ten-Ten Universe. I'd been away from my mother for only four days, and even though my father was able to take care of her, I felt selfish for stealing the short honeymoon, and guilt pressed on my stomach like a piece of wedding cake that had hardened to cement. The morning of the fifth day, we woke in our mostly ordered bedroom. Cal went to work, and I readied the house and myself to return to Red Leaf and my mother. I was almost out the door when my cell rang. Mom's weak whisper plunged a knife through me.

"Come," she said. "As soon as you can, Zoe."

I arrived ninety minutes later.

In the living room, my father slumped on the sofa in a silent stare, tears streaming down his face.

His haggard eyes met my own. "She's had a bad day."

I went to her bedside and knelt beside her, my face close to hers. The paper eyelids fluttered open. In the four days since my wedding, the disease had claimed its prize; she'd been holding it at bay until I'd said 'I do.' When I saw her face as pale as the moon, the flagging smile, and breathed in the thick odor of decay, all the misgivings I'd had about rushing the date of the wedding evaporated.

"Zoe. So glad. Love you, darling. So glad."

"Mom," I said, "don't try to talk. Save your strength. It's okay. I'll stay here."

She twitched her head side to side on the pillow. "No. No use." She stopped a minute and closed her eyes then opened them again. "Must tell you what to do. I must tell you."

"Tell me what, Mom?"

The light had hurt her eyes, so we kept the curtains closed, and now, the dark air filled with something else, a presence maybe. And I thought about the ancient image of Death wearing a hooded black robe and carrying a twisted staff. Ridiculously, I glanced around the room to find Him, but I saw only the furnishings I'd known since my childhood. Despite the warmth of the room, a chill wormed up my spine.

"In the top drawer," my mother whispered. "Back."

I glanced to the night table and she nodded. I pulled open the drawer and surveyed the contents: a small box of tissues, some nail clippers, a pen and paper, a pair of earplugs to shield her from my father's snoring before he'd moved to one of the upstairs bedrooms. I knew the contents of that drawer. I'd been nursing her for months and stored pain pills and spoons and extra cloths inside it.

"What is it, Mom? What's here?"

"Reach back. The mints."

I did as she asked and brought out a tin of Sucrets.

She nodded. "Yes. Open it."

Her breathing came hard; she was anxious I do this for her. Did her throat hurt? Was she desperate for relief? I popped the lid and saw dozens of pills, different colors, shapes and sizes.

"What are these?" I asked.

"Zoe, you must feed them to me. Now."

I'd known it, because she'd talked three years ago before the relentless destruction of the disease and how she'd be prepared for the end.

"No drugs at the end, Zoe," she'd said. "I don't want to die in a stupor."

"What about the pain?" I'd asked.

"I'll deal with the pain. But I don't want to be a mumbling zombie. Besides, I'll be the one to decide when the time comes. I've already started saving my pills."

I'd asked her what she meant by that, but she only patted my hand and let her eyes drift away from me.

I'd known what she'd meant, of course, but it was one of those things that even though I knew it, I didn't want to believe it. I tucked her statement into a remote corner of my mind and didn't think of it at again until that moment when I knelt beside her bed.

We'd both read about the ups and downs of the horrid disease, how it carried its victim to the edge of a yawning grave, but then suddenly would back off, leaving the patient praying for the suffering to end. I'd watched this cycle with Mom, and at first, I convinced myself she wouldn't die. But I knew now, as I held the tin of pills in my hand, that Rella Trueblood had never believed any such thing. She had prepared for death. She was ready.

I glanced toward the partially opened bedroom door into the living room. The door obscured my father from view, but I could see the toes of his shoes where he sat on the sofa. She watched me.

"No. He can't do it." She closed her eyes again and her lips bent up a little. "He can't." She opened her eyes, and even in her illness, I knew the stubborn set of that mouth. "You must. You must do this for me."

"Mom, how can I?"

"You must." Her breath came hard and ragged.

"But not today. Not now."

"Yes. Now." She closed her eyes and one tear made its way from the corner to her thin hair. "I can't do it myself. If I start and can't finish . . . It hurts, Zoe. Hurts so bad."

I fingered the box, closing and opening the lid a couple of times, my mind numb.

"Mom, I . . . I don't want you to suffer, but oh God." I closed my eyes and tried to black out what was in front of me.

"Don't worry, honey. Doc Wilkinson won't question you. I think he's surprised I've lasted this long. You won't have any trouble about it, Zoe."

Tears clouded my vision and blurred the stark pleading in her eyes. Even now, her final thoughts were for me, my well-being. She was asking this of me, and at the same time assuring me that as far as anyone else knew, her death would be the expected result of ALS.

And how could I refuse her? How could I whisper platitudes assuring her I'd rub her feet or brush her hair and then she'd feel better, when I knew it wasn't true?

But I didn't want it to be now. I didn't want her to suffer, but I didn't want it to be now. What if she still had some sage words for me hidden in the recesses of her unconsciousness? Words that would make my life meaningful? Words that would somehow explain why I had to lose her? Or if not words, a look or a touch. Another glance of tenderness, another stroke of affection from her hand that would tell me above all else, I was her girl. How could I give her the pills now and take a chance I'd miss that?

Less than an hour later, of course, I did give them to her.

I choked through my words. "Do you want to talk to Dad first?"

She shook her head. "No. We said all we need to. He can't

take much more. Please, Zoe."

I knew what she meant. Helping my mother to end her life was simply beyond my father's capacity to act. He'd loved her too much. It was up to me.

I examined her face and saw the starkest of her pain, something that until this point, my mother had never allowed herself to share with me. She'd always protected me, even as an adult, dismissed her own trials and tribulations as nothing, and then gone on to focus on me. And, God help me, I gobbled up her attention like a hedonistic child plunging into a bowl of sweets. Now I wanted the most personal part of her. I wanted to know every sadness that had ever pinched her heart, every disappointment and worry that had kept her awake during long black nights. I wanted to lean down and lick the tears from her face, swallow them, make them a part of my body, take her cells and molecules inside me to mingle them with my own. But I only touched her temple with my finger and wiped away the stream of tears, then looked back down to the tin box in my hand. I plucked one from the small mound and held it in front of her face for her to see it.

"Here it is, Mom."

She smiled at me then opened her mouth, a baby bird ready to be fed. I placed the pill on her tongue and she closed her mouth on it. It was started.

"I can do more than one. More than one, Zoe."

I plucked three and she opened her mouth again, then after I'd set them in the middle of her tongue, coated and dry, she closed her mouth over them. We'd kept a thermal bucket of ice chips on the night stand for her, and now I lifted the lid and with a teaspoon, scooped a few of the chips. She opened up again and I placed them in her mouth to melt the tablets.

"Do you want them all, Mom?"

She nodded. "Yes. And don't worry, honey."

I knew she was talking about the consequences of my actions again, the legal consequences. I didn't care if there were questions or not. They could come and haul me away in manacles for all I cared. I had no moral compunctions. Mom and I had spoken often about God, about heaven and about crossing to the other side. We had agreed dying was a natural part of life, and the next stage awaited. I figured God knew full well what I was doing, and He understood: I didn't want her to suffer anymore.

We'd been at it for about a half an hour—ice then three tablets then more ice, and in that time she asked me about Cal and about having children. She told me how much she loved me, and that when I had a baby, I'd understand the love a mother has for her child, and then I'd understand how she felt about me. They were soothing words, but her pain was so great that they were punctuated by her gasps and unconscious groans.

At one point, she opened her eyes, as conscious as if she'd not taken one pill.

"Pray for me, Zoe, that I have the strength to do this."

With that statement, I began to see death not as the gentle transition we'd discussed, but as the shrouded victor portrayed through history who snatched joy and life. Fear grew in me as I fed my mother death, but she maintained her rhythm: open mouth, ice on the tongue, close. And my admiration for that woman soared. She was a god to me, to do this, a lion-hearted soul who would meet the Henchman tight-jawed and clear.

About half way through the pills, her speech began to slur and her eyes closed, but she still opened her mouth, waiting for the tiny pellets that would transport her from the pain. She'd swallowed maybe fifty or sixty, when the bedroom door swung fully open and my father walked into the room. I had the box open on top of the side table, the teaspoon emptied of ice in my fingers. He stared hard at me, taking it all in. The muscles in his face worked silently. Finally, he spoke.

"You had no right. No right."

He turned and left the room closing the door behind him. I looked at Mom. Her eyes were closed, her mouth open and the bones in her chest rose in shallow even breaths. She'd go now, in just a little while.

And so I waited, I don't know how long, enough for me to hold the frail hand while it still had some life in it and remember the times that hand had soothed me and had given me what no one else could. Pictures scrolled through my mind; Mom smiling with the delight of a surprise, frowning with worry, listening to one of my adventures. Her eyelids fluttered open for a moment, but she was unseeing, then closed. I stood up from where I'd been kneeling and left her.

From his place on the sofa, Dad followed me with thick eyes as I crossed in front of him and lowered myself into Mom's rocker. I rocked for a few beats with my eyes closed, then stopped the motion and looked at him.

"She's sleeping now, and then she'll be gone," I said.

During the next minute or so, his expression mutated from helpless grief to blazing anger. Or maybe hatred.

"You had no right."

"Dad, she asked me to. She was suffering. I saved her from a few more hours of suffering."

"You don't know that. You're not God. She may have lived another few days."

"Lived? You call that living?"

"You had no right."

I knew he'd wanted from her the same thing I had: a few more words, another special look, some filament of connection.

"Dad, she had no more to give. Her time was up and she'd planned it all, with the pills. It was her time."

He shook his head and moved his eyes away from me. He

didn't say it again, but I knew he was repeating the refrain inside his own mind: You had no right.

It had been like that between us in the three years since that day; me trying to explain, tying to justify, him giving me nominal responses. And now he'd grown hard and cold toward me, bricked behind an unforgiving wall. The two people my mother had loved the most were lost to each other.

CHAPTER EIGHTEEN

The trunk lid of my Volvo slammed closed and, brushing my hands together to dislodge the dust, I turned to my father. He stood with his hands jammed into the pockets of his plaid wool jacket breathing clouds of frosty air, his face set in its usual grim determination. He'd helped me haul the bags and boxes of rescued memorabilia out to my car and together we'd loaded them. After I left, he'd return to echoing rooms finally devoid of every remnant of my mother.

I placed my hand on his coat sleeve. "You okay, Dad?"

"I'm fine," he said.

I watched his face in silence for a minute, but his expression didn't change. That was the thing with him; he could be miserable or ecstatic and unless he told me, I'd never know.

"Well," I said. "If you're sure. You're welcome to come back to Chicago with me. Stay at the house until you go to Arizona."

"No. I'll be fine here. I've got things to do. Lohan and I close on the sale January third. I'll be ready to leave after that."

"All right, then. I wish you'd reconsider and come to Chicago for Christmas. Cal will be home for about a week, I think, and you've never met Seth."

To my surprise, he tilted his head to one side like he was actually considering my invitation.

"That might not be a bad idea. I could drive up Christmas Eve and come back here the day after Christmas."

My shock was so complete, I'd lost his words after his first sentence.

"You would?" I said. "You really would come for Christmas?"

He barked a laugh. "What? Now you changing your mind about asking me?"

"No. No." I rushed to reassure him. "I'm thrilled, Dad. That's great. And Cal will be thrilled, too."

"You sure you got room for me?"

"Yes, plenty. I'll bunk you in with Seth. You can have the other twin bed in the guest room."

He'd never seen the house, our estrangement was so complete. I didn't remind him of that now. I didn't want anything to break the spell.

My father was coming to my house for Christmas!

I grinned at him and rose to my tiptoes to plant an impulsive kiss on one cold cheek.

He smiled at me and his face turned redder than the cold would have caused, but in the next instant he returned to his old gruff self.

"You better get going," he said.

I nodded, and with a final grin, climbed into the car. It hummed to life with a turn of my key and I lowered the window.

"I'll call you in a day or two, Dad. Don't work too hard getting the rest of the house packed."

He backed away from the car and with a smile and a wave, turned back to the house. I pulled out of the driveway with a hopeful heart.

The afternoon had grown darker and low clouds scudded in from the north. I cranked up the heater and turned on a CD, Jann Arden again, which I knew would help to dispel the melancholy that I'd dredged up with the memories of Mom's death. About ten minutes later, one of those pregnant lady cravings blindsided me: A hamburger. Thick and juicy with ketchup, mayo and dill pickle. My mouth watered, my stomach grumbled and thankfully, the Heartland Steak House was just ahead. Another ten minutes and I found a parking place in the crowded lot, swung open the restaurant door and inhaled the tantalizing aroma of cooked grease.

Saying hello to a couple of people I'd known most of my life, I made my way to a booth in the far corner. I took off my coat and threw my purse in beside me, then scooted in with my back to the wall, facing out. Two of my favorite things were in store for me: a great burger and the chance to people-watch.

The waitress placed a large glass of water in front of me, but bustled away before I could place my order. I was about ready to call her back when Gus Lohan stepped from the hallway that led to the restrooms and caught sight of me. He walked toward my booth with an expression on his face that said he was genuinely happy to see me. The nubby sweater he wore, in shades of deep green and teal, highlighted his hazel eyes, and his even grin deepened the hole in his chin. He slid in opposite me.

"What're you doing outside of bad old Chicago?" he said.

"I came out to the sticks to slum it for awhile. Wanted to see how the hicks lived."

His grin widened, and he took his time looking over my face.

I felt myself heat under his scrutiny. "I wanted a hamburger, all of a sudden. You know. The pregnant thing."

He nodded and smiled. "They do have good burgers here."

Relaxing back against the tufted vinyl of the booth, he rested one hand on the table. A beautiful hand, I noted, defined and strong with long fingers squared at the ends. An artist's hand.

"You still feeling okay about everything?" he said. "Still want to go through with the sale of the house?"

"Oh, definitely. No, I won't change my mind on that, you can count on it. Matter of fact, I just came from Red Leaf. I packed

197

some things to take back to Chicago with me and acted like I wouldn't be back to the house forever. I felt bad about pulling the wool over Dad's eyes, but unfortunately it can't be helped."

I thought of the warmth of our parting when I left the farm a half-hour ago. Maybe there was hope for us yet. Maybe over Christmas, we'd mend enough of our relationship that I could tell him I was buying the house.

Gus cocked his head to one side. "What happened between you guys, if you don't mind my asking?"

I shrugged. "Oh, it's a long story. When Mom died . . . I don't know. Things just somehow went bad."

That was all he was getting from me. He didn't press it though, only nodded.

"So you planning a big Christmas this year?" he said. "One last blowout before you become a Mom?"

Yes, I was planning one last blowout before becoming a Mom. And then we'd move to Uganda and Melissa Delany would be there. And then my world here would end. And I couldn't come to the Heartland Steak House to have a hamburger or plan Christmases with my father for a long time in the future. And Cal would be working working working and I would be—where? An important part of his life? Or a bother? A lump had sprouted in my throat. I looked down at the table, then spun my water glass in its damp circle.

"Hey, Zoe. Hey. What's the matter? Is everything all right with the baby?"

Gus's voice was solid and sure, like Dad's, I thought, only without the cutting edge of criticism. A voice to count on. A voice that would know what to do in any situation. A voice that would know what to believe and which way to turn. I felt his hand on my arm and looked up to meet the hazel pools brimming with genuine concern and a little alarm.

This was not the hard focused businessman I'd met before.

He was warm and willing to listen.

"Oh, yes," I said. "The baby's fine. No, it's not that. It's only . . ."

I thought of Seth and Neva and Cal a world away and my father and how I missed my mother. I swallowed again and met Lohan's eyes.

"You okay?" he said.

"Yes. Yes, the baby's fine. Sorry. I think I'm having a delayed reaction to everything. Lots of things." I glanced to the chiseled hand resting on the table in front of me. "It's just that with Cal gone, I don't know, it's harder than I thought it would be."

"Yeah, I can imagine, doing everything yourself."

He leaned forward, wanting me to have the solace of his words. Wanting to make me feel better. Caring about making me feel better. My pulse throbbed in my throat.

"I know when Charlene moved out," he said, "and the divorce was final, it was a real blow. Living the daily life of it, you know. I mean—God, sorry. I didn't mean you and your husband were going through a divorce or anything. I'm just talking about the being alone part."

He looked away for a moment, his mouth scrunched up in embarrassment. "Shit," he mumbled.

I laughed. Long and deep from my stomach and it felt good. The people at the next table caught my explosion and cast suspicious glances our way.

"Sorry," I choked out between the dwindling giggles. "I appreciate you trying to help, I really do. It's just that you were trying so hard, and it struck me as funny."

"Oh, thanks a lot." But a smile lifted one corner of his mouth.

"No, I'm sorry," I said. "I appreciate your effort."

"I just meant . . ."

He looked away from me then back again and burst into laughter at the same time. After we'd quieted, he started again.

"Nothing like stumbling over the 'I'm sorrys'," he said. "What I was trying to say is I know first hand how hard being alone is."

With his index finger, he traced a circle on the gray Formica table top. "Actually, Celeste went through a divorce last year. It was rough, especially at first, but she'll be okay. I never liked the guy."

"Really?"

He scooted up straight in the seat, and his face opened in a grin, ready to tell me a good tale.

"The first time she introduced me to him, now I'm the prospective father-in-law, right? So I'd flown out to California to see the girls—did you know they both live there? San Francisco area."

"I knew they lived in California, but I didn't know where exactly. How'd they end up there?"

"After the divorce, Charlene packed them up and took them out there. They were mostly grown though, seventeen and nineteen, so I flew them home every few months. But they like it out there. And now Sybil's married and expecting my first grandson next month, and Celeste is getting her feet on the ground. We're still pretty close."

Warm pride came into his eyes, and I knew where his soft spot was. This would not be a man to leave his wife for a job on another continent.

The thought was on me faster than a gunshot, and I squirmed a little; my subconscious was betraying me.

"So anyway," Gus said, "I go out there to meet my prospective son-in-law, right? And I told Celeste to make a reservation someplace nice, downtown or something, so I can take her and Millard, that's the guy's name if you can believe it, to dinner. Celeste chooses the Mark, very posh and expensive. So the three of us get there and we order drinks and everything is copasetic and the guy seems okay, a little prissy for my tastes but okay."

I recalled how I'd watched Cal fold his cashmere sweater as carefully as if he were handling an ancient papyrus. Prissy, was Gus's word. Prissy.

Gus leaned toward me on his elbows. "About half-way through the appetizers, Millard excuses himself from the table. He comes back after a little while and as we're starting on the main course, I begin to suspect that this guy is absolutely blotto. His words are slurring and he's breaking out in weird laughter every once in a while. I glance over to Celeste and I see she's noticed it, too. She gets this tic around her mouth when she's upset or nervous, and I see her little mouth just a-workin' like crazy. By this time, he's talking about some big lawsuit he's filing, he's a big-shot lawyer, and I look over at him and he is so wiped, he's talking with one eye completely closed. I kid you not. One eye open and the other one closed."

To demonstrate, Gus reached to his right eye and held the lid closed, then with his other hand, stretched his left eye wide open with his thumb and index finger. I'd started laughing midway through his recital, and now giggles bubbled out of me unchecked, and I covered my mouth with my hand.

"What can I get for ya?"

The waitress stood beside the booth, impatiently rapping her pencil on her order pad. I signaled to her with one finger held in the air to give me a minute. Finally, my face flushed from laughing, I looked up at her.

A thin woman wearing a Budweiser tee shirt and jeans slumped beside us, her eyebrows, black and bushy enough to hold water, pulled together in annoyance. The pencil stopped its drum roll and hovered over the pad. I turned to Gus.

"Would you like to join me, Gus?"

"Oh, no thanks. I gotta get back."

He glanced behind him to the front of the restaurant. His head bobbed back and forth, looking for his table.

"I don't want to keep you," I said. "I mean, if you need to get back."

He waved away my concern and shook his head.

After I'd ordered my burger, rare and loaded with the works, the waitress turned and flounced back to the kitchen window.

"Lady has some definite eyebrows," he said.

I laughed and Gus watched me. I felt a little self-conscious under his intent gaze. I searched in my mind for where Gus had left off with his story.

"So I guess Celeste married the one-eyed drunk anyway," I said.

"Yes, unfortunately. It's over now, but not because he had a drinking problem. That was the only time I saw him do that. Celeste said he was so scared about meeting the old man, he'd stopped for a few belts of gin on the way to the bathroom." Gus laughed again. "God, he was a mess."

Our laughter died down and we felt the awkwardness that comes with waiting for someone to take the next step. We started to speak at the same time, and after more laughter, I spoke.

"I'm not faced with a one-eyed drunk, only a less-than-stellar stepson."

I had intended to say something about drunks at parties, but the statement about my stepson was out of my mouth before I realized it.

"Your husband's son? How old?"

"Twenty-one. But Cal has never lived with him."

I gave the shortened version of Seth's background and his drop-in appearance twelve days ago. When I was finished, Gus thought a moment before he spoke.

"So what's the kid doing that's so bad?"

"I shouldn't have mentioned it, really."

He waited for me, patient and focused.

"It's just that I have a neighbor, an eighteen-year-old girl, who's very unhappy, a misfit and a loner. And, I'm embarrassed to say, Seth has been having sex with her."

"Geez. Does he like her? Or is it all about the sex thing?"

"Oh, it's the sex thing, one hundred percent."

And it all spewed out: Neva's visit, the pictures, my attempt to talk to Gladys Reckart, and Seth's promise he'd leave Neva alone.

"Hopefully," I said, "his word will be good. But I'll wait to believe it when I see it."

He shook his head. "That's not a good situation. What does your husband say?"

Shame and embarrassment made me squirm in my seat. I was sorry now I'd brought it up. I thought he'd let the question drop when the waitress, black eyebrows drawn together in an irritated frown, appeared with my burger and fries, but as soon as she'd left the table, he repeated the question.

"So what does your husband say?"

Suddenly, I was exhausted with it all: Cal, Neva, Seth, my father. Melissa Delany. I was pregnant and alone and hanging on by my fingernails. A sudden "what-the-hell" feeling came over me.

"My husband," I looked Gus in the eyes, "told me to handle it."

The hazel eyes widened in momentary shock and he was silent and staring for half a beat. My statement had thrown him off balance, but whether it was Cal's response to me or the fact that I admitted it, I didn't know. I lowered my eyes to my hamburger.

He reached across the table and covered my hand with his own. Rough calluses, from farming and the hard work of wood-shaping, heat, and a firm pressure. Not a tentative touch. Not a touch given by a man who was tortured with his own demons. A touch by a man who knew himself, knew his place in the world and knew he had enough in him to give to others. I raised my eyes and saw his troubled face.

"You're a strong woman, Zoe. You can handle it."

He'd unknowingly repeated Hattie's words. But I didn't feel strong. I felt confused and afraid.

Our eyes locked into each other and we froze in that position. My insides swirled like a tornado: anger at Cal, anger at myself that I'd blurted out Seth's sordid story, and on the bottom layer, a velvety kind of wonder at Gus Lohan. Who was this man? Where had he come from, and why now?

"Gus, everyone's waiting for you. Are you coming back to the table or should we eat without you?"

We jumped apart. She stood beside the booth, slim and elegant, one of those that could have been anywhere from thirty-five to sixty-five. Manicured, coiffed, perfectly made up and wearing a turquoise and silver necklace and earring set that must have cost the house payment. She moved like a woman who got what she wanted without asking for it. Tended, as Sabrina would say. Well tended.

"God, I'm sorry," Gus said.

He slid out of the booth and stood beside her. They made a striking couple.

"I got carried away with a story," he said to her. He turned to me. "Zoe, this is Bethany Fox. Bethany, this is Zoe Trueblood. Er, I mean Sterling."

My smile elicited a cool nod.

"Listen, I apologize," he said. "Zoe and I have some business together and I just got carried away."

She gave him a flick with her luscious eyes, then turned them on me. "No problem." She smiled and turned her back. "See you in a sec." She walked away from the table.

"Sorry, Gus," I said. "I didn't mean to keep you."

He leaned down to me. "Don't worry about it. I hope everything works out okay. I'll talk to you about the house soon. But it's been a pleasure, Zoe."

With a nod, he was gone.

I ate my burger in a kind of numb but pleasant trance. After a bit, I looked down to my plate and realized I'd eaten every single morsel, including the lettuce and parsley garnish. A mother's body will rule, I supposed. Steppenwolf wailed from the jukebox in the far corner, and conversation buzzed at a level that indicated most people had downed two or three drinks. In a few hours, the room would empty of dining patrons and the hard core drinkers would take over. I finally stood and sauntered to the front of the restaurant where the cash register sat on the end of the bar.

Casually surveying the room, I searched for Gus and found him at a table in the back with another man and two women. Keeping a friendly look on my face, just a neighbor looking around the local hangout, I studied the people with him. The other man was older, gray-haired and hunched through the shoulders, and I assumed his partner was the round woman with a smooth gray cap of hair and a matronly smile. The stunning woman sat on Gus's right. He either didn't notice me, or if he did, he kept his attention focused on the people at his table. The cashier dropped my change into my outstretched palm, and I pushed open the door into the winter afternoon.

During the two hour ride home, a lightness filled my chest where for days I'd been hauling around an anvil of worry. Suddenly, rather than half-empty, my glass was half-full. Seth said he'd stay away from Neva, and for now, I was going to believe him. Cal would be home in thirteen days for Christmas. My father had relented to come for a visit. I would own my mother's house, and thanks to Gus's arrangement to hold the mortgage for me, I'd own it all by myself.

I reached over to the passenger seat and dug in my purse. Like steel to a magnet, the foil-wrapped chocolate drop jumped into my fingers. I unwrapped it and savored the creamy sweetness on the roof of my mouth and my tongue. Before I got home to Universe Street, I'd eaten all five of them.

CHAPTER NINETEEN

The next several days passed in the usual routine: Hattie reading, knitting and listening to her radio, me upstairs in the office working, mainly on the ever-present Griffen account, Seth sleeping late, staying in his room until early evening then leaving until the wee hours of the following morning. I spoke with Cal every day, mostly for five or ten minutes, one time fifteen minutes. He was frantic and pushed to his limit, but loving every second of the challenge. He mentioned Melissa Delany only a few times, and each time in the context of her work. Several times a day I'd feel the green-eyed monster overtake me when I thought about her presence there, but mostly I was successful in fighting down the taunting images of my imagination. I missed my husband, but in a way, my world was more peaceful than it had been in months. I hated to admit that to myself, and I put it down to the fact that I didn't have the stress of worrying when Cal would be home, worrying I might be continually disappointed that at six o'clock in the evening, the phone would ring and Cal would tell me he simply had to work late—again. Besides, I reasoned, I was busy with my work and getting ready for Christmas; I'd baked two more batches of cookies for clients and a local women's shelter I liked to support, and Hattie and I had spent one cold but festive afternoon shopping in the local stores.

After breakfast seven days before Cal was due home, Hattie went to her room to read and listen to the radio while I cleaned the kitchen of our coffee makings and a few scattered crumbs. I heaved the trashcan from under the sink, grunting a little as I tugged the plastic bag mounded with trash from the bucket. I cinched the ties and with a clatter dropped it on the wood floor. It was heavy, and I wished Seth was here to take it out for me, but I'd checked the driveway earlier and seen that the white rental car was gone.

He'd gone out last night, as usual, and even though I didn't hear him come home, I knew he had. When I'd passed his room upstairs, I noted the bed covers had been jostled to a different position than the day before, and a different pair of pants, khakis rather than jeans, sprawled near the perpetual pile of dirty clothes he mounded on the floor by his closet. What did he do with his time? Where could he go for seven or eight hours every evening until the early morning hours, and then leave again early enough that I'd miss him? Had he met a girl? I assumed his friend Jason was still in New York so Seth wasn't hanging out with him, but now that I thought about it, I'd ask him. If Jason was back in town, maybe Seth could stay there—although he'd been no trouble to me, especially since I'd seen no more evidence that his tryst with Neva had continued.

I snapped open a new plastic bag, looped its edge over the trash bucket and re-stowed it under the sink. After throwing on the quilted jacket I kept on the hook by the back door, I lifted the bulging bag and headed out the back door into another dingy day.

We stored the garbage cans on the side of the garage nearest to the Reckarts' house. The tall privacy fence divided our property, but it wasn't one of the more expensive fences with the overlapping boards; Cal had gone discount, so the slits between the boards provided a sliver of a view into their yard and visa versa. Their utility shed stood only a foot or two away from the fence; we could see its metal roof from our yard. The bag of trash rattled when I dropped it on the ground in front of the garbage can. The metal lid came free with a tug, and the bag echoed with a crash when I dropped it into the empty bottom. My own cloudy breath swirled around my face when I bent to retrieve the lid, and I glanced to the fence section beside me. A pink form blinked between the spaces. The door of the shed opened, closed and then opened again. More movement—a pink sweat shirt. I replaced the lid and moved closer to the fence.

I hadn't seen Neva since I'd gone to her house. I had no idea how she'd react to me, but I still wanted to develop rapport with her, or at least attempt to.

"Hello, Neva. It's Zoe. I heard you over there when I came out to empty the trash."

A shuffle of footsteps through dead grass, then the fence moved a little and one brown eye peered through a slit in front of me.

"Hello," she said.

"How are you? Off work today?"

"I don't have to work until five. I get off at midnight. Is Seth around?"

Oh dear God.

"No. He's gone today. But what about you? Doing anything interesting?"

After a moment, she answered. "No. I gotta go."

The pink sweatshirt disappeared and I headed back to the house.

I stopped before climbing the back steps and tuned to survey the backyard. Left over from the early twentieth century, the apartment above the garage was called a carriage house, a place where a chauffeur might have lived above the cars he tended to. Sometimes, when I stood in the driveway and looked up to its crusty windows, I imagined gleaming Packards and ladies in fox stoles waiting for James to take them to cocktails. Now, I kept it locked and the key inside the porch light mounted beside the door. Cal used it for storing old furnishings from his university days and out-of-date medical texts. Electricity powered the apartment and because we decided not to replace the ancient coal oil heater until the renovations in the main house were finished, Cal bought a space heater, and, a few weeks later, a second-hand refrigerator. When we were first married, he'd climb the old wooden steps to the raggedly retreat, start the space heater, fix himself a drink and thumb through his memories. His cave, he'd called it, something that every married man needed. A few days after Seth had arrived, he'd shown the apartment to him as a means of sharing his college experience with his son. I privately wondered if in his own subtle way Cal was trying to pressure Seth into rethinking his career choice of being a scuba instructor for tourists. I'd thought once of converting the apartment to my studio when several hoped-for children would occupy every available bedroom in the house, but now, with Cal's plans in Uganda . . .

I spent the next several hours revamping the logo and new graphics for Griffen. Finally, I rested back in my chair and surveyed the result. I was pleased with my accomplishment. I closed the file and went down to the kitchen to fix Hattie and me lunch.

I opened the fridge to get the sliced ham and mustard for sandwiches when the phone on the kitchen desk rang. I automatically checked the time in Uganda: 9:12 PM.

"Hi, Zoe," Cal said.

"You sound exhausted."

"You have no idea. We've had meetings all day, and we're scheduled for another one to start in a few minutes."

"At nine-fifteen at night?"

"Crazy, isn't it? But we're pressed for deadlines from the

Mechin people from their damned tax crap so they can get all their ducks in a row before the end of the year. And on top of that, the Ministry of Health here wants—sorry. You don't want to hear all this."

I sank to the chair and rested my elbows on the desk top cradling the phone against my ear. "No it's okay. At least it gives me a chance to share something in your life. Tell me."

He did, a convoluted tale about certificates and screening procedures for another doctor from New Delhi. He finally ended with a push of air from his lungs, exasperated.

"I'm beat," he said. "Just beat to the bone."

"I'm sorry, sweetheart. I wish you could come home. I'd rub your back and you could take a long hot shower."

He cleared his throat. "Yeah. Well. That's not going to be possible."

"I know. Wishful thinking, I guess. I worry about you."

"So how's everything there? How's Seth?"

How was Seth, exactly? Exceptionally devious and morally corrupt? Or a good kid who'd made a mistake he'd taken care of?

"I've handled it. Everything's fine, Cal. I talked to him and—"

"Listen, Zoe. There's something I need to tell you and I'm just putting it off."

"What is it?"

"And before you throw a fit, just know I did everything I could, I really tried, to make it come out differently, but this is just the way it's got to be."

My heart pounded in my ears. Whatever was coming, I didn't want to hear it.

"It's about Christmas," he said. "I can't come home."

Was there a part inside me that had been expecting that? Had I buried my head in the sand shielding myself from subtle hints? Had a whisper in the back of my mind or an odd feeling warned me?

I felt like the shit had been kicked out of me.

"Zoe? You there?"

"Yes."

"Honey, look, I'm sorry, but there's just nothing I can do about this. You just have to know that I want to come home, I really do, but I just can't."

Deep breath in. Exhale slow and even.

"Well then," I said, "maybe I should just fly over there. I could look for an apartment and plan our move. I'll make all the arrangements for Hattie and—"

"I don't want you to do that."

"Why not?"

"I—I'm very busy right now and like I told you before I left, I'm just not sure how this can all work."

"Me coming over there for Christmas?"

"I mean you coming over here at all. I'm so swamped, you gotta understand that. Let's put it on hold. We can talk about it later, when I get the clinics up and running."

A long smothering silence.

"You there, Zoe? Say something."

"I don't have anything to say."

"Oh shit. Come on, Zoe. Don't be like this."

My emotions charged through me too fast for me to pinpoint. I clenched my teeth, wadded the hem of my sweater and crushed it in my sweaty palms.

"I've got to go, Cal."

"Come on. Don't do this."

"I'll talk to you later."

I ended the call.

I let my eyes wander the room, silent except for the faint drone of Hattie's radio program from her room and the ticking of the miniature wall-mounted grandfather clock behind the kitchen table. The sandwich makings rested on the counter where I'd left them when the phone rang, reminding me of what I was doing before the world tipped.

Time was an odd thing. Sometimes, the clock would mark its only passage, and sometimes, like now, time had nothing to do with the clock and everything to do with some kind of cosmic shift, a jump from one level to another because of a particular experience. And during that moment, time shifted for me—or maybe something inside me shifted. Because although I didn't think Cal was lying about how hard he'd tried to come home for Christmas, I knew that ultimately, it had been a choice. His choice. Once again, I'd come in second. And on top of it, for him not to want me there—

I was angry and frustrated and sad and humiliated, and I knew I was approaching an invisible marker within myself, like a channel marker in the midst of a vast ocean; a marker signaling a split in my journey.

What was I thinking about? Ending my marriage? Divorce? Or was this one of the bad times in marriage? The "worse" side of the "for better or worse"? I should call him back now, insist I was coming over there with or without his blessings. I should make all the arrangements, call the airlines and go. That's what I'd do. Now.

I slapped together a sandwich for Hattie and served it to her in her room, poured myself a Coke and raced up to my office. But instead of clicking on a website to check for an airline ticket, I dove into my design work with a concentration I hadn't mustered in weeks. But after a while, the jitters got to me. I finally clicked off the computer in frustration. I lay down in my room to nap, but twenty restless minutes later, I gave up.

Exhausted, I heated soup for Hattie and me and we ate in front of the fire I'd started in the waning cold afternoon. I managed half of my serving, but left the rest to get cold. Hattie threw me a questioning glance and asked if I was tired. I nodded, then stacked the few dishes and plodded my way to the kitchen. As I cleaned up, the back door opened and with a burst of cold air, Seth entered. Goldie's tail bounced on the floor and he reached down to scratch her ears.

"You're home early," I said. "Hattie and I just ate, but you can fix yourself some soup if you want."

"No thanks," he said. He unbuttoned his coat and pulled his arms out. "I just picked up my car from the shop, and I ate out. I have some things I want to do on my computer, then this guy I know might call. I'll probably go out later."

His boots clomped up the steps to his room.

He had his car back. And with Cal not coming home, there was no reason for him to stay. I thought I'd feel relief at the prospect of Hattie and me having the house to ourselves, but I didn't. I didn't feel much of anything.

Watching an old 1940s movie with Hattie numbed my chaotic thoughts for two hours. I retreated into silence, not pouting or melancholy, just a silence that would allow me to simply exist for the evening. Hattie gave me several sharp glances, no doubt picking up with her usual sharp intuition that something was wrong, but she said nothing. About ten o'clock, we said goodnight. I checked the lock on the back door, turned out the light and headed through the echoing hallway and up the stairs.

When I got to the landing, I stopped: Music, heavy hard rap, but muffled. Whenever he was on the computer or doing whatever he did to occupy himself in his room, Seth played music on his iPod speakers. His usual choice was R and B, a lot of Alicia Keyes and Beyonce Knowles, music that I enjoyed, too. But tonight the rap ground out. Odd. I'd remembered Seth making an offhand comment that he hated rap, and yet here it was coming from his room. I crept up the rest of the steps and stopped outside his door.

It was cracked open, and when I pushed it wider, I saw him with his back to me sitting at his desk in front of the window. The music wasn't coming from his iPod player, but from outside the house. His laptop was open and his fingers rested on the keyboard, but they weren't tapping. Seth was looking across the top of the computer screen to the view out his window.

Across from him, light shone from Neva's bedroom window, and Neva Reckart, naked, waving her arms above her head, undulated in the spotlight. She grinned, a one-sided grin because her hair covered one eye, a cheek, and half of her painted red mouth. The rap pounded on, and to its beat, Neva's breasts, loose and meaty, swayed and rolled. Small brown nipples protruded from her alabaster skin, and below the billowing flesh, the patch of pubic hair had been shaved. The full nakedness, the look of a little girl on the swollen body of a developed woman shocked me more than anything. I gasped, and Seth spun around to face me.

His eyes widened, and he stumbled to his feet, knocking the desk chair on its side.

"Jesus Christ," he said.

"Pull that window shade. Now."

He turned from me and reached up for the pull. Neva, evidently now understanding what had happened, stopped in mid-shimmy, her arms arced above her head. Seth pulled the shade down and turned back to me. The rap music pounded for a moment more, then abruptly ended. A painful silence stood between us.

"She did that on her own," he said. "I didn't ask her to. She did it."

"Oh stop it, Seth. Just stop it. I don't care about that. I'm just so . . ."

I stopped to take a breath. I knew my nausea sprouted from not only Neva's pathetic display, but Cal's announcement to me earlier in the day, a kind of delayed reaction. Maybe that was the channel marker I'd sensed this morning: I'd crossed a line with Cal and also with his kid.

Talons of anger gripped me.

"I'm over this, Seth. You've come into this house and have done nothing but create havoc."

He walked toward me, holding a hand out as entreaty. "Zoe, I'm sorry. I didn't know anything like this would happen."

"But you should have. After what we talked about. You've been seeing her all along, haven't you?"

He lowered his head, at last shamed.

"I see Regan. Neva just shows up."

"You're an adult, Seth. Your actions have consequences and those consequences affect others. You cannot go through life blithely seeking your own satisfaction without considering others. Well, you can, but it won't be in this house."

"What can I say other than I'm sorry? Everything just, I don't know, it went to crap before I knew it. I was only messing around. I didn't mean . . ."

He looked at me, and his eyes began to redden around the rims. So. This told me something. The kid wasn't as self-serving as I thought he was. That was something for him anyway. I felt the anger loosen its hold a little.

"You've acted very irresponsibly, Seth. Cal will be so disappointed."

"Oh shit. Don't tell him, Zoe. Please. Come on."

The appeal in his voice, the frantic darting of his eyes, his expression all told me he was sincere. But I wondered if his panic was rooted in embarrassment rather than shame: embarrassment that he'd had sex with Neva rather than some beautiful creature Cal would approve of.

"I'm not going to call him right away," I said, "but he needs to know. This has gotten serious. You're thinking Neva is some

216

lark, along with that Regan, but she's very disturbed, Seth. And for you not to understand that is beyond insensitive. It's selfish and self-centered to the point that I'm seriously beginning to doubt your character. And I think Cal will feel the same way."

I was amazed at myself that I could call up Cal's name so quickly, to use now without a clutch of pain.

His reddened eyes blinked in genuine shock. The tick in his jaw and the thick swallow told me he was fighting back tears. He ran a hand through his hair and then reached it out to me in an appeal.

"I'm sorry, Zoe. I . . ." He stopped a minute to compose himself. "I can't say anymore than that. I've made a mistake. I was wrong. I didn't realize she'd do something like this. I just didn't think."

I like a person who can admit when they're wrong, and for a twenty-one-year-old kid, he was doing a good job of it. For the first time since he arrived, despite this thing tonight, a seed of respect was sown inside me.

"I know you haven't thought, Seth. But I have, long and hard, about Neva and this whole thing with you. It's been worrying me sick. I'm going to try to talk to Mrs. Reckart again tomorrow. I think it's gotten to the point where we need her mother's help to intervene."

I didn't know what good another talk with the woman might do; my hunch was that Neva had a mother who would refuse to help her. I didn't know what I'd do next, but for now, I had to try.

I took a deep breath and slumped against the door jam.

"Seth, why don't you just get in your car and go on out to California? There's no reason for you to stay for Christmas anyway. I didn't want to tell you like this—actually, I was going to suggest to Cal he call you and tell you himself, but since it's come up now—he's not coming home for Christmas."

A little boy's wide eyes and open mouth gaped at me. "He's not?"

"No. He can't get away."

"Will he be home after Christmas? I mean, like maybe around New Year's or something?"

I sighed. "No. I don't know when he'll be home. We haven't discussed that yet. But given that he had been scheduled to start the clinics in January anyway, I doubt he'll be home for . . . I don't know when. I think you should go ahead to California."

He looked down to the floor and stayed silent for a long moment.

"Yeah. I guess so."

A sudden rush of pity threatened to overwhelm me. I examined the curls on the top of his head. He was still so young, emotionally still a boy, but living in a body and a culture that proclaimed him a man.

I stepped toward him and laid my hand on his arm. "I think it's for the best at this point. When you have a break from your school, let Cal know, and if he's home, he'll fly you back here then."

"Okay. But can I stay until day after tomorrow? When I drove the BMW home from the dealership today, the steering pulled a little. I want to take it back in and have them check it tomorrow, and I don't know how long it'll take, or even if they can get me in. I mean, I hate to get on the road with it and have it messed up. I mean, if it wouldn't be too much trouble if I stayed just another day or so . . ."

Contrite, pleading, humble.

A side of Seth Pruitt I'd not seen. And I side I knew had been manufactured over the years for the benefit of an indulging mother, lenient teachers and now me.

But there was nothing more for me to do about a relationship between myself and my stepson. In two days, he'd be leaving, and whatever would be between us would be determined sometime in the future.

"Sure," I said. "Get your car fixed and then we'll plan on you leaving the day after tomorrow."

He nodded at me again, crossed his arms in front of his chest and looked at the floor. Still playing the role.

A fierce wave of exhaustion crashed through me.

"I've got to go to bed," I said. "I'll see you in the morning."

I stood up to leave and he touched my elbow.

"Hey, Zoe? Thanks."

I gave him a weak smile and closed the door behind me. Walking to my bedroom, I nearly melted with relief.

CHAPTER TWENTY

The next morning, I climbed out of bed, padded into the closet and with gentle fingers, like an archeologist exploring pieces of treasured ruin, touched Cal's clothes. I smoothed the shoulders of his shirts and sports coats, adjusted by a millimeter their proximity on the wooden rack. Lifting a shirt collar to my nose, I inhaled his unique odor. I remembered doing the same thing to Mom's clothes, after she died, to hold her presence. And now I was doing that with Cal's clothes.

But my husband hadn't died. He'd made a free and conscious decision to stay in Uganda and work on his clinics—without me. Maybe one day, some day, he'd make the decision to come back to the house on Universe. He'd open the front door, alive and well and fully breathing, and enter my life again. When he decided.

I left the closet, walked into the bathroom and surveyed Cal's side of the counter. The last time I'd cleaned in here, I'd dusted the few bottles of his abandoned cologne, empty except for an inch or two of amber liquid. They clinked together as I scooped them up and stored them on the bottom shelf under the cabinet. Good, I thought with a streak of defiance, more room for me.

I showered and dressed, all the while puzzling about the logic of my own actions: holding on to my husband while rummaging through his clothes, pushing him away by stashing his cologne. Was I trying to remind myself Cal was still my husband, still the father of my unborn child, or was I pulling away from him, separating my emotions from him and from our marriage? My own actions were like those of a stranger, someone whose motivations were a mystery to me.

It was eight-twenty in the morning here, four-twenty in the afternoon in Uganda. Before going downstairs, I phoned Cal; I had a point to prove.

"Hey, Zoe," he said. "God, I'm beat today and we've got a dinner tonight with a group of French scientists that'll be providing some of our lab work. How's that for an exciting evening?"

"Oh, it doesn't sound too bad."

"Well," he said. "How's everything?"

"Good." I sparkled. I shined. My voice crackled with positive energy.

"Hey, glad to hear it. Everything okay with Seth?"

"Yes, everything's fine. I think we've got things pretty well smoothed out at this point."

In that instant, I decided not to mention Neva's disturbing dance exhibition or my ultimatum to Seth. I'd crossed some line, a line I hadn't even known was inside me. Usually, I would have rushed to elucidate all the details of the latest events; now, I just wanted to handle The Seth Situation, as I'd begun to label it in my mind, by myself. I felt the internal change of my perspective, like the shifting of a fault line beneath the earth.

"I'm glad you got things settled," Cal said. "That's great, honey. Seth's okay, really. He's just a typical randy kid. Listen, Zoe. I'm sorry, you know, about not being able to come home for Christmas."

"You've already apologized, Cal."

I sounded cool and mature, even to my own ears.

A surprised pause, then he spoke. "I want you to know how much I appreciate your patience. We'll talk about everything else later, okay?"

"Sure. Actually, I'm very busy right now. My father will be here for Christmas day, and Hattie and I will prepare for a nice holiday. I really don't have time to dwell on anything but that right now."

I was amazed with my words and the smug pride that I could come across like I wanted to, but my emotions were at war. One part of me—the part that only an hour ago had rummaged through his clothes—wanted to plead with him to throw me a scrap of evidence that our marriage was still intact. But another part of me sat on my shoulder and whispered in my ear: You are handling things very well. You're fine without him.

I stuck to the topics of Cal's business and a few odds and ends about the house; a bill for a roof repair that would require taking money from the savings account, Hattie's health, a few Christmas cards from unexpected senders. We finished up our conversation and Cal promised he'd call again the next morning.

The day returned to the usual patterns of the household: me working in my office and Hattie reading and knitting, listening to symphonies in her bedroom. Seth left in his car mid-morning, I assumed to take it back to the dealership to get the steering checked. I didn't see or hear from him for the rest of the day, although, there was nothing unusual in that.

That night, through the fog of my dreams, I heard Seth come in, but I plunged back into sleep. Later, something woke me. I turned to look at the digital clock on the bed table: 7:32 A.M. I'd overslept, but after a quick review of my coming day, I realized I had nothing pressing, so I curled the covers beneath my chin, closed my eyes and tried to finish my dream. Sabrina and I had just drizzled pancake batter over the top of Tom Twellman's enraged face. A door slammed outside of the house, and I realized it was the sound that had awakened me a moment before.

Was Neva going through the side door of the garage that led to Cal's workshop? Propping myself up on my elbows, I listened closely and heard the slam again. That wasn't the side door; that door had a damper, Cal had called it, that prevented the door from slamming closed. This door sounded like an old wooden screen door with a simple spring that released and closed without hindrance—like the screen door of the carriage house over the garage. I threw the covers off, padded to the back window and pulled the cord to open the drapes. Through the slit between the sheer panels, I peered through the dreary morning.

The garage occupied a space about fifty feet behind the house. The leaves of a giant elm would have blocked my view in the spring and summer, but now between its bare tangled arms, I could clearly see the wooden staircase on the side of the building leading up to the apartment. Above the two garage doors, three windows provided the light to the apartment's small living area, and at that instant, a shadow moved across the panes. Someone was inside. I stepped away from the window, ready to get dressed and investigate, when I saw the screen door open and Seth step onto the stair landing. The door slammed behind him and he clumped down the staircase. He reached the small stone walkway and trotted across the backyard toward the house. In the kitchen below me, the door opened and closed.

I tore off my flannel pajamas, threw on a sweatshirt and a pair of elastic-waist sweatpants then pushed my feet into my slippers and hurried from the room. Halfway down the hall, Seth met me and stopped. He looked at me a moment, then turned inside the guest room that he'd claimed as his own. I stood in its threshold.

"Seth?"

"Oh, hi Zoe."

He grabbed the strap of his duffle, hoisted it onto his shoulder and took a couple of steps toward me. His eyes held mine for a moment, then flicked away; I held my ground, blocking his way.

"I, uh, just thought I'd move out to the carriage house," he said.

"What in the world? What are you doing?"

He shifted his weight, planted himself, and adjusted the duffle strap, and a smirk bent the corner of his mouth. "I told you. I'm moving out to the carriage house."

I stared at him, and his eyes bored into mine, steady and defiant.

"I thought," I said, "we had all of that decided. I thought you were leaving for LA."

"I am. In a few days. And I figured maybe I wouldn't annoy you as much if I moved out to the carriage house. That way you could have your house back."

"We didn't agree to that. You were supposed to leave today."

He shrugged. "I decided to wait a couple of days. Kind of kick back for awhile."

Sudden anger snapped in my chest.

"Don't try to make this out like a casual thing," I said. "I don't appreciate this. This isn't your house, and what you're doing is beyond rude. It's presumptuous."

"Presumptuous?" He smirked again. A challenge loomed in his eyes. "Presumptuous? You know what Zoe, I don't think you'd be saying all that if Cal was around. I don't think he'd call it presumptuous at all. I think he'd tell me whatever I wanted to do would be fine."

"Have you talked to Cal? Did he tell you to do this?"

"No. But I know he would say it was okay."

"That just goes to show how little you know of him. Cal doesn't like rude people. And he wouldn't like it, just staking your claim to live in the carriage apartment without talking to me about it."

"Cal wouldn't care. And you know it."

"I know no such thing. You just don't do this, Seth. And I can't imagine that a kid who was raised in a nice home like you were doesn't know better than this. You just don't take over someplace that belongs to someone else, like you're a squatter or something."

He laughed. "Squatter? Shit. I'm his son. I don't think that qualifies as being a squatter."

I glared at him a moment, letting my anger show on my face and in my voice. "So you plan to move into the carriage house, for as long as you want, regardless if I want you to or not."

"I'm not ready to leave yet. Maybe in a few days or something, but not yet."

He took a step toward me, leaned in, and I was reminded of his first night in our house when he'd made the phone call to Mexico; how afterwards, he'd pushed into my space, intimate and disturbing. Now, his eyes narrowed and his breath brushed my face.

"Call Cal if you want," he said. "He'll back me up. Excuse me."

He moved his shoulder to the side and passed me, leaving me gaping with disbelief at his audacity.

"Cal? Can you hear me?"

I'd placed the call to his cell phone, and despite the fact it was 2:15 A.M. in Uganda, he answered on the first ring.

"Sure I can hear you. What's the matter?"

I paced in front of my bedroom window and watched Seth climb the stairs to the garage apartment. Balancing his duffle and a cup of coffee, he swung open the door and disappeared inside.

The emotion that for a week had lived in the pit of my stomach rose to my throat. Suddenly, it was too much for me:

the "handling" of Seth, this life Cal had decreed for us, the uncertainty of the future of my marriage. I heard my voice quiver with tears.

"Oh, Cal. Everything's just—"

My throat clutched and I stopped to swallow.

"Look, honey," he said. "Is everything okay? Because I'm right in the middle of something here. I'll call you in the morning, about five or six more hours."

"No," I yelled. I gulped back my panic and tried again. "Cal, I need you to hear me."

After a pause, he replied. "Okay. Just a sec." Resigned. Inconvenienced.

I heard his palm cover the receiver and muffled voices, then Cal came back on the line. "Okay. What's up?"

"Who's there with you? Isn't it late there? I mean early, like two AM or something?" I wondered if I'd gotten the times mixed up.

"Yeah, well, Melissa and I still have some things to talk over before tomorrow. We've got one of the funding committees flying in tomorrow for a review. You know. Just the typical hassle when the moneymen show up."

"Melissa Delany is with you?"

His laugh, a deep throaty sound I'd always loved, crossed the thousands of miles between us.

"Of course Melissa's with me. I told you we've got a big meeting tomorrow. What did you want, Zoe? We've still got a bunch of stuff to iron out."

My anger at Seth and his move to the carriage house dissolved into mist.

"You're meeting with Melissa Delany at two o'clock in the morning? I find it hard to believe that you can't accomplish what you need to during regular business hours."

"Regular business hours? Honey, there is no such thing now

as regular business hours." His tone was light, amused at his silly wife. "Melissa's my right hand man. What?" Scuffling and scraping of the receiver again, then Cal's laugh from far away, again through the palm of his hand.

He came back on the line. "It's nothing. She's just complaining because I called her a right-handed man."

His voice grew louder. He turned away from the phone and called to her again, evidently across a room. "I know very well you aren't right-handed."

He laughed again.

Nausea overwhelmed me and I sank onto the chaise lounge. I thought for a minute I might be sick, but I closed my eyes and took a couple of deep breaths while he finished laughing. The nausea subsided.

His voice spoke away from the phone. "Oh, Christ. That's right." He spoke into the receiver again. "Zoe, honey, I gotta go. I'm sorry, but we're just swamped here."

"Cal, wait." I pleaded, a little girl begging her parent for a special privilege.

I stopped myself, stunned while my rollicking emotions formed themselves into coherent thought. Wait a minute. That was it. I was begging my husband for the privilege of his attention, begging him to listen to me.

Anger hurtled through my chest and hardened in my throat, along with a bitter realization: If I railed at Cal, demanded his mindfulness, it would accomplish nothing—except to provide Cal and Melissa with a good chuckle about the wife back home.

No matter if we divorced or not, I would not allow myself to be the object of ridicule.

Divorce. A cold hopelessness settled into my chest.

"Zoe? Zoe, let me call you later today."

"No, don't bother." I said.

He heard the flint in my voice, I was sure, even on the other side of the world.

"What did you want?" His voice had softened. "Is Seth all right?"

"Yes, he's all right."

Angry panic got the best of me, and the words flooded out despite scrunching my eyes shut to keep them in.

"No, actually, he's not all right because he's moved out to the carriage house, and I want him to leave."

"Leave? Why?"

"Because he . . ."

How could I explain all this over a long distance call—the fear, the sense of foreboding I carried with me, foreboding that darkened every day? How could I tell him that his stepson and his selfish dalliance with our unstable, desperate neighbor sickened me, made me feel like I was peeping at obscene behavior through the knothole in a fence?

I wished I'd kept my mouth shut, but I hadn't, so I plunged ahead. "Seth's carrying on something awful with Neva. You know, Neva next door?"

He laughed again. "Jesus. Not this again. She's not my cup of tea, but hey, to each his own."

"Cal, stop this! I mean it. It's awful and wrong and Seth is just using her for sex and it's perverted."

He laughed. "Christ, Zoe. Come on. He's a kid. A young man. What do you expect him to do, be chaste?"

"No, you don't understand. It's not right. And—"

"Zoe, I have to go."

"I want you to talk with Seth. He got his car back, and I want you to tell him to go on to LA. He needs to leave."

Anger nipped his voice tone. "I'm not going to tell my own son he has to leave my home. If he wants to live out in the carriage house, let him."

I wasn't getting through to him, and now that I'd started my tirade, the situation swelled with urgency. "Cal, listen to me. Seth is wild and out of control. I'm uncomfortable with him here. I'm pregnant and stressed and upset. I need you to do something."

My voice had risen and the thought flashed through my mind that I sounded like a banshee unleashed. His voice, low and calm, broke through my panic.

"Okay, okay. Now listen. If you're upset, just ask him to leave. Just tell him you want him to go, that's all."

I kept my voice as calm as his, I hoped. "I've told him to leave, but he won't. He says he wants to stay out in the carriage house. But I want him gone."

His voice exploded over the line. "Jesus, Zoe, I do not have time for this now. I don't. What's the big deal? He's got plenty of money, so it's not like he's asking for us to support him. He wants to live above the garage. That would be a good place for him, come to think of it. He could hook up that old stove and the space heater's up there. He's not hurting a thing by staying up there for awhile. Jesus, don't bother me with this bullshit. Please."

I stared at the dark spot on the brown shag carpet, a spot I'd made when I spilled a cup of tea a few weeks before Halloween. That had been right after I'd found out I was pregnant. I was so happy, and Cal was solicitous and concerned. I'd taken up the spill as best I could, but a faint stain remained.

A stain. A stain that would be there forever.

I heard Cal's voice again, and I blinked myself back from numbness.

"Listen, I gotta go. I really do. I'll call you later today."

The line went dead.

CHAPTER TWENTY-ONE

I turned off the phone and placed it back in its cradle hardly conscious of my own actions. Nausea bubbled up again, along with a conscious thought: My marriage may be over.

Was he having an affair with Melissa? I closed my eyes against the onslaught of visions: Cal smiling tenderly at her; Cal kissing her, stroking her check; Cal's mouth lowering over one of her nipples, his fingers gliding down her stomach to the dark tangle of pubic hair.

I shook myself out of it. Don't be a fool, I scolded myself. Of course he was having an affair, or at least was on the way to one. And soon . . . very soon. Hadn't I feared this, dreaded it for months, on some level below my thoughts? I'd heard other women say the same thing: I knew it, I just couldn't believe it.

Dear God. I was forty-one years old, pregnant and looking into the face of a bungled marriage.

Maybe it wasn't over yet. Maybe Cal would come to his senses after a while, after his affair with Melissa. I suddenly saw my place as third in line, behind Melissa and his relentless ambition that had always been my competitor. My husband was gone, in terms of miles and experience, to someplace that would never include me. Renewed rage burst through me, I felt my heart pound, and for a moment, the air in the room appeared crimson.

The bastard. The ruthless, selfish bastard.

Hattie. I wanted to talk to Hattie. Had to talk to Hattie.

I hurried from the bedroom and clamored down the steps. I staggered down the back hall, using my outstretched hands to feel my way along the walls. After knocking at her door, I turned the knob.

She sat at her table with a book opened in front of her and a mug of coffee steaming at her elbow. She'd already dressed for the day in crimson velour pants and turtleneck pullover and black house slippers with gold-stitched curlicues and colored stones scattered across the toes; slippers for a dainty royal personage. Faint roses perfumed the air, and her scrubbed face and brushed silver hair glowed with good health. When I inhaled the scent and saw her sitting at her table, calm and accepting, I felt like I'd entered another world, a world of reason and order and love. I stood in her doorway and sagged with relief.

"Come in, Zoe, come in."

I managed to make my way to one of the other chairs at her table. I lowered myself into the seat like an invalid who'd walked too far, then gripped my hands together in my lap. She placed a ribbon to mark her place, set the book to one side and waited for me. After several false starts, I drew a deep breath and glanced out to the backyard, half expecting to see Seth dance down the stairs from the carriage apartment, but then I realized his car was gone.

"He left a few minutes ago," Hattie said.

Once again, she'd missed nothing.

The words flowed out of me, gushed out like stale and putrid water that had sat to long in a rusty tank. Seth. Neva. Cal. Melissa Delany.

I'd been dry-eyed and logical through my recitation. But now, ending my story with Cal's call this morning and his curt dismissal of my concerns, I heard my voice quiver as it made its way through my cramped throat.

"I'm afraid, Hattie. I'm afraid I've lost Cal and my marriage.

I'm afraid of being alone. I'm afraid of being a single mother. And I'm afraid I've failed."

She reached a knotty hand across the table and gripped my arm, a surprisingly strong grip. Tears stood in her weathered eyes.

"You will prevail, Zoe Marie. You will. I know of loss and hardship and broken hearts, and I know about the character that it takes to prevail. And you will."

My tears came then, and I plucked a tissue from the box she kept on the table and wiped my eyes.

"But it's so unfair. How could he do this to me? He's left me high and dry and I don't know what to do."

I tried to catch my breath, but the air I took in only seemed to generate more sobs.

"I don't know what to do," I repeated. "And I'm sorry. I know I'm talking about your grandson. I know this must hurt to hear."

She folded her hands on top of the table and interlaced her fingers. Her eyes clouded and she turned her head to look out the window.

"Yes, it hurts. But it hurts to think of what my grandson has done to you. It hurts to see you being harmed by him. I have seen this for weeks. My only regret is I could not stop it."

A new wave of tears threatened to break through, but I held them at bay. I pressed the back of my hand to my nose, then plucked another tissue from the box.

"I've never told you," she said, "about my young years. In Romania, during the war."

I knew she was speaking of the war that had defined her life: World War Two. Her voice took a wistful tone. I dabbed my nose and eyes again and shook my head.

"You know I'm Gypsy, Cal is part Gypsy."

I nodded.

"What many do not realize, is that during the war, the Nazis not only persecuted Jews, but many people, Gypsies included. And I had both things against me. I was a Jew, at least in their eyes, and a Gypsy."

She'd been looking at me, but turned away now and stared again out the window. I followed her gaze to the bedraggled yard. Spiked yellow-brown weeds fringed the base of the garage. The windows of the carriage house were black and silent rectangles set into the gold hue of the siding, the same color I'd chosen for the house. It had dusted snow last night, I hadn't noticed until now, and it had begun to melt in swirls and streaks on the hard earth, like a slab of arctic marble. One tiny wren flitted from the carriage apartment roof to Hattie's feeder and then darted into the gray heaven.

I looked at Hattie's profile as she gazed out the window and into her past. "I knew you lived in Romania as a girl, but you've never told me any details."

"Ah, God in Heaven, it was another world. Another life. I don't like to talk about it."

She turned her eyes to mine and I caught a gasp in my throat: The gentle dark eyes I'd come to love like they were my own grandmother's were filled with hate.

She lowered her eyes, hiding what she'd already exposed.

"Please don't then, Hattie. Please don't talk about it for my sake."

"No, I want to tell you a thing I learned. I want to tell you."

I watched the movement of her face, the eyes that grew sadder as she spoke.

"I was in a concentration camp. Mauthausen, in Austria. I lived, I existed, in a dormitory for the women. On a cold wooden bunk."

I'd read about concentration camps and studied about the persecution of Jews, and others, by the Nazi party in Germany during the second world war. The conditions of the concentration camps were subhuman, the worst in history. Hattie was choosing to share her memory, she was on the verge of opening that repugnant door, for my sake. Through the turmoil of my own pain, a sudden humbleness came over me. I didn't want her to suffer anymore than was necessary, and the haunted look in her eyes told me she was suffering.

"Please, Hattie. You don't have to tell me."

Her gaze rested on the winter scene outside the window and her voice cracked when she spoke again.

"I lived there for two years. I knew a man there, a man from my village, who in the old days would never speak to the Gypsy daughter of a farmer. But now, we had all been reduced to the same animal level. We, all of us, lived in the same pile of excrement."

Narrowed eyes and the flint in her hoarse words told me the bitterness had oozed its way to the surface. Her clasped hands trembled, the knuckles whitened with her grip.

"But at Mauthausen, now this man would deign to speak with me, when he went to the infirmary across the yard. It was beside my dormitory, and when I saw him crossing the compound, I went to wait outside in the cold. He went to the doctor many times at the end, when he got sicker. But of course it never mattered. He was always sent back to break the rock. He died there. Died breaking the rocks for the Nazis."

Resting a moment, gathering herself, she took a deep breath and then went on.

"He told me about a teacher he'd worked with in Vienna, before the Nazis. And how this teacher, a Jew, lost his position, his family, everything when the Nazis imprisoned him in a concentration camp. The teacher's name was Victor Frankl. Have you heard of him, Zoe?"

I shook my head.

"I learned later he survived, like me. After the war, he went on to become very famous. He wrote books. But while he was in the camp he became famous, too. Because he taught others. He taught the inmates about dignity. About making choices."

I sniffled again. "What do you mean?"

"Doctor Frankl taught that no matter what the circumstances, no matter how horrible a person is victimized, how powerless they think they are, they still have choices. Even in the face of terrible torture and humiliation, people have a choice about their attitudes, about their beliefs. They can choose to cower and become like animals, let their emotions rule them, let their fear define who they are, or they can choose not to do that. They can behave with dignity. They can choose to deny their torturers control over their souls."

"But how could that be? If someone is torturing you, hurting you, forcing you to do things, you don't have any control."

"You don't have control over your body, true. But you have control over your soul. Your dignity."

"I don't understand how."

"One day, long after his release from the Nazis, Frankl had a student in one of his classes ask him about his philosophy. He said to Frankl, 'You are wrong, Doctor. Sometimes you have no choices. If someone holds a gun to your head and is ready to pull the trigger, you have no choice.' And Frankl said, 'Yes you do. You can choose how to die. Whether with dignity or cowering like an animal, you can choose how.' "

Her black eyes met mine. "You have choices, Zoe. You are a victim, but you have choices for how this will shape your life and that of your child. Look for your choices."

I left Hattie an hour later, humble and grateful for that wonderful woman. She'd traveled back into the dark decades, told me things she'd banished from her memories long ago. And she did it for me.

I had choices. I could choose to crumble under the fear of a failed marriage, or I could choose to live one day, one moment, one phone call to Cal, at a time. Right now my job was to take care of my baby, take care of me.

And I had the choice whether to surrender to failure or not. Maybe my marriage could yet be saved. Lots of marriages survived distance and affairs. I wouldn't chalk this up as a done deal, not yet.

I had another choice, and I picked up the phone to make it a reality. After several electronic directions and responses on my part, I finally heard a human voice.

"American Airlines. This is Monica, may I help you?"

"I'd like to make reservations for the twenty-sixth of December. To Kampala, Uganda."

I'd wait until after Christmas, for Hattie's sake, then I'd fly half way around the world to see my husband face-to-face. I'd need to talk to Sabrina about having Hattie stay with her for the week I'd be gone. She'd offered before, and I knew that she and her family were planning a quiet Christmas, just Mitch, herself and Devon, so I didn't think that under the circumstances, she'd mind Hattie joining them for New Year's. My passport was up to date. I'd call the kennel to make a reservation for Goldie. Seth would certainly be long gone by then. I made my reservations fully intending to carry through with the plan, but at the same time, conscious that if I backed out of the trip, we'd forfeit nearly two-thousand dollars. Cal could afford it. I'd not spend another moment thinking about money.

And I might back out. I might decide tomorrow or the next day or the next or the night before I was set to leave to forget it, to let it go for now, to wait it out and see how things shaped up later into January.

Or, I might decide to forget the trip and move out of the house for good.

I had choices.

I thought of my mother, how difficult it must have been for her to get past the hard shell my father usually wore to the soft place inside him where he could be loved. I saw now, with the distance of maturity, how his blunt criticism must have lacerated her heart. But she'd never wavered in her love for him, even when she didn't like him, even when she couldn't stand to be near him for one more second. I remembered how after his scathing tirades, she'd slam from the house and march out to the wash house. She'd stand inside the old shed and gaze out the window onto the prairie. If I opened the door and tried to intrude on her reverie, she'd look at me over her shoulder and say, "Not now, sweetie. I'll be back inside in a minute." And later, I'd find her fixing dinner or folding laundry without a hint of pain on her delicate features. When I'd asked about her alone time, she'd say, "Don't worry about it. Everything's fine."

My mother had always been such an icon to me, someone to admire and model. I remembered what she'd said about working both halves of her marriage, but I realized that I had one thing that as a woman, she'd never had at her time in history: I had choices.

CHAPTER TWENTY-TWO

I wandered through the rest of the morning in a hazy dream-state reliving conversations with Cal, Seth and Hattie. I still wanted to talk to Gladys Reckart about Neva's bizarre dance performance last night in the window, but it would have to wait; when I checked out my kitchen window, I saw their car was missing from its usual spot in their driveway. If their usual pattern held true, Gladys had taken the car to work. I'd keep an eye open for her to return. I wondered if Neva was in the house or if she'd walked to the bus stop at the end of the block to go to work. I thought about going over there and if she was home, having a private word with her, but in the end, I decided against it; I imagined the encounter disintegrating with Neva's closed hostility. Besides, I wanted to suggest professional help for her, and if Gladys Reckart would at least listen to my suggestion, with her endorsement, I could make the arrangements. Without her endorsement, well, I didn't know what my options would be; I'd have to face that when the time came.

Besides, right now I had enough to handle with getting the details arranged for my trip to Uganda.

If I went.

My stomach gave the alarm a little before noon that it would not be ignored. Despite the tornado of thoughts and emotions swirling inside me, I was hungry, and I knew Hattie would be, too.

I crossed to the pantry and glanced out the kitchen window

in time to see Seth pull his BMW into the driveway. He popped the trunk, lifted out a couple of plastic grocery bags, then closed the trunk and trotted up the steps to the apartment.

The power was on up there, Cal had never turned it off, so I was sure the space heater provided Seth all the warmth he needed. And the old refrigerator would be adequate to hold enough beer and snacks for a couple of days.

How special, I thought. Just home sweet home.

The gate in the back fence slammed. Neva hurried across the yard and with the back pockets of her jeans wobbling from side to side, climbed the steps to the carriage house. When she got to the top, she knocked once and entered. The door closed behind her and in the next seconds, two figures moved across the apartment windows that faced the kitchen where I stood. Cal had placed an old sleeper sofa just under the windows, and through the thick black mesh of the screens and the thin piece of fabric that had served as a curtain for the past owners, I saw the two of them sit down. Another moment, and the deep base of Seth's stereo system thumped through the air.

I fixed a couple of sandwiches for Hattie and myself. I opened her door to invite her to eat with me, but she'd crawled on top of her bedspread, pulled a coverlet over her, and had fallen asleep. I tiptoed in, covered her shoulders and turned out the light she'd left burning. Bless her dear heart. The recounting of her grim memories had exhausted her. I returned to the kitchen, wrapped her sandwich and put it in the fridge, took my own sandwich and a glass of milk and mounted the steps to my office loft. Since it faces the front of the house, I could neither see nor hear the activities in the rear. I clicked on the computer and stared at the bouncing cube of my screensaver for a minute.

Choices. What were my choices?

I could call the police, but I realized the second the idea crossed my mind that it would be a drastic step. Instead, I picked up the phone and called Amanda Crawford, our attorney. After a twenty minute conversation, she told me what I'd silently predicted.

She asked if Seth had damaged the property. I said no. Had he paid rent? I said no again, although he had given me some money a couple of weeks ago for food and "bother." Could be construed as rent, Amanda said, but there was no paperwork. So, she informed me in her best lawyer-like tone, I could obtain an eviction order if I chose to, which I could file through the court. That legal process would take a week or more.

"Let me ask you something," Amanda said. "Why do you really care if the kid, what's his name, Seth?, stays above your garage a couple of days? What's the big deal?"

"It's a long story. I haven't told you the whole thing, but it involves my next door neighbor. A young girl."

"Say no more. He's screwing her, right?"

"You think like a suspicious lawyer."

"I think like a lawyer who's paid to see reality. Is the neighbor girl a minor?"

"She's eighteen."

"In the eyes of the great state of Illinois, she's old enough to decide who she screws."

"Yes, but Neva's not . . ." I tried to think for a minute of a word that would distill her personality, but I couldn't. "She's got a lot of problems and Seth is taking advantage of her."

"Has she been coerced or threatened?"

A picture came to me of Neva jogging across our backyard and bouncing up the steps to the carriage house. Freely, enthusiastically, willingly climbing those steps.

"No. She's not been coerced or threatened."

"Then here's my official attorney advice. Ready? Because you know this won't come cheap. Leave it alone. Do you really want to cause a legal hassle, much less alienate your husband's son?

Is the issue really worth it to you? Seth said he'd be leaving in a few days. Let it go for now. With any luck, he'll pack his things and be out of there within forty-eight hours."

With Amanda's sound advice for comfort, I could concentrate on the Griffen project for the afternoon. Hattie and I ate dinner, chili I'd made and frozen a couple of weeks before Thanksgiving, and then Hattie announced she wanted to retreat to her room. The visions she'd dredged up for my benefit earlier today stayed with her, I surmised, but when I asked if she'd like my company, she assured me with a tired smile that what she needed was time to herself. We retreated to our respective rooms. I read a chapter of a regency romance I'd been reading, a book whose images transported me to another world. About ten-thirty, I turned out the light.

Unlike many people, when I had trouble in my life, my appetite and sleep time increased rather than decreased. Sabrina was the opposite; she didn't recommend personal angst as a weight loss program, but, I reminded her, at least she didn't blow up a size or two during times of turmoil.

I'd fallen into a twilight sleep, teetering between reality and floating dream images I couldn't put a name to, when the thump-thump from Seth's stereo dragged me back to the present. I turned over on my back, opened my eyes to the dark and listened for a moment to the low vibration.

Great. Just when I felt in control of the situation, Seth blared the stereo. And it was loud enough that if I didn't put a stop to it, one of the neighbors would take matters into their own hands. I imagined blinking police lights, darting beams of flashlights across my front porch and the pounding of official fists on the door.

This was ridiculous. I felt intimidated in my own home. I flung the covers to the floor, pulled my sweatshirt over my pajama top and hitched my sweatpants over the bottoms, then shoved my feet into my clogs. Flipping on lights as I went, I hurried downstairs.

I silently opened Hattie's bedroom door and peeked inside. The nightlight showed her form in bed, and the light from the hall illuminated her sleeping face. At least the music hadn't bothered her. The door clicked softly as I closed it. Well, I'm glad she can sleep through this, I thought, but I can't. I headed through the kitchen and to the back door. When I pulled it open, the base of Seth's stereo vibrated in my ears.

The flagstone path between the house and the garage glowed like giant silver discs set in the earth, and I gazed at the sprinkling of stars above me. My breath clouded the air and for a brief moment, the ache in my heart that had begun with Cal's call two days ago eased a little; a transcendent peace flowed through me.

"God's in His heaven and all's right with the world."

The instant evaporated even as I clutched at it.

In the apartment windows above me, a blade of light sliced between the closed curtains. The wooden steps cracked and squealed as I climbed and the throbbing music intensified with each rung up. On the landing at the top, I balled up my fist, and with the side of my hand, pounded on the door.

The music continued and now along with the beat of the base, I could make out a rapper's fierce rhymes. I couldn't understand all the lyrics, and I wasn't familiar enough with rap to even guess at the artist, but my ear caught some of the phrases and they were hard and mean and nasty. I hit the door again with the heel of my hand, waited a moment then turned the knob and pushed. After an initial stick, the door swung inward. I crossed the threshold and then halted mid-step: blasting rap, someone's groans of ecstasy and the pungent odor of pot.

The small alcove where I stood held an old two-burner stove and a sink with one scarred cupboard beneath it. The bathroom was to my right, and a quick glance told me its door was open and the light off. The small L-shaped entryway led to the main room, and although I could hear a girl's laughter—or was it two girls?—I could see nothing through the dull light except the threadbare chair Cal had saved from his medical school days. I crept forward, leaning my head to one side to peer around the corner.

I knew I should leave, go back inside the house and either call the police myself or wait until one of the neighbors did. Or at least I should call out Seth's name, give him a few seconds and wait for his reply. But I didn't. The curiosity, the fascination with the foreign activities of other people drew me to that peep hole in the fence I'd thought of earlier, where perversion might live.

I stepped forward with the full stealth and intent of the voyeur.

One table lamp in the corner lit the scene. They'd pulled the sofa bed open, and at first all I could make out were naked arms and legs and bare butts and torsos. And laughter.

A girl spoke, not Neva, a girl whose voice was hoarse and low-pitched. "No, dumb shit. Not that." Then a groan. "Uh-huh. That. Oh shit, yes."

Winding its way through the thump of rap, were the pervading grunts and moans and slurps and smells of humans having sex.

I don't know how long I stood there. At least a half a minute, maybe more. Suddenly, I caught sight of a face in that writhing mass: eyes blackened with makeup, a swollen red mouth, and goth-black hair, twisted and matted from rough sex. The undulations continued, and she peeked at me through gaps between arms and legs and smiled.

"Hey," she laughed, "want to join in?"

Seth's head came out to one side of the fleshy bundle, and he stared at me a second.

"Oh fuck."

The black haired girl laughed again, harsh and loud. "That's what we're doing, man."

I saw Neva then, she'd been on top, and now heaved her body off the pile and perched on her knees, looking at me over her shoulder, staring at me, her eyes dull and blank.

I turned and ran from the room, clattered down the steps and bolted into the house.

A minute later, the music subsided to a dull thud, and I crawled back into bed. I spent a sleepless night, exhausted and haunted by visions of naked people and writhing snakes and smiles with pointed teeth. At seven, I forced myself out of bed, crept to the window and peered outside. The morning was still black, and no lights showed from the carriage apartment. I wondered when Neva and the black-haired girl, who I assumed to be Regan, had left. I craned my head to the side in order to see our driveway. By the reflection of the streetlight in front, I saw that Seth's car was gone.

I showered and changed, got some breakfast for Hattie and myself. Through the window beside the kitchen table, I surveyed the Reckart's side yard and the section of their driveway in the dawning light. Gladys Reckart's usual parking place was still empty.

With Hattie, I kept silent about the night's activities. Seth was her great-grandson, and as unshockable as I knew Hattie to be, there was no point in telling her this latest episode. We chit-chatted through our coffee and toast, then I climbed the steps to my office.

The computer hummed to life at my command and I automatically checked its clock: 8:48 AM. Cal would be just finishing up his day. The phone beside the computer sat silent and tempting. If I'd told him about last night, wouldn't it finally shock him enough so he'd intervene, he'd talk to Seth? But on the other hand, did I really care at this point? I slumped back into my chair. He was with Melissa. They were working together every day, all day, and I knew in my bones their affair had either begun or was destined to begin at any moment. Did I still want to go to Kampala the day after Christmas? Was there any reason to try to salvage our relationship at this point? I didn't know, but Christmas was five days away and my ticket was the day after. I'd better decide pretty soon.

Christmas. Dad would be here. I needed to shop, plan a dinner, finish wrapping a couple of presents for Hattie and one for my father. But the event I'd looked forward to stared back at me with hollow eyes. All the pleasure had gone from the season, frozen as hard as the ground around our house.

I stared at the bouncing blocks on my computer screen, and thought of Neva. Poor pathetic Neva. Was there anything, any one thing, that I could do to help this girl? And why did I want to? What got to me about her? I thought about what Amanda Crawford had said: She's old enough to screw who she wants to. She was not some helpless child. There were lots of people to feel sorry for in this world, lots of people who needed help desperately, so why had I focused on Neva? I didn't know. But tonight I would talk to her mother again, as soon as she got home from work. For my own satisfaction, I had to at least do that.

But right now, I'd had enough. I was tired and lonely and depressed and I felt like a failure. I'd been cramping again, and I worried about the baby, about Cal, about Seth, about my life. Just as I was about ready to give in to another jag of crying, the phone rang. Since there was no caller ID on this phone, I wondered if was Cal. And I wondered what in the world I would say to him. I answered with a whispered 'hello' on the third ring.

"Hi, Zoe? Gus Lohan."

Something like relief caroused through me.

"Gus. Hi."

"I have the contract ready for the house sale. I need your address, and then I can drop a copy in the mail so you can take a look at it."

A wonderful idea occurred to me.

"I'd rather just drive out there and pick it up. Would that be okay?"

"Sure. Come on ahead if you're sure you want to make the drive." He sounded genuinely delighted.

"I want to. I'll be there in a couple of hours."

We said good-bye, I turned off the computer and hurried down the stairs and into the kitchen. I filled my thermos with left over coffee, stuffed a granola bar and seven chocolate candies into a brown bag, gave Hattie a brief run-down, tended to Goldie, grabbed my coat and purse and ran out the door.

CHAPTER TWENTY-THREE

During the two hour drive to the Lohan farm, visions of writhing bodies tumbled through my mind. As worldly as I'd been in my single days in Chicago, to witness three people having an orgy shocked and upset me. I would have been disapproving, if truth be known, even had the participants been mature adults who'd made the decision to indulge in that form of sexual experience; but this particular episode saddened me more than it sparked my disapproval. The sexual partners were kids—irresponsible people who had no notion of the consequences of their behavior. Seth was spoiled, immature and an opportunist. I didn't know anything about the other girl, who I assumed was Regan, but she came across as hard and cynical. And of course Neva. Seeing her participating in the sex scene last night, when she'd looked at me with those resigned, weary eyes, jarred me to the marrow of my bones.

Bare oak limbs canopied above me as I drove down the dirt lane leading to Gus's house, and eventually the vista opened to the sweeping rock and timber home perched on the rise. Taking a moment to enjoy the view, I pulled to the side of the lane and called him on my cell phone to let him know I'd arrived. By the time I'd parked in the semi-circle drive in front of the stone walkway, my concerns about Neva and the disturbing images of last night had receded into a dim memory. I parked, slammed closed the car door and trotted up to the stone porch. The door opened before I knocked, and Gus grinned at me.

"Good to see you, Zoe."

His open face, the genuine delight in his expression, his focused attention inspired my own smile; I felt like a drought-wilted garden that had just received blessed rain. He stepped aside and I entered his world. My memory had failed me; the house was even more welcoming and beautiful than the first time I'd seen it. Only now because it was somewhat familiar, instead of delightful surprise when I surveyed the room, I responded with an internal sigh of calm.

He led me to the leather sofa. I tucked myself into one corner and propped two tapestry pillows behind me. Like the last visit, a fire crackled in the grate. He'd made one concession to the coming of Christmas: a child's paper-chain of multi-colored construction paper looped across the mantle.

I nodded toward it as I got comfortable. "Is that your decoration for the season?"

"The girls made it years ago. I don't put up a tree just for myself, but I always hang that paper-chain. Reminds me of the fun holidays we had when they were young."

He smiled at me, leaned back into the middle of the sofa and brought one jean-clad knee up as he turned to face me. One arm stretched across the back of the sofa; his hand came within inches of my shoulder.

The knot of tension in my stomach released even more as I relaxed, and I studied the warm hues of the room, the wood paneling and the stone fireplace. Gradually my gaze came to the tree-trunk coffee table in front of me. The ceramic bowl decorated with riotous daisies, the same one I'd admired during my first visit, sat beside a few issues of Architectural Digest and Midwestern Farmer. An odd but intriguing combination, a combination that befitted a multi-layered man: a magazine filled with fine design and luxury beside a publication which carried an article about the newest grain silos. I inhaled the scent of the room: wood smoke and something pleasantly natural, but mysterious. The house and this room had transported me to another world. I had an overwhelming urge to paint. If I'd had my watercolors and a paper with me, I would have been hard pressed not to pull them out now, set up an easel and begin creating what I was sure would be a magical image.

"What smells so good in here?" I said.

"Probably that group of candles on the mantle. Sybil sent them to me a week ago for Christmas. She said they're supposed to smell like a California redwood forest."

"I've never smelled the California redwoods, so I don't know about that. But they're nice. Not too perfumy."

He smiled and nodded. "I liked them."

"Will you stay here for Christmas?" I said.

"No. I'm flying out to Montana on Christmas Day. A friend of mine has a house out there. We're going to do some skiing. You ski?"

"I've never tried it."

"You should some time. You look like you have the strength for it."

I blushed under his frank perusal, and at the same time wondered if the friend was the stunning woman I'd seen him with at the steak house. Thankfully, I caught myself before I blurted out the question.

"I mean, of course, after the baby comes," he said.

I blushed again and squirmed in my seat. I felt delightfully unsettled. And that bothered me.

"So," I said, "tell me about this deal you've drawn up for the house."

He brought a folder from the desk in the corner of the room and fanned the pages on the tree-root coffee table. We discussed the house sale for thirty minutes or so, and I grew more convinced of his fairness and decency. Finally, he sat back and laid his arm again across the back of the sofa.

"Do you think you could live with all that? You get what you want: the house and yard. I just need the well access, but the water will stay the same for the house."

"You don't have to convince me, Gus. You've been more than fair, and I appreciate it."

"Great. We can close the deal after the farm sale, which is the first week of January. You mentioned before that your husband wouldn't be a part of this. That still hold true?"

I nodded, and a cold sharp point of something poked me in the stomach.

"What is it, Zoe? Can I get you some water?"

I shook my head.

I struggled for a moment with what to tell him and what not to. My situation with Cal was really none of his business; we had a business connection, not a personal one. But I remembered the open listener who'd sat across from me at the Heartland Steak House—and the connection that had sparked between us. And right now, I wanted to spill my guts. I needed someone to talk to. A friend.

He waited, silent and focused.

"Cal has decided to stay overseas for awhile. I'm not sure when I'll join him. It might not be until after the baby comes."

Unexpected emotion jettisoned up from my stomach and swamped my face. My eyes burned with waiting tears and my throat closed. All the mature control of a second ago slipped away.

"Sorry," I said. "I'm upset about it, as you can probably tell."

"I don't blame you."

He leaned toward me a little and the low comfort of his voice smoothed my frayed emotions.

"It's just hard right now," I said, "because his grown stepson, the one I told you about, is living in the carriage house we have over the garage, and he's—it's hard to describe. I just don't like what I'm seeing."

"So tell him to leave."

"It's not that easy." I told him what Amanda Crawford had said about evictions.

He shook his head. "Unbelievable. But listen. If I can do anything, let me know. I can see this upsets you."

I nodded and felt his hand drop onto my shoulder. He rubbed it a minute with his thumb and I watched his face.

"So does your husband have to stay overseas for the sake of his work, or is it something else?"

"What makes you ask that?"

"You said he decided to stay. He decided to stay overseas, not that he had to stay overseas."

"Oh. Well. I guess I did."

I could have added, and my scolding conscious told me I should have added, that I'd already made reservations to visit my husband after Christmas. But at that moment, watching the green eyes and his full mouth, hearing his breathing a foot away from me, the pop of the fire in the grate, the cocoon of warm wood that encased me in that room of art and light, I wasn't sure I'd keep those reservations after all.

I heaved a sigh, then shrugged and gave him a half-smile. "Honestly? I feel like if he wanted to push for it, he could have come home, at least for a week or two, without doing real harm to the project. I think he made a choice to stay."

Tenderness shifted the lines of his face and the hole in his chin softened. He watched me for a minute and the hand that had rested lightly on my shoulder increased its pressure. He was going somewhere with his emotions; I'd seen it coming, had waited for it.

"Gus—"

He shook his head. "Don't, Zoe. Don't say anything. I'm not

here to take anything or make you do something you'll be sorry for. I'm here, that's all. I really think you're a fine person, and I'm just here."

I stared at him, dumbstruck.

He smiled and gave a little off-hand shrug. "Always have thought you were special. I should have scooped you up when you came back home to live years ago. But I knew you were torn up, watching your mother die. And I figured you wouldn't give me a chance anyway."

"Why not?"

He shrugged again. "Our age difference."

He was almost like a boy, asking if the girl next to him in class liked him. I smiled at him.

"You don't look all that ancient. How old are you?" I said.

"Fifty-four."

"So? I'm forty-one. Thirteen years isn't that much."

What was I doing, flirting with this man? Here I am, pregnant and married and flirting with him. I must be going insane.

But I knew I wasn't insane. I was vulnerable and lonely and feeling like a failure. My emotions weren't clear, and I didn't trust myself.

I scooted forward. "I better go."

"If you need a friend, I'm here."

I nodded, grabbed my copy of the agreement and fled the house.

Chapter Twenty-Four

I pulled into the driveway and came to a stop in front of the garage. Neva was at the gate heading into her own backyard.

"Neva," I called. "Wait. Please."

She watched me approach, her face neutral.

The thought crossed my mind that my hope of making headway with Neva was naïve; she was a girl with serious mental trouble who needed serious help. And I didn't like how she looked. Her face appeared puffier than usual, the eyes swollen and bloodshot, and there was a sour odor on her breath from last night's liquor. Her hair was dirty, and the thin greasy strands tangled together in the back, like she hadn't brushed it out this morning. She looked more unkempt and troubled than I'd ever seen.

She tucked a strand of hair behind her ear, and her sleeve inched up; raw welts and bruises marred her wrist. Without thinking, I reached out to touch her hand.

"Are you all right, Neva? Those look like they hurt."

She didn't withdraw her hand from my touch, but again her voice was clipped. "I'm fine."

"You know, and I've told you this before, if ever you want to talk, I'm here." I bent down a little and tried to catch her eye between the curtain of stringy hair.

"You don't have to worry about me," she said. "I can take care of myself."

"I know you can. Of course you can. I just—"

"Just what? Pity me? I don't need your pity."

She said this last without the fire in her voice, a mere statement of fact.

Before I could say anything, she spoke again. "Besides, you got enough on your mind."

"But I have time to be a friend."

She snorted a laugh and her foul breath clouded the air between us. "Sure you do. Just like Seth. Always such a good person. Taking pity on a poor fat girl who needs friends."

"Neva, no. Please."

"Oh yes, Neva, yes," she mocked. "Seth and you and Regan. All pity the poor fat girl."

"Neva—"

"She was no friend of mine. Oh sure, she was a friend until she got close enough to Seth to get him to fuck her." She looked up to the gray sky. "I should've known."

At the tone of her voice, a cold fear slithered into my throat. Her eyes, ancient and bone-weary, drifted away.

I couldn't think what to say. I should have been more prepared for the bitterness; she'd caught me off guard. The fear hardened into a low vibration of panic. I placed a gentle hand on her shoulder.

"Neva, please come in the house. I'm worried about you, sweetheart. Please come in and let's talk for awhile."

She gave me a blank stare. "About what?"

"About you. About getting you to be a happier person."

She smiled a little and shook her head like she was taking pity on a person who couldn't understand. "Oh, Zoe. Ever the do-gooder."

She started to say something else but the sound of an engine in the drive stopped her.

Seth was back.

She glanced at his car, then at me and pulled her coat closer to her chin.

"I gotta go," she said.

I caught her arm. "No, please, Neva. Please don't go. Let's go inside the house. Just the two of us. He won't bother us. He's leaving soon. He's got to get to LA for school."

My words came in a quick ramble, sharp with desperation. Anything, anything so she wouldn't leave. But just then, Seth got out of the car.

Neva glanced at him, then at me. "I gotta go."

She kept her eyes on the ground and slipped through the gate.

Seth walked toward me, wide-eyed and somber.

"I didn't know she'd be here," he said. "I wouldn't have pulled in if I'd known."

I touched his coat sleeve. "Seth . . ."

He looked at me.

"I'm absolutely worried sick about Neva," I said. "She's not doing well at all. And after last night—oh, God, Seth. I'm so just so terribly disappointed in you."

He had the decency to look embarrassed, and I watched the color climb to the curls on his forehead.

"She barged in on me and Regan. It was her fault. I told you I wouldn't talk to her anymore and until last night, I hadn't."

Rage tore its way up from my stomach to my voice. "This little-boy sulkiness is old, Seth. Grow up. What you did last night was stupid and hurtful and disastrous to Neva. It was despicable."

"Hey, I told you I'm leaving and I am. Then you won't have me to worry about any more."

"I'm not worried about you. I'm worried about Neva. Worried enough that as soon as Mrs. Reckart gets home this evening I'm going over there again. Her daughter is ill, and by God, she'll either do something about it or I will."

"What are you going to do?"

"I don't know. But something. I have to do something. After all, if it wasn't for my stepson, she wouldn't be feeling like this."

"Oh, sweet. So it's all my fault. Great. Well nice to meet you too, step-mommy. You know what, this whole scene is just one big hassle. I'd leave right now but I gotta wait for Jason in the morning 'cause we got a deal going. But don't worry, I'll be gone after that. Jesus."

I briefly wondered what his "deal" was with Jason, but at that point I didn't really care. He could be working drug deals for all I knew; I just wanted him gone. This had gotten so out of hand. I felt sick to my stomach, for me, for Seth and for Neva. My head spun for a moment, and I closed my eyes.

"Hey, I'm sorry, Zoe. Sorry." He put his arm around my shoulder. "Come on. I'll help you into the house. Jesus Christ. I'm sorry. I keep forgetting you're pregnant. Jesus. You okay?"

The dizziness subsided some. I nodded.

"I'm fine. I just need to go in. But," I watched his eyes, "please go, Seth. This has gotten so bad. Please go."

"I will." Contrite and accepting. "I will."

He turned and left me on the back stoop, and then he trotted across the yard and climbed the stairs to the apartment.

I didn't care what Cal would think. I didn't care if I ever saw Seth Pruitt again, but of course, if Cal and I stayed married, I would. I stopped in my tracks; regardless if Cal and I stayed married, Seth would be my baby's half-brother. I felt sick all over again.

I gazed across the cold lawn through the smoky evening. Gladys Reckart kept odd hours, but surely she'd be home before midnight. It must be five by now. Only a few more hours and I'd get Neva some help one way or another.

When I sat in my office loft and turned my chair from its usual position of facing the computer, I could see over the half-wall, across the space that rises above the foyer and through the high window. Our front yard, the street, and a small part of the Reckart's drive was visible to me, and I glanced away from the computer screen every few minutes watching for Gladys Reckart's headlights that would tell me she'd arrived home. I'd decided that when I saw them, I'd drop whatever I was working on, probably another draft of the promotional pamphlet for the Griffen account, and hurry over there, no matter how late it was. I yawned and glanced again at the clock on the toolbar of my screen. 10:15 P.M.

I glanced at the phone that sat on the desk beside my computer: early morning in Uganda. Should I call now and tell Cal about his son conducting an orgy above our garage? I reached toward the handset then dropped my hand to my lap and sighed. I was tired of trying. And there was certainly no message waiting for me when I'd returned from Gus's. Besides, I had the sinking feeling he'd brush aside my worries as a needless distraction to his precious work.

His all-important, all-consuming work. He'd been honest with me about the demands of his career before we'd gotten married, but I thought I could handle it. And, I admitted to myself, I hadn't looked too closely; I'd minimized the impact of his dedication. Like a menacing insect I held in my palm, I kept the issue at arm's length, too fearful of what I'd see to put it under a mental microscope. I'd loved him, and he'd loved me, but Mom was dying, and I wanted to get married before she was gone. I wanted to make her happy. Would I have looked closer at the impact of Cal's career on our lives if Mom had been well? I didn't know. I closed my eyes against the onslaught of my own embarrassed shame. I'd been so silly. So stupid and blind and silly. And now, I was bringing an innocent child into the middle of this.

I opened my eyes at the sound of a car passing in front of the house, but its beam of headlights faded into the ebony night as it traveled its course down Universe. I checked the clock. 10:21 P.M. Did I really want to wait up for Gladys Reckart's return? I was tired, and she might be working until after midnight—

A shot.

Oh my God, a shot? A gunshot?

I hurried down the steps, trotted to the front window and pushed aside the curtain. Nothing. Calm and cold, the night broken only by the pool of light from the streetlamp two houses south of us. I opened the front door and leaned outside. Nothing. I closed the door, locked it and hurried across the living room to the back hall. Maybe Hattie had heard it. I opened her door and peered into the dark room; from the covered form in her bed came the steady rhythm of her breathing. I closed the door softly and bolted toward the kitchen. Had I imagined it?

Goldie stood at the back door, waiting to go out. She looked at me over her shoulder, but her tail didn't move in its usual welcome. She focused on the door as I came toward her. I parted the slats in the blind that covered the back window. Seth's lights in the carriage house were on, and after a moment, I detected the faint beat of rap music.

I opened the door and stepped onto the back stoop. I'd heard a shot, I was sure. I ran down the two steps, across the yard on the stepping stones that led to the stairs and grabbed the hand railing. The music intensified with my rise upward. The door was open a couple of inches, revealing only a slice of yellow light from the main room.

"Seth?" I called.

A rapper's poetry was my only answer. The door hinge chirped when I pushed open.

The smell of leftover marijuana registered with me and the ever-present musty odor of the old apartment, but not freshly smoked pot. No shadows moved through the light, and I wondered briefly if Seth was up here. Maybe he'd gone out tonight. But his car was parked in the driveway. Why would he leave the door open? I stepped the two or three steps around the L-shaped little entry and entered the main room.

Neva lay on the floor, crumpled on her side. Her face was forward, pressed into the carpet. She wore a hat on her head, and her hair spiked out from beneath it. A viscous liquid, which in the dull light of the old table lamp looked like oil, seeped from her head and was spattered across the floor and on the walls. A languid glob of it moved slowly down the wall. I blinked away from her and looked at the sofa. Seth huddled in the corner of it, nearest Neva, his knees drawn up to his chin and his arms holding them tight to his chest. His face was blank, looking at Neva with a puzzled expression, like he was trying to cipher some sense from a confusing problem. The rap music pounded on, a man's voice rhyming and swerving to the beat. An odor came to me, something living, but spoiled or decomposing. I opened my mouth to breathe.

"What's the matter?" Seth said.

He'd lifted his eyes to me, and I stared back at him for a moment, then took a step toward Neva. She'd fallen, passed out maybe, and spilled something.

"Help me get her up," I said.

He didn't answer me, but I started toward her and the toe of my clog nudged the sole of her sneaker. Solid resistance. A dead weight.

I crouched down at her feet, and put my hand on her thick solid ankle and gave it a shake. "Neva?"

But her leg jiggled only a little. I looked at her closely then, followed the rolling contours of her body. She was wearing her pink sweatshirt and jeans. She loved that sweatshirt. She always wore it. It was absent of a logo or printing or pictures. Just a plain pink sweatshirt. I'd always kind of liked that about her, that she didn't wear some attention-getting picture or an almost-appalling message printed on her shirt, that the sweatshirt was plain. The bottom band had scrunched up around her hip, and I straightened it for her, then sat back on my heels.

I surveyed her hair that matted the side of her face, and I knew then. The hat on her head was not a hat. It was the top of her skull, black with her blood, that had been blown off with the gunshot.

My voice came from somewhere other than myself, and a sharp vice squeezed my chest. I stood and looked at Seth who'd remained frozen on the sofa.

"Did you do it?"

He stared back at me for a minute and smiled, then shook his head no.

"Where's the gun?"

He pointed and I followed his finger to a rickety end table I'd used in my first apartment. A black pistol lay underneath it.

The rapper's beating words, the ripe odor of fear and death, Seth's stare, his vacuous smile: the surreal scene had altered my reality. Like feeling for a light switch in a dark closet, I groped for logic. Eternity passed, then it came to me: Help. Police. I had to get an ambulance. Don't panic, don't panic. My hand found the wall, I stumbled to the entry and toward the door. Don't panic. Call emergency. Just go down into the kitchen and call nine-one-one. Yes, call the police. That's the thing. Quick.

My hands found the threshold. I stepped outside on the landing, and the cold air slapped me across the face. Dear God. Dear God. What had he done? Oh my dear God.

I grasped the handrail. Run. Run down the stairs to the house. The phone. Get to the phone. My foot slipped through the air, my shoe flew off and I felt myself turn through space. A punch on my shoulder, then my head, then the back of my neck. I heard the clatter and the clamor of my weight skidding down the wooden steps, and before I hit the bottom, I realized exactly what was happening to me.

I was falling, falling, falling; and then I floated into a black mist where I was suspended between my mother and my baby.

CHAPTER TWENTY-FIVE

A quiet snore. A soft whir of a machine. A dull cramp in my uterus.

I fluttered my eyes open. Butter-yellow walls, daylight through the film of a window shade, a ceiling of lighter gold: a warm cocoon. I inched my head to the right and pinpointed the source of the snore. My father, chin on chest, slumped in the recliner chair beside the bed. Sunlight glinted on the few strands of his hair and transformed them to a silver gossamer cap. His chest rose and fell, and as I watched, the index finger resting on the bulge of his belly twitched.

I took my time surveying the hospital room, a room that could have been a professionally decorated bedroom in a private home. In the corner opposite the foot of my bed, a bouquet of baby's breath and crimson roses swarmed a small table. Huge. Ostentatious. Beside it, on another table, perched a clutch of daisies in a hand-thrown vase that reminded me of rolling meadows and a soft spring day on the prairie. I remembered that Gus Lohan had visited, remembered smiling at him through a haze of pain and painkillers, remembered his green eyes and the daisies. He knew I liked daisies, he'd said. He'd remembered I liked the ceramic bowl on his tree-trunk coffee table in the middle of the soul-filled room of his prairie home. I was flattered he'd remembered—and at the same time, it didn't matter.

"You're awake," my father said.

He stood beside the bed, and when I lifted my eyes to his

face, I caught his expression of relief; the frown lines beside his mouth were softer than I'd seen them in years.

I reached for the cup of water that stood on the bedside table, but he lifted it and brought the straw to my lips. I sipped, rested and sipped again, then nodded. He sat the cup on the table.

"Feeling better?" he said.

"I think so. Still sore."

He nodded and spoke again after a moment.

"Cal called again. Did you remember he sent the flowers?"

I did, and I studied at the gaudy display again. The perfectly arranged stems struck me as false and arrogant, exploding with their own importance, but then maybe I only thought that because I knew they were from Cal. A veil of sadness slipped over me, and I pressed my head back into the pillow and sighed.

"He did call again, Zoe. He's called every few hours for the past two days. He's very concerned."

"But not concerned enough to come home, is he?"

Dad lowered his eyes to the edge of my bed and adjusted the cotton blanket, even though it was fine.

"Could I have some more water, please?"

He hurried to do my bidding, and I finished the water. He filled the cup from the pitcher on the table, offered it to me, then when I shook my head, set it back in place.

Maybe I was wrong. A sunbeam of expectation surfaced through the grog of painkillers, and I looked at Dad again.

"Did he say he was coming home? Getting on a plane?"

Dad lowered his eyes again and shook his head. The sunbeam faded.

"I didn't think so," I said. "Even losing the baby wasn't enough. Wasn't enough to hold him to me and wasn't enough to bring him home."

"Zoe—"

"It's okay, Dad. I'm really sad right now, but I'm clear about one thing: Cal made a choice, and I'm not it."

"Honey, maybe you should rest now."

I blinked at him. This was unlike my cards-on-the-table father. Before my fall, if I'd made a comment about Cal not choosing me, he would have said: "Well, ya made your own bed, now you gotta lie in it." The fall down the stairs, the loss of the baby and the d and c must have scared him. Poor man. He thought he'd almost lost me.

"I'm okay, Dad. Dr. Heller said I could go home tomorrow. Rest. That's all I need. Please don't worry."

He pressed his lips together and his chin quivered. Dad, on the verge of tears? For the first time since Mom died, he'd allowed me to see his anguish. That was hard for him. His hand still rested on the edge of the blanket and I covered it with my own. He squeezed and gave me a weak smile.

"I hired a nurse to stay with you for a couple weeks," he said. "Every day from seven to seven."

"That was nice of you. Thank you. But I don't know how Hattie will take to an interloper."

He smiled and squeezed my hand again. "Well, you can let her go before the two weeks, it's up to you. But you'll need someone for the first week anyway."

"Yes. That's great." I paused a minute. "Have you . . . have you been to the house? My house?"

I meant the carriage house, of course, and he knew it. He pulled himself a little taller and took a deep breath. When he spoke, his voice tone was the usual gravel.

"Yes, I was there. I don't want you to worry about all that. I hired a service and they cleaned up the place. They threw away the rug and some pillows. Uh, they were, um, ruined."

The picture flashed again in my mind, the picture that hadn't been erased even with the slug of drugs that caroused through my veins: Neva lying on the floor, the blood, her exploded head, her sweatshirt curled up along the bottom edge. But what brought the fist into my stomach was the remembered feel of her when I'd shaken her ankle, trying to wake her up—how her leg was so heavy and solid and final.

Neva. Oh, Neva.

"Now don't get upset all over again," he said.

A tissue dangled before me, and I took it from him and dabbed at my eyes.

"I won't. I won't."

And, I vowed, I really would not. I needed to get well. I wanted to get well. I wanted to see Hattie and Goldie and have lunch with Sabrina. I wanted to get back to work on my accounts. I wanted to see my mother's house at Red Leaf.

All the pieces of my life. I had to somehow bring them together, to make a new life—a life that a year ago I would not have envisioned. Sudden exhaustion overwhelmed me, and I closed my eyes.

Dad patted my arm. "I'm sorry you had to go through all that. But Seth's gone now."

I opened my eyes to watch my father's face harden.

"Where did he go?" I asked.

"Beats me. Cal said he was staying at a friend of his."

Jason, I thought.

"Did the police talk to him?"

"Yes. They're ruling it as suicide. She left a note, and the gun belonged to her mother."

"Neva," I said.

"What?"

"Her name was Neva."

"Oh." He paused a moment. "The police want to talk to you, but I told them they could wait until you were discharged from the hospital. They didn't give me any problem about it."

I smiled at him. My hero.

"What about a funeral?" I said.

"The mother didn't want one, evidently. Just cremation. No ceremony."

I shook my head. Poor Neva.

"That doesn't surprise me," I said.

The telephone chirped, and Dad picked it up.

"Hello?" A pause. "Yes, Cal. Yes, she's awake. Hold on."

He handed me the receiver then left the room.

"Hello, Zoe. Are you feeling better?"

My husband's voice entered my ear, my brain, my numb heart.

"Yes, better. Still tired though."

"Good. Good. I talked to Sam Tuttle. Suzanne Heller consulted with him. You remember Sam and I went through residency together?"

"Sure. I remember."

"Yeah, well, he said that the results from the d and c look very good, healthy tissue. No problems."

"That's what Dr. Heller said. She said I could go home tomorrow. Dad hired a nurse to be with me for a week or two."

"Yes, he told me earlier when I called. So that's good. And Hattie will be there, of course."

"Yes."

"Uh, Zoe. I'm sorry I couldn't get home. We've run into some problems with one of the clinics, the doctor from New Delhi was supposed to start last Tuesday, but he never showed. We tracked him down, and there's some kind of a problem with his visa. Meanwhile, I've had to personally take up the slack."

"You mean you're actually practicing medicine again?"

He laughed. "Yeah. Can you believe it?"

I waited. I didn't know what to say, but I wanted to try.

"Cal, I want you to know how I feel." I swallowed the lump

before I continued. "I'm very sad and very disappointed that you didn't come home to be with me."

The words sounded weak and childish and incredibly understated.

"But I told you, I couldn't leave. And I knew your dad was there and I know Suzanne Heller is a very good gynecologist and I told you I talked to Sam Tuttle, so it's not like I could do anything anyway."

His voice stayed hard and defensive to the end of his rationalization.

"Cal," I said, "please. I know more than anyone in the world how much those clinics mean to you. You've done a wonderful thing, and the clinics will make better lives for thousands of people. It's—" I tried to formulate the words. "I realize now that those clinics, or the next project after this, or the next one, will be more important than me. I'll always be in second, or even third place."

A long silence. "You know, I told you before we got married how important my work was. I never lied to you about that."

"I know, and I'm not saying this is all your fault. I was willing to accept second place to a noble cause, but damn it, I wanted it to be a close second."

And, I admitted to myself, if Mom hadn't pinned her happiness on my getting married, and if I hadn't been so desperate to grant her that one wish before she died, I wouldn't have taken second place, even a close second, to anything.

Another silence, then his voice came soft and low. "I'm sorry, Zoe. Sorry for all this. I do love you, you know. I . . ."

You're just weak and narrow and selfish. Brilliant in your field, but disappointing as a human being.

"I'm getting tired again. I think I better go. I'll talk to you later."

He blurted his answer. "I'll call tomorrow, Zoe, same time.

I'll talk to you then, okay?"

A plea for acceptance. But the exhaustion of talking to him, of slogging my way through the muck of my emotions had caught up with me. I told him I'd talk to him later and punched the button to end the call.

Dad entered the room. He must have been watching through the window in the door. He took the phone from me, sat back in the recliner, laced his fingers together and looked at me.

"Any change?" he asked.

I shook my head. "He can't get away. He has important commitments."

He glanced over to the bouquet of roses, then back at me.

"Well," he muttered.

A nurse entered the room and thrust a paper cup of pills under my nose. Dad handed me the water, and I gratefully gulped them down. He settled back into his chair, I pulled the covers to my chin and drifted behind my closed eyelids.

When I'd first moved back to Red Leaf to nurse my mother, I kidded myself that she'd live—not the life we'd always imagined, but she'd live. But there came a time when my mother and I began to understand she'd die. She'd had a string of difficult days, of choking and spasms. She was hungry and couldn't eat and exhausted and couldn't sleep. Sometimes, since then, I'd wondered if that was the period when she'd decided to take the pills. I think the certain knowledge came to her that she was going to die, and after that day, like stepping through a kind of portal, she never turned wistful eyes back to what might have been.

Now, thinking about my conversation with Cal, I felt like I balanced at the edge of my own portal. I didn't want to cross into a new life, but at the same time, I couldn't picture myself turning back to the old one.

"I do love you, you know," he'd said.

But not enough. Not enough.

I closed my eyes and potent drugs dragged me into sleep.

CHAPTER TWENTY-SIX

Hattie was waiting for me inside the back door along with Goldie who grinned and wagged like she'd rediscovered a lost friend. I inhaled the aromas of my kitchen: blended spices and decades-old wood. Dad helped me settle in, then left for Red Leaf promising he'd return for Christmas. Even though he'd been wonderfully solicitous toward me, he was still the same old Dad: restless and impatient. I knew it was best for all of us that he leave.

I spent the next few days stretched out on the sofa snuggled into my knitted throw in front of the fireplace, sipping hot tea Hattie brewed for me. Every so often, she'd come to my side and cover my folded hands with her own gnarled dry ones. I'd stare into the fire, thinking of everything and nothing, drifting and reliving.

Sometimes, I'd fall asleep only to wake with a start at the imagined sound of a gunshot. I dreamed of climbing the carriage house staircase, pushing the door open, Seth's numb eyes. I dreamed of myself twisting and turning down the sharp edges of the steps, the punch to my stomach as I landed. I thought I remembered shouts and sirens and a policeman's voice, but I couldn't be sure. I dreamed them anyway. But I never dreamed of the scene I'd stumbled into. Only awake would I sometimes picture Neva's crumpled bulk, the wrinkle in her pink sweatshirt, the black liquid flowing from her head, the solid weight of her ankle. I was able to picture the scene without fear or terror or gasping for breath, but I'd come back from my reverie wearing a mantle of sadness, tears stinging my eyes.

The hired nurse left after a few days; Dr. Heller told me to climb the stairs carefully, but whenever I was ready was fine. And with Hattie's care, I began to strengthen. She even managed to carry in logs for the fire, one or two at a time, and with a gas starter, we kept a fire burning from morning until deep into the night. She laughed and told me how a few logs to haul were nothing compared to what women in her girlhood village used to do; wood not only to haul, but to split and trim, too.

"Life those days . . ." She pressed her lips together and shook her head from side to side. "A lost world, Zoe, and thank God for that. I had enough hard labor in my life, and the women of my family before me. Still, there are some things about those days I miss."

Tears pooled in her tired eyes, and with a hearty squeeze of my hand, she told me to disregard the ramblings of an old woman. I teased her that all she'd ever be was a Gypsy camp woman at heart. She took it as a supreme compliment.

As he promised, Dad came for Christmas and brought dinner with him. For the first time since the accident, I crammed myself full of food: ham, mashed potatoes, green beans with toasted almonds and homemade rolls that Sabrina had brought over the day before. Dad spent Christmas night at the house, and then went home to finish his packing. His plan was to head to Arizona the last part of January, and he promised he'd stop by before he left.

On the Wednesday after Christmas, low clouds skidded over the rooftops of the houses up and down Universe. In the early afternoon, I bundled my coat and scarf around me, pulled my knit hat over my ears, and stepped onto the front porch. I inhaled the sharp cold air and exhaled a cloud of icy smoke, then sat on the edge of the porch railing. Too cold to snow very much, but a few flakes dropped from the flat sky and drifted to the dead grass. I perched there for a moment, alone with the icy day and my aching heart.

I looked to the curb in front of our walk. Right there. Right there Seth had parked the first day he'd come here and strode up the front walk. Had it really been only a few weeks ago? A picture came to me of his grin as he introduced himself; the arrogant ebony eyes, the buttery leather jacket he wore. What had I been doing before that? He'd arrived late in the day, five or so—the nursery. I'd been in the nursery doing my little ritual tour. Neva had been ducking through the firethorn hedge, sneaking around, afraid to come to the door and knock.

I let myself look over to the Reckart house. The closed blinds colored the windows a dull yellow. She'd moved, Hattie said. A man in a pickup truck had pulled into her driveway, and Hattie had watched from the back stoop as the man and Gladys Reckart loaded a few boxes, a dresser and a rocking chair into the truck bed. I wondered if it was the scarred rocker I'd seen in the living room. There could have been another one somewhere in the house, but in my mind, she'd taken that one.

Gladys Reckart. A sad, sad woman in a sad, sad life. I wondered what would happen to her, and immediately had a vision of a hoary crone perched on a bar stool hunched over a whiskey in one of the hundreds of corner bars that dotted the old neighborhoods of Chicago. Would she be capable of making sense of her daughter's life and death? Would she even try? It exhausted me to think about, and I turned around and went back into my house.

It was odd, the serendipity of life, how one event, one happenstance led to another. If Cal and I had not moved to the house on Universe, I would have never known Neva. Seth may have entered our lives, but if we'd lived anywhere else, he simply would have made his appearance, then left for California.

Eventually, we would have integrated him into our lives, and more than likely, it would have been an uneventful integration. We would have been one of the many millions of blended families that would assemble for holidays, a divergent brood spanning multiple generations. Our clan would have grown with the addition of our child and more than likely Seth's own wife and children. But because we'd moved into this particular house on the corner of Universe and Stargazer, Neva was inextricably threaded through my life—and Seth's.

I huddled on the sofa, my wide and staring eyes locked into the embers that burned in the fireplace grate. And as often happened with me when I roamed the pattern of this type of thinking, letting one event lead to another, I gradually chewed into the seed at the center of the fruit: my marriage to Cal.

I've often wondered where I'd have to travel to know myself absolutely. It wasn't a place, a physical location, like a city or a landscape or a particular chair in a particular room; it was a place inside me, a place I'd glimpsed from time to time but never had the patience or maybe the fearlessness to explore.

I loved Cal, and I'd loved what we'd dreamed of together. But if my mother had been well and whole, would I have proposed to him, insisted on us marrying as fast as I'd done three years ago? Was my mother's hope for me the reason I hung on and hung on to a man who for almost our entire married life had found something more important to do than to be with me?

I heard the swish of Hattie's slippers as she crossed the living room, felt her weight shift the cushion on the sofa and then a warm dry hand pressed my own icy fingers.

"Time to talk," she said.

The creases in her face shifted and deepened, and her eyes moved away from me.

"What?" I said.

273

"Time to talk. Time for me to talk to you."
And she did.

CHAPTER TWENTY-SEVEN

In the fall of 1934, outside of a small village in Romania now paved over by a stretch of European highway, her father lay on his bed, gasping for his last breaths on earth. Fourteen-year-old Hattie Gottesman cupped her palm around his cheek and stroked the gray wire of his beard. As the eldest daughter in a household with no sons, it was she who sat beside him as death crept through the bedroom, then hovered in the dark corner. Hattie's sister, Triana, would come later, but because she was only twelve, her vigil wouldn't be as long as Hattie's. Or as heartfelt, Hattie thought. Triana was a silly child, a child who should be preparing to be a woman now, but her wild ways and wicked charm kept her young in her father's eyes. She'd been protected and indulged.

"Harriot," her father whispered.

"I'm here, Papa. I'm here."

"Promise me. Promise."

"What? Promise you what?"

"You will take care of Triana. Take care of her as if she was your own child."

Hattie stared at the ashen face. She owed this man much, her life as she knew it. But Triana? To care for Triana as her own child? God help her.

In the years after his Gypsy wife had died, Aviel Gottesman had hired a series of housekeepers to care for himself, his little girl Hattie, and his newborn daughter, Triana. But by the time she was ten, Hattie had taken over the care of the family, so that now, at fourteen, Hattie knew more about the farm and house management than her father. Triana was encouraged to continue school, which was only right. Triana was, after all, her father's natural child while Hattie had been the five-month-old baggage attached to her Gypsy mother.

Hattie's mother had been twelve years old when she conceived Hattie, the first month after her first menstruation. She never confessed who had planted the unwanted fetus in her womb. After Hattie's birth, the Gypsy tribe had traveled to the farm of Aviel Gottesman, a Jew in western Romania who owned rolling acres of cherry trees. They'd traveled the same route for years knowing that each summer, the men would be hired to pluck the bursting fruit from Gottesman's trees. When the lusty old man caught sight of Hattie's mother in the Gypsy campsite on the outskirt of the orchard, he begged her to marry him, promising he'd provide well for her and her Gypsy baby. The young mother bundled her infant in an embroidered shawl and with a disdainful look thrown over her shoulder at her debased half-brother, left the tribe and married a Jewish farmer.

Holding to his promise, Gottesman gave the baby girl his name and spent two years happily rutting with his Gypsy woman-child. The birth of Triana sucked every ounce of strength from the mother who had just turned fifteen. She died, and Avril Gottesman was left with a contemplative three-year-old Gypsy girl and a newborn. In the following years, until the fall evening on his death bed, Aviel Gottesman kept the promise he'd made to his young bride. He adored his natural child, Triana, but Hattie kept the special place in her father's life as his eldest adopted daughter.

Hattie had no illusions as to how much she owed this man, and as she pressed a damp cloth to his forehead, she leaned forward and whispered next to his ear.

"Don't worry, Papa. I promise. I swear on Mama's grave I'll take care of Triana."

After he died, Hattie used the proceeds for the sale of part of the farm to keep Triana and herself fed and clothed. But by the time Hattie was sixteen, Triana's fourteen-year-old spoiled appetites had blossomed into daring escapades, all in the name of getting what she wanted. Did Hattie love her? Of course, like a full-blooded sister. But she didn't like her. And for the first six months of 1935, whenever she went into town, Hattie overheard the neighbors talk behind their hands about the Jew's wild daughter. Despite Hattie's daily pleas and lectures, Triana Gottesman was turning into a tramp.

On a soft summer night of that year, Hattie awoke in the room that she and Triana still shared, turned to her side, and by the light of a full moon, saw Triana's empty bed. She threw her mother's quilt to the floor, pulled her housedress over her head and shoved her feet into her shoes. She'd had enough.

During the mile walk to town, Hattie rehearsed the speech she'd drill into her sister: She'd sell the remainder of the farm, take them away from here, pull Triana from school and make her go to work. Hattie would shackle her sister to the heavy walnut bedstead, if necessary, and bring her a plate of food every evening. She'd use the money from the farm to get visas, and they'd go to America or Australia. Besides, a war was coming, even the ignorant peasants knew that. And a person heard stories, stories about the Nazis who'd recently commandeered the local police department—how they hated anyone whose veins ran with just one drop of Jewish blood. That would mean Triana.

It was time to leave.

A quick walk down the familiar main street of Platzentoff told her the shops and homes were buttoned up for the night. She stopped in front of the greengrocer's, the same grocer to whom Aviel Gottesman had sold his cherries for decades, and listened. A thin steam of laughter and guttural voices floated in the air. Triana's laugh. Hattie surveyed the vacant street. She meandered in the direction where she thought the sound might be originating, but was greeted only by the dead night. When she came to a corner where an alley intersected the main street, she stopped. The alley cut through to Perstyn, a notorious section of town where she'd never had occasion to venture—a section whose businesses traded in liquor, gambling and prostitution.

Voices wafted by her again. She turned the corner and followed Triana's shrill laughter. Light from an open window of the second story of a faded Victorian tenement drew her gaze upward while Triana's laugh floated down. Odors of cooked cabbage and unwashed bodies assaulted her as she climbed the stairs. A light showed from under the wooden door at the top of the steps, and her sister's squeal sounded within. Hattie turned the knob and pushed open the door.

A phonograph in the corner played American jazz, and the stench of cigarette smoke and whiskey permeated the room. Triana sat on a man's lap. His four companions surrounded a small round table. They held playing cards in their meaty fists, and at the sound of the door opening, glared up from their game with rumbled protests. Each of the men wore the uniform of Nazi Germany. Hattie didn't know about insignias and ranks and the influence inherent in the symbols, but the thick squared shoulders of the uniforms, the shining silver swastikas on the collars and the glimmering buttons, now unfastened in casual debauchery, told her the men were important and powerful. She froze, her hand still resting on the knob.

"Triana," she said, "come home with me at once."

Triana's smile of disbelief, the snort of derision and knitted eyebrows told Hattie that her little sister had at last grown into a woman; a woman who would pilot her own downfall.

"What are you doing here?" Triana said. "Go home."

"No. Not unless you come with me."

Triana jumped to her feet and her dress swung open in the front, held only by a single button at her waist. She gathered the edges together in one hand and the other hand balled into a fist of defiance.

"How dare you. Get out. I'm old enough to make my own decisions. Get out."

"You are fifteen. That is not old enough. You'll come home with me now."

The man who'd been holding Triana on his lap stood. He was as brutal as a wild boar, sloped in the brow, a large hooked nose, and a slit for a mouth. The other men stared at Hattie with amusement glowing in their eyes.

"She wants to stay," the boar said.

Hattie met each of their eyes. Fear fluttered in her stomach, but she was determined to do her duty.

"I'm her sister. I'm responsible for her. She must come home with me."

Boar-man guffawed, rocking back on his heels, his hooked nose pointed to the grimy ceiling. He looked down at Triana.

"Do you want to stay?" he asked in German.

Triana smiled up at him and let loose the edges of her dress. It opened to reveal her white cotton slip and the outline of a long young thigh.

He glowered at Hattie. "I think she wants to stay."

A knot of anger, humiliation and terrible fear tightened in Hattie's stomach. She turned from the room, hurried down the stairs and onto the street. She stared up at the second story and listened to her sister's shrill mirth and the hoarse guffaws of the men.

Triana wore a cool detachment during the next several weeks.

She came and went as she pleased, when and with whomever she chose. Gilda Happestott, their neighbor who'd served as caretaker until Hattie was old enough to manage the house on her own, talked to Hattie.

"Let her go, Harriot. I know she's your sister, but she's trash. And the Nazis . . ." Gilda crossed herself. "God save us from them. But she's under their protection."

But Hattie would not, could not for the sake of her promise to her father, let go. And over the next few months she hammered at Triana while she made arrangements to sell the remainder of the farm. Maybe her sister would have relented. Maybe she would have stopped her despicable behavior before it was too late—except that one morning, Triana confessed she was pregnant.

"Now," Hattie said, "I'll go to this man's commanding officer. I'll tell him you're a child. He must be punished and then we'll go away to have your baby. We'll start over in Australia or America, like I promised."

But Triana would have none of it. And Hattie, with her promise to her father pulsing through her, vowed to save her sister. She finalized the sale of the farm to a neighbor, practically gave it away, but she didn't care. She'd do anything, suffer any hardship, to fulfill her duty to her father. Gilda Happestott again begged Hattie to let go of Triana.

"She's the age of many young women who marry and become mothers. If she doesn't want to go with you, then go alone. But cut loose of her, Harriot. Let her go."

But the promise held her.

One night shortly after the sale of the farm, Triana had gone to town, as usual, and Hattie was alone in the fall evening, sorting through her father's keepsakes stored in the attic. They wouldn't be able to take much with them. She'd planned to leave in a week, but now, as she tossed aside old photographs and documents her father had saved from his home in Russia, an urgency burned inside her. She wouldn't wait, they'd leave quickly. The day after tomorrow.

A pounding at the door.

Triana. Something had happened.

She flung open the door and faced four Nazi soldiers, their black caps decorated with shining military symbols pulled low on their brows.

A stout man in front of the pack spoke. "Triana Gottesman?"

"She's not here."

The worst flashed through her mind. The brutal one, the subhuman one—

"Is she all right? Take me to her."

"You are Triana Gottesman, daughter of the Jew Aviel Gottesman."

"No, no, I'm Harriot Gottesman. Where's Triana?"

A soldier shouldered his way forward from the back of the group. He tipped his hat upward and revealed his leering grin. The boar.

"Your sister told me you would say this, Triana Gottesman. As part Jew, lying is in your blood."

"What are you talking about? You know Triana." A fierce anger fueled by a sliver of terror flashed through her, but she steeled herself to be brave in the face of the pig. "You've fathered her unborn child."

Narrowed eyes told her she'd hit the mark.

The boar spoke again. "You are Triana Gottesman, Jewess, and you're under arrest for conducting an illegal sale of Jewish property that is owned now by the Republic of Germany and for conspiring to subvert the Fuhrer."

He stepped away from the group and clasped his hands behind his back.

"Take her," he commanded.

The stout one grabbed her arm and pulled, but still it didn't sink into her thick brain, a brain clogged with promises to the dead.

"What are you talking about? Where's Triana? Let go of me."

But of course they did not. And for the next two years, until her escape from the Mauthausen concentration camp, a bitterness grew inside Hattie that warmed her through the coldest winters and filled her starving belly with revenge.

When she escaped, hidden under a tarp draped over a wheelbarrow, an escape purchased from a guard with the use of her body for six months, she scrounged like an animal to live. She eventually found Triana in a Warsaw tenement, prostitute to the occupying Nazi army. And sick. Dying, in fact.

Triana begged and cried for her forgiveness, but Hattie withheld it. Triana died six months later, her dissolute face shadowed by Hattie's unforgiving gaze.

I watched Hattie through a film of tears that had come to my eyes.

"What happened to her child?" I asked.

"Stillborn."

"And then after that, where'd you go?"

Hattie took a ragged breath and the anguished eyes shifted away from me again.

"After the war, I managed to get in a refugee camp." Her accent had thickened with her memories. "I was sent to England. I lived there for two years, where I met my husband at Cambridge. I worked there for him, I typed for him. He saved me. He married me. My son, Cal's father, was born there. And my other son, Edwin. We came to America later."

I fingered the fringe on my wool throw and watched the fire. Copper flames caressed the logs shooting sparks and sizzles upward into the black chimney, the winter sky that overlay our house and the heavens above the cloud cover. Maybe they floated up there forever. Maybe there were zillions of cinders from zillions of fires that had burned through the ages: fires from Gypsy tribes and fires from inside the cold dormitories in concentration camps. Who could say when the embers would die? Maybe they were like memories: out of sight, but always a part of our world.

I got up and added another log, then returned to the warmth of the sofa.

"Are you cold, Hattie? Do you want me to get your shawl for you?"

She shook her head and stayed silent.

After another bit, I spoke again. "That's an incredible story. It's incredible what you went through. Did you ever tell Cal that story?"

She shook her head no, then looked at me and sighed. "It's too hard to talk about. Too hard to see the pictures of the memory."

She leaned toward me and pushed up the sleeve of her sweater. Using her index finger of her opposite hand, she traced the faint scar on the inside of her forearm, a scar that in the past I'd noticed but dismissed.

"I had the numbers removed. I couldn't stand to live with them."

She smoothed her sleeve and sat back in the chair. "My regret, my biggest regret is Triana died without my forgiveness. You remember when I told you my baby son died how I could not forgive myself? And how I could not forgive one other? Triana was the other. She died thinking I hated her."

"Did you?"

"Yes, for years. I'm ashamed to tell you it took me twenty years to let forgiveness enter my heart."

"No one could blame you, Hattie. I'm honored you told me

the story. Thank you."

"I told you because our stories are the same."

"Because of the promises?"

She nodded and I turned from her, gazed at the fire for a moment and listened to the muted pops and hiss of the logs. I took a deep breath and let it out slowly.

"We both tried to please our parents," she said, "me by giving a promise, you by trying to live to your mother's expectation. And we held on to those ties long after they should have been released."

I watched the fire again and after a little while, nodded. "Yes."

"My father loved me, as your mother loved you, and I know now he looked down from heaven on my travails and cried angel tears for my pain. He would not have wanted me to keep the promise at the dear cost I tendered for it." She leaned over to me and gripped my arm with her veined hand. "And your mother would not have wanted to bind you to her wishes either, Zoe. If you love Cal, and want to dedicate your life to him and your lives together, then do so. But do not love him for any other reason. Do not make a commitment to him because of a death promise."

Tears dripped down my cheeks, and I blinked through them. She was right. She was so right.

We were silent awhile and visions of Cal and my mother and our wedding day floated through my mind. I saw her illumined face, the tender peace-filled smile—all because she thought I'd found love, thought I was finally going to be settled in a home with a family.

But I knew I couldn't do it anymore. I could admit it to myself now: I had loved Cal when I married him, but I married him for the wrong reasons. Love was the reason to get married, but when the inevitable hardness of living set in, maybe it wasn't enough. Maybe there had to be other things, too, like commitment and courage and the ability to sacrifice heartfelt desires for another person.

It seemed so clear to me now, so obvious that my marriage was over. I thought about the ticket to Kampala that I'd purchased, now unused and forfeited, how I'd teetered on the edge of running to Cal to give us one last chance to reconcile. It had been a desperate move, and now I understood my visit wouldn't have made a difference. For the first time, I allowed myself to put into words what had been lurking in the darkest corner of my heart: It had been wrong from the beginning. I'd been wrong from the very start.

Chapter Twenty-Eight

Cal called daily. We'd chat on the surface, never referring to the swirling morass of our relationship that lay at our feet. And on New Year's Eve, two days after Hattie had told me her story, he called again, about six in the evening my time.

"Happy New Year, Zoe."

"You beat me to it. You're two hours into the new year."

He laughed, and in the background, I heard other rumbled laughs and murmur of conversation.

"So you're at a party," I said.

"A few of the staff and . . ."

And their wives, I thought. Their wives who live in Uganda with their husbands.

"It's business stuff," he said. "Always business here."

I was silent for a moment. I really tried, even pressed my lips together, but the words came out without my permission.

"I suppose Melissa is there."

Silence for a moment, then finally, "She's a part of my staff, Zoe."

"Of course."

Even across the ocean and half the continent, I heard his sigh.

"You know," he said, "I just caught myself about ready to say 'I'm sorry' again. That's all I say to you: I'm sorry, I'm sorry."

"You're right. And I'll tell you what: Those aren't the words I want to hear."

"What are the words? Tell me and I'll say them."

"You can't. It's too late. Weeks ago, if you'd said, 'Come with me. Come be with me and you and me and the baby can be in Africa together'—now those are the words I would have loved to hear. But it's too late now."

"But the timing wasn't right. I had so much to do. I couldn't open these clinics and tend to a pregnant wife." His voice held a quality that I'd heard before, but could never pinpoint. But I could now: he was whining.

"Let's not go into that again. It doesn't have anything to do with the timing. It has to do with you. You don't want me cramping your style. Because if I'm there, you have to be accountable to me. You'd have an immediate and local responsibility to me. So please, forget trying to convince me of the logic of your decision."

He was silent for awhile, and I wondered if he hung up on me, but I hadn't heard the disconnect that would have left me hovering over thousands of miles.

"If you could just wait. Wait a while and let me do this. Let me have the time to do this. Then we could go on from there."

"You mean if I could wait until you finish your affair with Melissa Delany?" Except for the background noise, a thundering silence.

"How long has it been going on?" I said.

Another silence, then: "It's not like that. It's not. She's a part of this, part of the challenge—"

I laughed. "Remind me to give her some pointers."

"I didn't mean that. It's complicated. There's a lot more to it than what it looks like."

"Spare me the 'complicated' details, Cal."

We were silent again, and a bleak exhaustion overwhelmed me. But I needed to know one thing. "Why did you marry me?"

"I've told you. I loved you. I did then, and I do now."

"But why did you marry me?"

"Because . . . because I love you, and because your mother was dying and you had something you had to show her about your life. And I felt so sorry for you. I mean, I've seen ALS patients, worked with them. I felt so sorry for you."

Pity. He'd married me out of pity.

"And I don't mean I married you out of pity. I didn't. I loved you, I thought we could make it work. And if you hadn't gotten pregnant, it might have. We could have done this together."

"Conditional commitment, right? As long as I remain the same, you can love me."

"No, no. I don't mean that. I mean, I told you before we got married how important my career was to me. And you said you could accept that. And now all of a sudden you can't."

"What I can't accept, Cal, is that you left me here, alone, suffering the loss of the baby, losing Neva, everything, and you couldn't leave your 'complications.' You couldn't come home to me."

He started to say something, but I interrupted. "No, listen. I've been doing a lot of thinking. This whole thing, this . . . this failure was as much my fault as yours. We wanted two different things from life. Now, I accept that."

A long silence passed before he spoke. "Would it change things if I were to jump on a plane right now?"

I took a breath and held it. My heart thudded and my temples throbbed with my pulse. I didn't know how I felt. Did I want to try? Was there something left we could salvage from the tattered shreds of our relationship?

"I don't know," I said.

I heard a woman's voice in the background. Through the cacophony, I deciphered a question about how much longer was Cal going to be on the phone.

"I better get off here," he said. "I have to do the host deal."

I heard him cover the mouthpiece and mumble, then remove his hand and again the woman's voice. I didn't have to ask who. It was Melissa's.

"So are you?" I said.

"Am I what?"

"Jumping on a plane and coming home?"

A silence, then a final, firm, "No."

"Good-bye, Cal."

"Wait, Zoe. Wait a second."

"Not anymore. I'm tired of waiting for something I only imagined to be there."

I disconnected the call.

Over the next couple of days, a restless pacing took hold of me. I'd pace my office, sometimes stopping to open the Griffen file and attempting to work, but after a few minutes I'd close the file and wander again, down the stairs to the kitchen to the living room, up the stairs, to my bedroom and back down again. Even to the nursery. I treaded the parameter of the room, lifted the window shade and gazed on the hollow Reckart house and thought of Neva and Seth and Cal. And my mother. And my baby.

Over those dark hours, a crystal knowledge settled into me: I was alone.

I hadn't told Hattie of my conversation with Cal, how I'd all but ended our marriage, but I knew she sensed it with that amazing intuition of hers. And I was sure she'd also sensed my own torturous thoughts. She knew guilt was making me twist my hands and stare vacant-eyed out the window. Guilt for rushing into a wrong marriage. Guilt for not being able to reach Neva.

Guilt for feeding my mother the pills of her death.

On the third afternoon of my pacing, I emerged from the

nursery drained and wrung dry and cold and shivering. I'd rattled the bars of the cages beneath my soul that held wild dogs with bared teeth and distended claws. And I wondered if the locks would hold. In those frigid moments, when I looked inside myself with obsidian eyes, I wondered if God had punished me with his dictum of an eye for an eye: my baby's life for my mother's.

I huddled again in the corner of the sofa, drawn into myself, until I felt a gentle touch on my forehead.

I looked at Hattie, and she must have seen something of my ragged emotions because her eyes widened in shock and concern, but she kept silent. Finally, I cleared my throat and spoke.

"Hattie," I said, "after a while, how did you, I mean, how could you come to terms with your sister's memory? And all that happened to you in the concentration camp—how did you get past it all, go on with life?"

I was thinking of my own horror, of course. The horror of accepting the consequences of my decisions. A horror incomparable to hers, but one that I owned.

She sat on the opposite corner of the sofa and smiled, her face softening into the dear countenance I'd grown to love. "There is only one way to bear unimaginable pain: forgive everyone. Forgive everyone of everything. Including yourself."

Her words tumbled through my mind. Forgive everyone of everything. Was that possible? Forgive every single person for every single thing?

"If everyone practiced it, that would change the world, would it not?" she said.

Tears came to my eyes, and I nodded in agreement.

With fresh appreciation, I perused the lion-hearted woman beside me who'd turned her head in profile and watched the smoldering fire in the hearth. She'd had to forgive much in her life. It took twenty years, she'd said, to forgive her sister. Twenty years. I didn't want to hold on to bad feelings for Cal or Seth or myself or anyone for twenty years. I didn't want to hold to them for another day. I was sick of living under the pall of turmoil. I wanted to get on with life.

I got up, tossed the throw on the arm of the sofa and headed for the kitchen to heat soup for our supper. Stopping in front of the living room window that looked at the Reckart's house, I watched a sparrow flit from the firethorn hedge to Neva's window sill then away. Dusk, hushed and heavy, blanketed our corner of Universe Street. A sweet sacred peace rested on my heart, and I craned my head to look at the sky between the houses.

"Look, Hattie," I said, "it's starting to snow."

CHAPTER TWENTY-NINE

When I woke the next morning, it was to a ribbon of sunlight across my eyes. I tossed off the blankets, padded over to my bedroom window and pulled aside the sheer curtains. The snowfall had continued through the night, and a white coating lay pristine under a crystal blue sky. I inhaled deeply. At last, the sun.

As I dressed, I kept returning to the window time and again to take in the glowing backyard. The sight of the snow on the roof of the carriage house apartment gave me a feeling of having all that bad energy covered with purity.

I'd been in the garage to get the Volvo in and out since I'd been home from the hospital, but I hadn't mounted the steps to the apartment itself. Let it sit, locked and silent, I thought. I was in no hurry to open that door again and relive the scene of Neva's death. Now, looking out at the idyllic scene in my own backyard, the horror of that night seemed to retreat, along with the visions of Hattie's story.

Hope. That was it. For the first time in what seemed like years, I felt hope.

Hattie and I chatted through breakfast, and afterwards, I scurried up to my loft to finally work on the Griffen account. Sabrina had called to ask how I was feeling, and also to tell me the account was still open for me. Beneath her cheery optimism, though, lay a nervous need for reassurance. She'd personally vouched for me to Elana Rodriguez and the marketing team. I promised her I'd make her proud. Parking myself firmly in my office chair, I vowed to myself that I'd remain there until I had a solid draft on the screen.

I hadn't heard from Cal in two days. I hadn't let myself burrow into the mire of unanswered questions about my future. For now, my instinct told me to just continue to heal. I paid attention to it.

When the phone rang, at first I thought it might be Cal. I didn't have caller ID in the loft, and if I was into a project, I'd usually ignore the chirps and let the answering machine get it. But since I hadn't opened the Griffen file yet, I picked it up.

"Zoe?"

"Hello, Dad."

I smiled into the receiver. Even though he'd been attentive and thoughtful since the accident, our conversations still had the characteristic of a stalled engine trying to crank to life.

"How are you feeling?" he said.

How was I feeling? Today, probably for the next couple of hours, very good. Better than yesterday. A little. But I didn't think he'd want to know the details of my emotional life.

"I'm fine. Matter of fact, I was just getting ready to do some work for my big account. It's been a long time."

"Well, that's fine, Zoe. That's fine. Okay if I come on by the house still this afternoon? I have a box with some things of your mom's I thought you might like to have."

He was on his way to Arizona, the car packed with whatever he wanted from the Red Leaf house. He'd left some of the larger furniture, thinking that Lohan was buying that, too. I still felt guilty about deliberately deceiving my father, but not enough so that I'd jeopardize losing the deal by confessing my scheme to him and then have him cancel the sale.

"Yes, sure Dad. I'll be home all day. What time?"

"How about around two or so?"

We hung up, and I went to work on the Griffen project.

Two and a half hours later, the front door buzzer sounded. Despite being slightly more comfortable with him, unease squirmed in my stomach. I kept my guard up with him, a prize fighter in the ring, waiting for his next swift and painful punch. He still held Mom's death against me, I knew, and I figured he'd die holding those hard feelings close to his heart. But I had changed. Now, rather than trying to do something about his feelings, I gave in. If he wanted things between us to be unsettled, that was his choice. No more would I live with false hopes for relationships, and never again would I beg for someone's love.

Gripping tight to my sentiment, I went downstairs and opened the front door. He entered along with a brace of cold sunny air, wrapped to his chin and carrying a small cardboard box.

"Let me take your coat, Dad. Come on in. There's a fire going in the front room."

"No, thanks. I can't stay."

"Well it seems silly to drive all that way and not sit at least for a minute. Have you had lunch?"

"Yes. I stopped and got a burger. I, uh . . ." he glanced around the entryway, "I guess I could come in for a minute. Get warmed up again."

He shrugged off his coat and followed me into the living room. I sat on the corner of the sofa settling in to face the armchair I assumed he'd take. But he sat next to me, not too close, but enough so that I got a whiff of the Avon aftershave he always wore. He held out the box to me.

When I opened the flaps, gold-colored metal embossed with delicate white flowers shined up at me: my mother's jewelry box.

"Where was it?" I heard the smile in my voice, felt it in my chest.

"Buried in the back of Mom's secret drawer."

"But I looked all through her dresser, after she died and again a few weeks ago when I packed."

"You didn't look in the false back."

I laughed. "You're kidding."

He grinned at me. "I'm not. I put a false back on that dresser for her years ago. You know how she had her thing about secret places for hiding presents. I did it as a joke, really, and when I showed her, she thought that was the funniest thing. It wasn't big enough to hide much, but she got a kick out of it."

I turned the box in my hands and lifted the lid. Tinkling music, the Tennessee Waltz, filled the space between us. Mom's locket rested in the black velvet. I lifted the chain and let it dangle from my fingers.

"Oh this is so wonderful. Thank you, Dad."

"I honestly forgot to look in that false back when you were there last. I really did."

I smiled again, directly into his eyes. "I know you did. We were both upset."

He nodded. "There's something else in there for you."

I reached into the box and withdrew a pink diary; a Girl's Secret Friend scrolled in raised letters across the cover. With a delicate touch, I traced the letters. Oh Mom. Only you would keep your womanly thoughts in a girl's book. When I clicked the metal button on the lock, the pink tab fell away. I opened the book and flipped through the pages. Mom's graceful hand covered the pages for about two-thirds of the way, then her handwriting deteriorated into scribbles, then blank. I flipped to the last entry, six months before she died.

"I guess she got too tired to write in it after that," I said.

"I suppose."

We stayed there a minute. I felt my own sanguine smile as I arranged her treasures back inside the box.

"Zoe—"

He had a look on his face that I hadn't seen in years, the look he used to give me when I first moved back in with them to care for Mom; the look that had been followed by the words, "I'm so glad you're here."

He cleared his throat and swallowed.

"I want you to know. I read that," he nodded to the pink journal in my hands, "and she talked about wanting to die. She wrote about what she would ask you to do and how she'd already collected the pills. And she wrote that she prayed that you'd do it for her. One final act of love, she called it. So, I guess . . ."

A lump the size of downtown had formed in my chest, and I knew what he was going to say: I forgive you. I forgive you.

I put my hand on his arm. "You don't have to say it, Dad."

He nodded and looked down at my hand then covered it with his own. He rubbed it for a minute then looked back up at me.

I smiled and heard Hattie's gentle refrain again. Forgive everyone for everything. Something stretched and yawned awake inside of me, and I felt calm, light and peaceful, like I'd just awakened from a much-needed sleep.

"And I forgive you too, Dad."

He stared at me a minute, like he might tell me he'd done nothing to be forgiven for, but he didn't. After a moment his face relaxed and he smiled. "Well, guess I better be going."

"Wait a second. I need to tell you about Cal and me."

He shook his head. "No need. I imagine you've thought enough about all that. I don't want you to go through it again on my account." He stood and adjusted his belt. "Tell me in a letter."

"I'd love to have you stay. I mean it."

And for the first time in ages, I wanted to simply sit and talk with my father. But he shook his head. "Nope. Gotta go, Zozo, got to go."

I held his arm tight against me as we walked to the front door, held his coat for him while he pushed his arms in, then I wrapped his scarf around his neck and tucked it in.

"Don't want you to get frozen before you get to Arizona."

He kissed me on the forehead and put his hands on my shoulders.

"Maybe you can fly down next month or so. That is, if you're not too busy fixing up your mother's house."

I opened my mouth and gaped like a kid caught sneaking in the back door past curfew.

"You know?" I said.

He nodded.

"I'm sorry, Dad. I—"

"No more sorrys. Nothing to be sorry about."

He reached in his pocket and withdrew an envelope.

"The deed to the house. I renegotiated the deal with Lohan. He was glad things worked out like this. He's a good man."

A picture flashed through my mind of Gus's kind eyes.

"Thanks."

He waved me away and put his hand on the knob, then turned back to look at me.

"But you'll fly down, soon, won't you?"

"Yes. Real soon."

He reached across me and opened the door ushering in a blast of wind.

He pulled me to him in one quick hug, and then turned to leave. As he clamored down the steps, I called after him.

"Call while you're on the road, okay?"

He waved without turning around, and I wondered if it was

because he didn't want me to see the tears in his eyes.

Too late. I already had.

Chapter Thirty

I flipped through my address book, located the number I wanted and punched it into the handset. After the third ring, I got an answer.

"Hi, Gus. It's Zoe."

"Zoe."

He said my name smooth and a little drawn out. I imagined his smile, his eyes softening with affection. I sensed he was savoring the moment.

"My father just left here. I got a nice surprise."

"Let me guess: the deed to the house."

"You sly devil, you."

We laughed together.

"I'm pleased for you, Zoe. He made me promise not to tell you when we closed on the farm. I never would have agreed to hide anything from you except he told me if I told you he'd throw manure down the well."

My father's love of Zane Grey westerns was showing. I laughed again. "He's an ornery one."

"So," Gus said.

"So."

More laughter, the kind of laughter that came without a punch line, came from two people who heard the unspoken whisper of promise floating between them.

"That's great about the house," he said. "I'm happy for you."

"Thanks. But you missed out on a business deal. You don't

have anything to sell me now."

"Yeah, that's right. Do you feel like you owe me a favor?" A tease lifted the tone of his voice.

"Hmmmm. I don't want to say yes or no to that question."

He laughed. "Smart lady." He paused a moment. "Now that you don't have to meet with me to buy your house, I'm at a loss; I've got to finagle a way to get to see you again. When you're ready, that is."

The prospect filled me with warmth and my stomach, always the precursor of my emotions, flipped.

"I'd love to see you, Gus. But I have to tell you, I can't promise you anything. I mean, it's been a rough time, and I'm still trying to get my act together, you know?"

"Yes, I know. And don't worry about it."

The heat rose to my face. "I didn't mean to sound like you're waiting for me with bated breath."

"Oh, but I am."

I reddened again, flustered and flattered. We both laughed.

"I have to quit this giggling," I said. "I sound like a school kid."

"Sounds good to me."

A comfortable silence lasted a moment.

"I'll say one thing for you," I said. "You sure know how to turn on the charm."

"Is that what you think? That I'm turning something off and on to manipulate you? Because I'm not. I want to be very open with you. I want you to know all of me, from the top of my head to the tips of my boots, inside and out. I want you to know exactly who I am."

I caught my breath. "Okay," I whispered.

"So can I come up to Chicago to see you?"

"Sure. Any time. But by the first of next week you won't have to. I'll be living at Red Leaf."

"Wow. Really."

"Yes, really. I've decided I want to watch springtime come to the farm. Hattie and I . . . did I tell you about Hattie?"

"No."

"Cal's grandmother and the dearest person in the world. So Hattie and I and Goldie, that's my dog, will batten down the hatches here in a few days and head on down there."

"What about your work?"

"I can do everything I need to online. And for the few meetings I'll have, I can drive up to the big bad city once every few weeks or so."

"Sounds like you've thought it all out."

"You know, it's funny, because I haven't really. I'm just going with my gut reaction here. You remember how that goes, right?"

He laughed. "Sure do."

"And my gut tells me to lock up this house and get out to the farm. I have a lot in mind for the Red Leaf house, things to fix up and redecorate. I'm anxious to get started."

"And what about Cal?"

I should have known Gus Lohan would be direct. I'd gotten used to Cal talking around issues with me instead of stating them openly. For everything that Cal left unsaid, Gus would find the words.

"Cal has his life's work to do. No one can be a part of that." I took a deep breath and blew it out. "And I have my life's work: My mother's house. My job. My art. Dad and Hattie. Maybe love again. Some day."

He didn't say anything, but I imagined him grinning on the other end of the line.

"I'll see you at Red Leaf, then," he said. "First part of next week."

"Bye, Gus. See you then."

I wandered toward the pantry and entered the spicy haven.

My fingers found their way to the candy jar at the back of the second shelf and dived into the mound of chocolate drops. I withdrew three, put two in my jeans pocket, and unwrapped one. Placing it on the front of my tongue, I let it sit there for a second. Finally, I closed my mouth over the soft tip and let my senses sink into ecstasy. Wearing a contented smile, softly humming a nameless tune, I strolled into the living room. Hattie sat knitting in her favorite chair in the corner. I plopped into my fireplace chair and swung my feet up on the hassock.

"Did you start something new?" I said. "I don't remember you working with that yarn before."

Hues of yellows and golds interlaced her fingers. She nodded. "A sweater, I think. Do you like the colors? I think it would look lovely with your olive coloring and dark hair."

"It's delicious. Thank you."

She smiled and her needles resumed their clicking.

"Hattie," I said, "how would you feel about moving to Red Leaf for a few months?"

She lowered the knitting to her lap and smiled at me.

"I love farms. I'd like it very much."

About four o'clock the next day, the buzzer rang and I opened the door to see my friend smiling across a glittering red bow perched on the top of a wicker basket she held in her arms. I grinned back at Sabrina.

"Well, ask me in," she said. "It's colder than hell out here."

The aroma of fresh yeast and cinnamon meandered up my nose and I was suddenly in the grip of an enormous appetite.

"Hurry up and get in here," I said. "I can smell the goodies already."

She stepped inside and set the basket on the Chinese-style teak table in the foyer, shrugged out of her coat and waited while I hung it in the closet.

"Let's have your rolls now," I said. "I'll put on some coffee."

Grabbing the basket by its handle, we linked arms and headed through the living room. At the sound of the commotion, Hattie had rested her knitting on her lap and met Sabrina's smile with her own.

"Look what the snow blew in," I said. "And she brought her world-famous cinnamon rolls."

I lifted the basket for Hattie to see.

"They smell wonderful," Hattie said.

"The coffee will be ready in a minute," I said.

She nodded and picked up the saffron yarn from her lap. "I'll give you two a minute to talk, then I'll be in."

Goldie trotted ahead of us, crossed to her pallet in the corner and plopped down. She lifted her nose in the air for one last sniff before tucking herself into a ball for sleep. Sabrina sat at the table in front of the window where a view of pristine snow and a gleaming day formed her backdrop.

We chatted as I brought out butter and honey, then settled at the table surrounded by our feast. Hattie joined us long enough to swoon with pleasure as she ate a roll, then left us to our talk.

After taking one last lick of gooey cinnamon and sugar from my finger, I told Sabrina about my decision to go to the farm.

She nodded her agreement. "I think that's the best thing you can do now."

She'd have every right to say "I told you so." Three years ago she'd tried to tell me Cal was the wrong man for me. But she didn't remind me of that, which didn't surprise me about my classy friend.

"I figured," I said, "I can work the Griffen account just as easily from the farm as I can here at my office. And if I need to see Rodriguez or Twellman or you for a meeting, I'll just drive in for the day. It's not a bad drive."

"Don't worry about it. Everything's on hold," she said.

"They're going to postpone the new launch until April. So that gives you several months to get it together, Trueblood."

She'd referred to me by my last name for years, but after Cal and I were married, she made an effort to stop it and just call me Zoe. I noted the use of my maiden name now and wondered if in her own mind she'd made a shift in perspective. She'd tossed off the reference, like it was the natural name for me, and I let it go.

"I appreciate the extra few months," I said. "I'd hate to lose the account. Should I feel humble that the delay was because of me?"

"You should feel about fifty percent humble. The other fifty percent was a screw up by your friend and mine."

I laughed. "What'd he do?"

"Mr. Thomas Twellman, aka, Tom-Tom the Terrorist of the fourth floor marketing department, Griffen Uniform, city of Chicago, got fired."

"No."

"Yes. And you want to know what for?"

"Quit torturing me and spill it."

"He hit the 'send all' button for a dirty joke."

"It must have been a very dirty joke."

"Worse than dirty, it was personal. To Rodriguez."

"Tell me."

"It had a picture of a woman cracking a whip over this guy who's chained to the wall, ordering him to have sex with her. It came complete with graphic pictures of the woman wearing black leather and steel-studded boots snapping this whip over the guy with an enormous erection. He changed the names to fit Rodriguez and him, then to make matters worse, copied and pasted Rodriguez's photo over the face of the woman. Then the idiot hit 'send all' and there it went careening though the Griffen Uniform cyber space, along with several dozen customers."

"To Rodriguez, too, I guess."

"Oh yes. And when she got it, and also realized it had been sent to customers, she told Twellman to pack his shit and leave."

"I didn't get the joke. Maybe I wasn't on Twellman's 'send all' list."

"Yeah, that makes you a real social outcast, huh?" We laughed. "But at least you won't have to worry about him anymore. And I'm taking over the contracts for some of the vendors."

"Congratulations. Or is it?"

She shrugged. "Maybe. Give me until April and I'll let you know. I'll be handling your contract, though, so that's one good thing."

I grinned at her. "I'm proud of you, Reena. What does Mitch think?"

"He likes it. And it comes with a bump in salary which he likes too."

We talked for another hour about her son Devon, a few of the acquaintances from Griffen, my father and my move to Red Leaf.

"So are you considering this a permanent move?" she asked.

"I'm not considering it anything except what I want to do right now. I'm in no state of mind to make long term decisions, and by long term, I mean anything more than six months. Hattie and I will stay there through the spring at least, then I'll decide. I also have to see how it goes with Griffen and the rest of my clients. I can't afford to loose any business, especially now."

Especially now that I was soon to be single. Despite my optimism, a melancholy ghost wiggled inside me. Sabrina watched me for a moment, but didn't say anything. The ghost faded to mist after a minute, and I leaned over and gave my friend an impulsive hug.

"What's that for?" she said.

"Just because you're such a lousy friend." I grinned and

hugged her again.

She gathered her basket, leaving the last two rolls for Hattie and me to enjoy later. In the foyer, she zipped her coat to her throat then faced me with that see-to-the-center look of hers.

"You're going to be fine, Zoe. Just fine."

She kissed me on the cheek, pulled open the door and left.

CHAPTER THIRTY-ONE

Over the next several days, I readied the house for our move: stopping mail and paper, getting the utilities arranged, all the myriad details that run a home. When I'd done all the small things, I realized I could put off the inevitable no longer: I'd have to pack my clothes.

I stood at the threshold of my bedroom closet and surveyed the remnants of the life of Dr. and Mrs. Sterling at Ten-Ten Universe. I didn't run my fingers over Cal's clothes, like I had that one morning so many weeks ago; I examined them without touching. There was something about the intimacy of a closet, and mine felt both familiar and foreign at the same time, like re-visiting a childhood home after years of absence. The garments on his side of the closet had overlaid Cal's skin. The jackets still bore his scent. The shirts housed the cells of his body in the folds of their fabric. I recognized the clothes, even remembered where he'd worn particular garments, but they belonged to a stranger. I felt like an intruder.

A thought came to me: Already . . . Already I was beginning to detach.

I wheeled out my largest suitcase, opened it on the bench at the foot of the bed and began to pack with brisk, businesslike precision: this blouse to stay, these pants to come with me, this sweater to donate to charity. I'd leave most of my things. I'd be coming back and forth to Chicago anyway, so I could retrieve anything I'd need. For now, I'd take enough to be comfortable at Red Leaf—but not enough to feel like I'd moved out.

Pulling open a dresser drawer, I lifted three of my favorite bulky wool sweaters and placed them in the suitcase. I stopped for a minute and leaned against the bench at the end of the bed to steady myself. A hotness simmered behind my eyes, tears waiting in the wings for their cue. Even though I'd reminded myself I wasn't officially moving out, my emotions weren't fooled; packing was the concrete action that signaled the end of my life as Mrs. Cal Sterling. I hurried through the chore and concentrated on folding and fitting the clothes into the suitcase.

I stopped after a half hour or so, walked over to the window and after sinking to the chaise lounge, stared out to the backyard. Another iron day. Snow still remained on the ground, although now at the edges of Universe Street it had been heaped in dirty mounds by the plow. The snow magnified the frigid isolation of the carriage house. A shiver shot up my spine; something awful had happened there.

Neva had been on my mind. I hadn't climbed the stairs to the apartment, but now, I found myself rising from the chaise with the full purpose of going downstairs to the kitchen, wrapping my coat across my shoulders and marching out to the carriage house. I didn't make a conscious decision to go there, but I didn't make a conscious decision to stop myself, either.

The heels of my boots echoed in the empty hallway, and I stopped in front of the open door to the guestroom where Seth had stayed. When we'd first moved into the house, I'd purchased the guest bedroom furniture at a discount, merely something to put in the room, we decided, for visitors. Now, absent Seth's strewn clothes and blinking laptop on top of the desk, the room had been returned to its former sterile self. I was glad.

I trotted down the steps and turned toward the kitchen. It was a day for saying good-bye to the house, I guessed, because when I came to the nursery door, instead of passing it by as I usually did, I turned the knob and stepped inside the dim interior.

Since I'd been home from the hospital, each time I entered the room, a kind of curtain would drop around me, a mental barrier that cushioned still tender emotions from the onslaught of memories. Now, the curtain dropped again, but it seemed to me that rather than being thick and opaque, it was almost transparent. A kind of shivering sadness worked its way into my chest, but with a deep breath, I realized I was okay. Was I healing? Getting stronger so I could move on?

I flipped on the light and crossed to the shuttered window. Adjusting the shutters to the open position, I gazed out at the Reckart house. The firethorn hedge where Neva had crept around on the day Seth arrived was tangled and brushed with snow. I scanned the room and rested my eyes on the wicker bassinet, the panda pictures on the wall, the tiny diapers still stacked in a basket on the dresser. Yes, I affirmed to myself, I would be okay. I'd not mourn the loss of my baby forever. I was forty-one and I doubted I'd have a child in my life, but who knew?

Choices. I had choices.

I left the room and closed the door behind me. Hattie's radio symphony program filled the hall with the sound of a classic. I wouldn't disturb her. She'd be knitting and listening and enjoying her own place right now. I marched through the kitchen, grabbed my coat from the hook beside the back door and stepped outside.

I stood for a moment in the frosty air, engulfed by my own breath and stared up to the three windows of the carriage house. Turning back to the door behind me, I opened it and stuck my head inside.

"Come on, Goldie. Let's go girl."

She thumped her tail a couple of times, lumbered up from

her pallet and padded to the door. Her knowing eyes watched me a moment, then she scooted through the doorway and sat beside me. I stroked her silky head as I gathered my courage. We crunched our way across the yard on a layer of hard thin snow and mounted the steps. When we got to the landing, I unlocked the door with the key I took from under the porch light and pushed open the door. Goldie crossed the threshold and looked back at me over her shoulder.

"All right, girl. I'm coming."

A cold musty odor permeated the apartment, along with traces of marijuana. I tiptoed through the L-shaped entry way into the main room. My breath came in shallow puffs, my heart pummeled the walls of my chest and I gazed into the room where Neva had died.

The floor claimed my full attention. The area rug where Neva's life blood had seeped was gone; I remembered Dad said he'd had it thrown away. The wooden boards were warped and stained and the varnish had long since disappeared. I forced my feet to move to the center of the room. I stood where she'd fallen. The stains around my boots had seeped dark and deep. Were they blood stains? I didn't know. I didn't remember the condition of the floor before; we'd put down an area rug when Cal used the apartment for his cave, and I'd had no reason to look under it. The discoloration could be from blood, or from a can of spilled varnish that had darkened as it had aged, or from a cup of coffee spilled by a hired driver of a sleek Packard, a driver who had been provided the apartment to live in while he was employed at Ten-Ten Universe. Turning in a circle, I examined the walls and baseboard for stains, but there were none. Everything had been scoured clean by the professional cleaning crew Dad had hired.

The hide-a-bed was folded away like it had been the night I'd heard that terrible gunshot. I rested my gaze on the corner of the sofa, the corner next to the wall where I'd found Seth huddled and incoherent. A picture came to me: Seth's knees drawn up to his chest, the stunned odd smile on his face. Shock, of course. For all his spoiled, selfish behavior, the kid was still human. The fact that someone committed suicide in his presence would impact him forever. I knew that like me, no matter how far he'd travel from the house on Universe, he'd never be able to get away from that memory.

I didn't pity him, and I didn't excuse his behavior with rationalizations about how young he was, how spoiled he'd been all his life, about how he could easily be labeled by some as a victim of a hedonistic society. But even though I didn't make excuses for him, it made me sad to think of the vision he'd carry with him forever; how when he became an old man decades from now, he might croak out the whole sordid story to a grandson as a way of teaching another restless young man a lesson.

I took one last sweep of the room, called to Goldie and turned around and left.

Enough of the carriage house. Enough of poor doomed Neva. Life was going on and I wasn't going to miss it.

ABOUT THE AUTHOR

Rebbie Macintyre lives in Florida. This is her second novel.